THE
HARD SIDE
OF THE
RIVER

— A NOVEL OF ABOLITION —

JOHNNY RAYNE

TCK PUBLISHING.COM

Susan —
I hope the stories
carries you along.

ISBN: 978-1-63161-074-5

Sign up for Johnny Payne's newsletter at
www.johnnypayne.com/free

Published by TCK Publishing
www.TCKpublishing.com

Get discounts and special deals on books at
www.TCKpublishing.com/bookdeals

Check out additional discounts for bulk orders at
www.TCKpublishing.com/bulk-book-orders

To Betty Payne James, cousin, fellow poet, and novelist, hewn of stone. Born in Rockcastle, died in Lubbock, where, she said, "If you stand on a beer can, you can see the Pacific Ocean." Her ashes were scattered on the little farm we took turns owning.

MARCH 1831
CHEAPSIDE SLAVE MARKET
LEXINGTON, KENTUCKY
DAN BASKIN

I HAD WORKED EIGHTEEN DAYS STRAIGHT. It seemed everybody wanted to sell or trade slaves at Cheapside Market. Nobody liked what chattel they had and coveted the other'ns, so the pens got overcrowded and we was having to leave some chattel overnight in the backs of wagons where they wadn't secured; it became a mess really. Mid-March had fell, and the wind blowed hard, full of trash and grit, like it would never stop, expelling the remnants of winter in its jaws. One of the overseers acted partial to me; Rickman was his name. He said, "Baskin, I done seen you eyeing that Yoruba gal, she ain't but about seventeen, fresh as they come. Take her on home to your digs for a day or two, while we get this madness sorted out. Give yourself a well-deserved break. Nobody will be the wiser, and I owe you a favor or two. I know I can count on you to take good care of her."

Now I ain't called nobody Pappy in my life, and I wadn't about to start with him, but he did cast a fatherly eye on me in his quiet way. I figgered that in his old man way he wanted good things for me. I told him I didn't think it was such a choice idea, me alone in charge of a young strong thing, what if she escaped, how would I explain it, but he winked again and said "What if? The tussle is what makes it excitin'. I'm sure you'll find a way to overpower her if necessary. Ain't you a tracker by trade?"

I wanted to say no. The whole idea gave me a bad, unfamiliar pang in my gullet. But next thing I knowed, her and me was slipping out a side alley, me trying to act normal-like, though I could feel a spring in me winding itself tight. I got her home, pulled the shades, casual, as if that was my nightly routine. I turned the lamps down low and heated water on the cook stove. She sat stock-still with her rump parked on the edge of a straight-back chair, didn't say nary a word to me, even when I tried to speak a few Yoruba phrases to her. *Ki ni oruko re? Inu mi dun lati mo o.* Normally I can conduct a conversation at the most basic level in that language, a short one, but I got so tongue-tied she might not even have understood the words I was trying to say. I set a pan of water and a bar of lye soap in the next room, instructed her with a gesture to wash herself, and found her a set of clothes that a wench had left behind when she took off on me in the middle of the night with my week's wages, and I had swore then that was the last time I let any woman see the sun come up inside my house.

The Yoruba gal went to the second room and closed the door behind her, at first right tentative, then I heard the splashes a little harder and a little sloppier, like maybe the water was running off her legs onto the floorboards, then the splashes freer still, as if the water run down from yet some higher place. To turn my mind in another direction, I commenced to cook squash in my only pan, then I warmed two hoe cakes I had wrapped in brown paper for when I come home too tired to seek food in a tavern, and three strips of bacon that had set out a day or so but didn't look no worser for it. I wanted to tell her, if I'd had the proper words, that the fare was poor but wholesome, though I s'pose it would have sounded completely ridiculous, under the circumstances, in any language.

She come out wearing the white shift. It was a bit on the short side, and too tight in the bosom, but otherwise not a bad fit. I could sense that getting herself freshened up made her nervous by the very idea of it, as this wasn't something she often got asked to do, certainly not by no white man, but all the same you could tell that she enjoyed the sensation of being clean, her black hair wet and coiled and the droplets falling onto her shoulders. In the visible naked space of her shoulder blade between the end of the shift and her neck, I could see the tip of a scar where she had got whipped with a braided lash. Each kind of whip makes a particular scar, and though I have seen many and many scars in my day, I had to fight back tears, for I could not imagine why a master would have for striping this Yoruba gal.

Doubtless from the other side of the door she had smelled the evening meal being warmed up, for her eye fell on it with the tag beginnings of boldness. Any woman, no matter her condition, will sniff out the place where her stratagems with a man may begin, she does it instinctually, without even intending. I know this only because many a woman has done exactly that to me, always with disastrous consequences for myself.

I served supper on tin plates. Now I was the one perched on the edge of my chair, like an escaped convict at a stranger's funeral where he has ducked in to escape notice by the authorities, only to realize he owed the dead man money. It was her who settled back in the chair as if right at home and took almost an entire hoe cake into her waiting mouth, only a blunt end sticking out enough to make her lips part a certain distance from one another. I looked down at the floorboards, not wanting to make eye contact. Each time I peeped up, she was looking directly at me, steadfast, almost calm, while she crammed more food in her mouth, then she set to work on apples heaped in a wooden bowl on the table. I believe she ate about six apples in a row, the core and all, and I only wished I had more food so she could keep on eating the livelong night and I would never have to contemplate what might come next.

When she had finished off the apples, I took her by the wrist closest to me and pulled her straight into my lap. Her whole body was a-tremble. I couldn't say if it portended excitement or fear, lust or ague. Cornbread crumbs yet stuck to either side of that oversize mouth of hers, where she had ate the hoe cakes so fast. I pulled her mouth to mine like a man who knows the beer is good, meant to be savored slow, but can't help guzzling it in a single swaller. I tried to push my tongue as far down inside her gorge as I could manage. I know I ain't no expert kisser, I lack with women the steady patience and necessary slowness of movement I display when tracking. Could be that's why they up and run off with my money in the middle of the night.

Maybe the Yoruba gal was only trying to keep her balance on the chair, but if she hadn't looped her arms about my neck, I might have been able to satisfy myself with that one sole kiss. I'll never know. For as soon as she caught aholt of me, I stood up, she wrapped her shanks around me, and I walked stiff-legged to the bed, where I throwed her down on her backside and flung up that same white shift I had flung up once before on a different gal. Suffice it to say I entered the Yoruba gal with all whatever power I've got. I told myself she was sturdy and could take it. I told myself she'd been through worse and would go through worse still. But the truth is, I didn't need or ask for any reasons or permission to do what I wanted to do. That's all there was to it. Whatever a man could improvise to do, we done it.

Her body never did quite cease to tremble, which only excited me the more, and there come a time when we turned so weak we fairly had to drag ourselves out of the pool of our own waters just to keep from drowning. I don't know the first thing about pleasing a woman. And I cannot positively say she enjoyed herself, though she showed signs of ecstasy. There was no quiet in her, no mere yielding. Could have been an act, like the show the whores always tries to put on for my benefit, and the more I disbelieve, the more they holler. The Yoruba gal was aggressive in her own right. Quite possibly, she was coupling for her life. I never wanted to be parted from her vital reek.

In the first lull, as we lay drowsy, watching a thick shaft of light from the uncurtained window hit the cracks on the other wall, she rolled onto her side to face me, and she said very clearly, "*Mo nifẹẹ rẹ.*"

I answered her, "Don't say that."

She repeated the words in English. "I love you." No obvious desperation or guile lurked in the phrase. It was just as if she was stating a fact, like saying "Butter is yeller."

I wasn't sure whether I'd heard her right the first time in Yoruba, or if she knew exactly what those three words in English meant, if she had just heard somebody say them in another place, maybe her mistress speaking to her master. But she said it five or six times, "I love you," in plain English, and there was no way we could argue about it. She slunk down and fingered the parallel knife-cuts in my calf, all the same length, more than a dozen of them, and give me a questioning look, as if I might find the words in her language to explain to her how and why I got them. But I didn't explain.

For three days, we thrashed like blazes, sleeping only in fits, eating the same way. I went off and bought provisions at the store, leaving her completely unattended. When I come back loaded down with catfish, meal, taters, grits, corn, shucky beans, onions, flour, a wheel of cheese, a bottle of beer, cream, lard, crackers, peppercorns, and two bunches of radishes, spending all I had earned in those eighteen days, the Yoruba gal had not moved one whit. I halfway hoped she'd be gone when I returned, and the other half of me couldn't wait to look on her face again. I could smell us on the sheet, like somebody had died there and then come back to life. I thought she was going to use me up complete. The more puny I felt, the stronger she looked. I had always reckoned a man was to possess a woman, but this seemed more the other way around. Whatever power existed between us at that moment seemed to all come from her. I wanted to turn her out of doors, but I couldn't make myself.

Neither of us knowed how to cook. But as with the other act, I improvised. Whether the meals tasted strictly good or no, I can't take a vow, but as I lived it, those were the best shucky beans I ever ate. I don't know what I thought was going to happen after. We didn't think about nothing. Well, that's wrong. I reckon I should say I didn't think about nothing, because in truth, I had no idea what went through the Yoruba gal's mind. I wouldn't of been surprised had she took it on herself to plunge a kitchen knife into my neck while I slept. Maybe she was plotting her escape the whole time, waiting until the streets was empty before she made her break. Maybe she had thought to slip off while I bought the groceries, but couldn't find an opening just then. Maybe she thought she had misunderstood our laws all along, as they dragged her from pillar to post, and that now we would marry, or that I would buy her and keep her as a concubine. Maybe she thought I had done already bought her.

Which, on the third morning, I begun to reckon what I could sell—my pistols, a few sticks of furniture, my horse, and then what? My only skills was selling slaves and tracking slaves. Was I going to bring her into the family business? I wisht I hadn't spent my earnings on them groceries, but ruther we had starved and treated my small pay as the beginnings of a strange dowry. I wished I hadn't bet most of my last tracking reward three weeks prior on three jacks against another man's straight. That morning, while the Yoruba gal slept, them lips that had ate the hoe cakes now pressed together and pursed just the slightest bit, a shadow birthmark under her eye right where it met the pillow, and me beginning to recognize a certain way she had of snoring, silky, no trace of a rasp, the snore of a young person, the snore

5

of a tender girl, not like the deep snore I been rebuked with by a couple of women, keeping them awake half the night in a state of nerves, well, as I contemplated her, that was the only bad case of jitters I ever suffered, me who had never flinched from rifle-shot or a man's fist.

For I knowed that Rickman would happen by soon. He'd said a couple of days, without being overly specific, and some way or t'other he'd seen fit to cover for me thus far, perhaps deliberately miscounting or explaining away the absence of this gal, whose name I didn't even know. In her sleep she sometimes said "*Agbára, Agbára,*" while she wallered around, but that could have been her man's name, or her child's, or her grandfather's name, or her tribe's name, though I'd never heard it spoke before, but most likely it was any name beside her own, as we do not often cry out our own names in sleep unless we are calling ourselves to account. One of the times as she cried out them words, just having awoke, she pulled an ivory ring from her finger, carved with the figures of three birds, and slipped it on my pinky finger. I've never took it off since.

Sure enough, Rickman come by and let himself in the screen door, as I had done got up to open the main door before dawn, to release our heat and let her sleep the longer without discomfort. Rickman strode right in like he owned the place. I had drifted back off and nestled close to her body, but I woke up right quick and was ready to go for my firearm until I seen it was him. He sat in one of the straight-backed chairs, real relaxed-like, real chipper, looking downright pleased. "Hey, there, son. I do believe your holiday time is about up. Was you aiming to bring us back the chattel, or did you take her as a gift?" By this time, the Yoruba gal had sat up too. She recognized Rickman, who took special pride in never raising a hand or a voice, either one, to anybody, whether slave or client. I wouldn't call him refined exactly, but yes, even-tempered. He wasn't going to let himself get riled over nothing. Friendly and laid-back was how everybody who known him described him. That's how he got to be a boss. I watched her watch him, and it seemed like she was trying to make out the syllables he spoke, as if by main force she could will her mind over into the new language, and in that manner learn all she needed to survive.

"No," I answered. "I lost track of time, is all."

"Well, I'm happy to see that you made the most of your opportunity. You pure enjoyed yourself, and God as my witness you needed a rest in the worst way. You been working way too hard, Baskin, and I blame myself that I hadn't noticed until right then how wore out you had got. I apologize for the oversight."

I kept a keen eye on him in the half-dark, waiting for a transgression. I didn't even realize it at the moment, but I was prepared to kill him, if he gave me only the slightest provocation. I'll have to say, in fairness, he cast nary a lustful glance toward the Yoruba gal; Rickman never seemed to notice that she slumped against the wall, undressed, with only a bare sheet to scarcely cover her torso and breasts. Rickman had seen several hundred such gals. They was all chattel to him, I don't believe he was partial to their charms, and any sustained gaze he give them was only long enough to calculate their exact worth in United States dollars. He was about to retire, or so he had told me once or twice recently, and I believe he seen me as stepping into his shoes, always telling me I was the quickest study and the aptest pupil.

"I don't mean to hurry y'all, Dan, but this little escapade done got to draw to a close. The girl is needed back on the block by late morning, and we got to get her to step lively after you done took all the starch outta her."

All at once, she leapt to her feet, her face fierce, letting the dirty sheet fall to the ground. She began to cry out in her native language, speaking more quickly, heated, imploring, frenzied. I didn't want her body on display in front of Rickman, which was crazy because of course he could unclothe her any time he seen fit, if not here, then back at Cheapside, and he might well do so if that's what it took to fetch a fair price. Buyers have a right to inspect the goods. Still, I waited as her breasts swayed and her arms gestured, to see if her motion would arouse Rickman. I waited for him to make a nasty crack, or to lunge out of the chair, grasp her by the arm, and slap her face hard a couple of times, so that I could fly into a passion and pistol-whip him into a stupor.

But I knew he wouldn't do that; I only hoped it. Rickman plucked his moustache liken he was embarrassed by the whole situation, and not only did he refrain from ogling and coveting, he averted his eyes, like a man who has blundered into a domestic quarrel. In a soft, reasonable tone, he said, "Dan, you've got to calm this filly down. I'll wait outside if that's what is needed, while you dress her, but I've got to get her to the stalls in three quarters of an hour. I won't compromise on that." He sidled out the screen door, holding the frame until it shut, so it wouldn't bang.

I laid my hand upon the Yoruba gal. At once she settled down and clung to me. She was meek and obedient, and let me dress her back in her own clothes. The shift lay shapeless now on the mattress. Her body had gone about as limp. Together we walked out into the alley. I could smell trash burning the next street over. A Doberman, one I sometimes fed, hung around a few feet away, in case I might set out scraps. That dog has surely been kicked aplenty, for it won't come close, but must have smelled the cooking. Doubtless it belonged to a neighbor, but I don't know who.

"I want to keep her," I said.

"Baskin, you know I cain't give you her as a present. She ain't belongin' to me. If she was mine to give, you know I'd let you have her. I ain't stingy. Me and you, we're not of the stripe what owns slaves. We only help sell 'em."

"I'll buy her, Rickman."

He laughed softly, but I knowed he wadn't mocking me. It was more the ironical situation. It was his way of showing compassion for my plight. "Buddy, what with? You're worth about a hundred dollars yourself, all told. If I could auction you off bodily, I'd plumb do it, as I can see you've got an awful hankering for this Yoruba female. But Baskin, you won't fetch nothing on the open market, believe you me."

"Give me a few days and I'll come up with the cash somehow."

"If I thought you really could, I'd surely hold her for a day longer. I've done no less for favored, long-time clients, and no one could raise an eyebrow. But her owner already been on my case about where she'd got to, and I said I was keeping his property out of the fray, so she wouldn't get hurt in all these overstuffed pens. I said I don't abide poor sales conditions at market. I'm not sure he believed me, but he let it pass, as I've served him well on other occasions. If he knowed I'd lent her out to let you fondle her, I'd be retired right now, and probably destined for the Fayette County Jail. Men can be more finicky about their slaves than they is about their own wives. Wasn't it you yourself that told me that bit of wisdom once? So, let's not talk of this matter anymore. It ain't meant to be, friend. I thought I was doing you a favor, but I ain't so sure I done you a favor after all."

There wasn't much else I could say, by rights, so I kept my mouth shut. I either had to kill him and hightail it, then risk me and the Yoruba gal gettin' run down by a mob, because even with my stealth, we wouldn't make it to the edge of town, or do what he said. I know how to bring slaves back from open country, but I had never turned my hand to helping one get away. Rickman helped the Yoruba gal into the coach he'd brung along, wanting to be discreet about the whole affair, both for his sake and for mine. When we disembarked near the stalls, we had to step around a sow scratching her teats in the grainy dirt with a satisfied look. People let their livestock run around that way and wonder later where it went, or how it caught bush foot. The pens were not as crowded as when I had left. They was slaves enough, but the frenzy of buying and selling had settled down over the past three days, giving way to more or less a quietude. As we passed by the open pens, some of the slaves looked curious at the Yoruba gal, as if trying to recognize her with her head downcast, and others stared more hostile-like. During the short ride, she had kept her counsel, only now and then reaching out a hand to touch me, as if she needed to steady herself.

We came within sight of the block and I heard a murmur rise up, as the mid-morning customers caught sight of the Yoruba gal. They seemed to detect a special quality in her, almost as if they could smell it. I've always said that buying a slave is the most irrational act in the world. So often, the price that's finally given has nothing to do with anything; it's just a feeling that one is worth more than another, based on reasons no one ever really states, or else they make up false reasons in their mind to cover over the real reasons. Once she realized that her stay with me was over, she didn't cry out, as she had in my bedroom. I waited for that cry, but no, it never come out her throat. All she did was take the liberty of hanging on to me with all the force that remained in her. Rickman remained on the other side, waiting for me to hand her off. He don't usually take that march onto the block himself, but on this occasion, he wanted to spare me what he knew I couldn't tolerate, so without saying so much, he put out his arm to escort her the last few feet and help her up onto the block. I never knowed before then a woman could have so much strength within herself to hold on to what she wanted, or what she thought she needed. I believe she could have held fast to me for quite a long time, and that it would have took several men to pry her loose. But I turned to her, suddenly not abiding her touch, and said, "Woman, let me be," which was not the words I had meant to say at all. I had meant to say other things I never will be able to put into words. As soon as I had spoke my brief sentence, in a tongue alien to her, all the fight went out of her, and she let loose.

PART ONE
ABEJIDÉ

MAY 1833
DOWNTOWN LEXINGTON
DAN BASKIN

I HAD HER PUT ON THE white shift and we slipped into my bed. She'd cleaned up right before, but I could swear she still smelled of another man. Maybe it gets down in your skin and can't be washed out.

"I don't like to wear this gown. It makes me feel second-hand."

"I'm only going to pull it off you in a minute or two."

"All the more reason."

"Then don't."

"But you'll make me leave."

"That's true."

"I'm not giving up my pay. We're this far along."

"When did I ever hold back on you? I give you more than you ask, always."

"This is the last time, Dan. I swear. I ain't putting it on no more. You're thinking of another woman when you're with me."

"I never said that."

"You don't have to. Your eyes is far away. You spend more time watching that teakettle over my shoulder than you do me. I'm a fair piece, or ain't I?"

"Would it bother you if I was thinking of another gal?"

"Yes, it hurts. You think I got no pride? I want to satisfy you. If nothing else, I want to do my job right. Don't you like to do yours right?"

"I don't have a job anymore."

"So you say. They's been a rash of darkies running off these last weeks. You could make plenty of money if you wanted. Like before."

"And throw it all away later? I'm damn sick of the whole business. I told you that. I've been turning down offers of work."

"If you was to court me, say, take me to a music concert, I could give you a hint such as nobody knows."

"I don't go for concerts. Only music I hear is from buskers who wants a penny."

"Then buy me candy. A chocolate bar."

"I'll give you an extra coin, and you can buy yourself one."

"You are so hard-hearted. I want you to buy the chocolate for me. That way it tastes better. I'll wear the white shift. Give it to me."

She struggled into the shift, grunting. It wasn't a good fit. I had to grant that much.

"For Godsakes, I'll buy you a candy bar. Only don't talk no more." She yanked up the hem and begun to move atop me, brisk, not even providing her usual harlot's moan for atmosphere. Except for occasional little grunts, I was treated to a beautiful silence. My mind began to relax and I tried only to exist in the sparks between my legs as the pressure on my brain eased up.

"This fellow I mean jest busted loose a few hours ago and I know about it already. Maybe I'll go tell my story to another slave tracker, who will act more interested."

"Christ alive, Leora. Can you not hold your tongue still for three minutes until I can get shut of my little spasm? That's all I ask."

"You called me by my name."

"For the last time."

"I mean it, Dan. I got this information from a good source."

"In bed."

"Naturally. Where else would I hear such a thing? Most of y'all men, yourself excepted, will say every kind of words upon a mattress. I can't squeeze six good words out of you, no matter how creative I am."

"Okay, let's hear it then. Who is the source?"

"Fontenot."

"The Frenchman?"

"I gave him a toss last night, and he was so all-fired he let it slip. He turns extravagant now and again."

"That's a mighty big word for a little lady."

"I'm big where it counts and little where it counts."

"You was with Fontenot?"

"Have been several times. He likes it good and dirty."

"That man don't need to pay for sex."

"Neither do you, Dan. You're all man. Lots of girls would bed you for the fun of it. Only you don't let them. You're peculiar."

"Leave my mind-springs alone."

"He makes me do acts that most women won't, unless they is straight-out trollops. Acts I'd love to do for you as well, only you didn't ask me. Want me to show you?"

"You ain't ever mentioned Fontenot before."

"Do I talk to him about you when we're abed?"

"Heaven only knows."

"Well, I do not. That's called confidence to the client."

"What's the information?"

"A slave is being carried up the Maysville Road as we speak. He's belonging to Walter Brathwaite, a businessman."

"His loss. Ain't got nothing to do with me. They's lots of fellers wants a bounty. Brat, you said?"

"Yeah, that's what they call the owner. Jehosephat was his daddy, may he rest in peace."

"A real bastard, Brat is. Welches on his debts. Now you've got my interest."

"For once. I got a real good body, you know."

"What's the slave's name? Did he say? Brathwaite has several."

"For a kiss I'll reveal it."

"Woman, I am about to backhand you, more like."

"Would not. That's all bluff. His name is Pingrim."

"Jacob Pingrim?"

"I believe so."

I got quiet for a minute and Leora slid off my waist and squinted, trying to figger me out. I sat up.

I reckoned the situation. "The bounty is apt to be large. That slave is one of a kind. His mind is working all the time. You can see it on his face. Say he puzzled out plant hybrids and such for Brat, like one of them science experts. And nobody trained him."

"Maybe it's voodoo. He could of made a pact with the devil."

"His wife and child was took to Cheapside. Five year ago, it was. Mariah was the wife's name. And I heard him call his daughter Creech. But they never made it to the block."

"Why not?"

"Never you mind."

"Did they run away?"

"I ain't saying."

"I told you summit. You got to tell me summit back." But I begun to pack my tobacco pipe and she give a flounce on the bed, then flopped back on the pillow. "Fontenot has a message for you."

"I thought you said you never talked about me in his bed."

"Just this once. He brought it up."

"What's the message?"

"He said Pingrim knows where the woman is."

"What woman?"

"I don't know. Another slave that you sold, or helped sell, or something."

I sat up and took her by the sleeve. I could feel my brain start to burn. "What woman?"

Leora looked scared. "I don't know, Dan. Don't peer at me like that. I didn't do nothing."

"Did he say it was a Yoruba woman?"

"I ain't sure. Them foreign words sounds all alike to me. It might have been that. Yes, I think so."

My hands shook so I couldn't light my pipe. "I don't know what you or he is trying to do to me. But somebody is gonna get hurt if this is a prank."

Leora took the pipe out my hands and lit it for me, taking a long puff in her mouth without coughing. Smoke slithered from her lips like a wraith. She put the pipe in my mouth and continued to hold it for a moment, and coddled the back of my head with her other hand. "I wouldn't do you no harm."

I made myself puff, two or three times. It tasted like dung. "I know you wouldn't. Is Fontenot involved in the escape of Pingrim?"

"I reckon not. Some other woman told him about this and he turned around and told me. And no, I don't know who that wench is, nor do I want to know when and where she opened her heart."

15

"Did he say who would take the slave across?"

"There was no mention."

"You're sure about that?"

"It was me in bed with Fontenot, not you. Maybe you should go sleep with him yourself. I told you what I knowed, and it's a lot."

I slid out of bed and hoisted into my britches. "You've got to leave now. Our business is finished for tonight." I took her by the arm and fetched her up.

"Let me take off this shroud and get into my skirt, for pity's sake. Does this mean you're back in the trade? I thought you was going to go break horses in one of the territories out West."

I handed her a wad of bills without counting. "I ain't sure. I jest wanna find out more."

"Curiosity killed the cat."

"Don't get philosophical, Leora."

"Will if I want to."

"I'll tell you one thing. Next handful of money I get, I am off to Oklahoma to break horses."

"That's what you say now."

"Have you told this piece of news to anyone else?"

"No."

"Keep it to yourself."

"If I'm in bed with another tracker, I'll keep my mouth shut. Is that what you mean?"

"This bit had better not be some whimsy of yours."

"And if it is?"

"I'll come back and marry you. That should be punishment enough."

"As if you would. Fontenot also told me whilst we was drinking wine that he'd marry me."

"Don't listen to that nonsense. He don't mean it, Leora. He'll only hurt your feelings later."

"As if you don't." I buttoned my shirt as she turned her sulky face toward the candle. It was pretty, if a little spent. "Dan."

"Yeah?"

"I sure wish you would marry me."

"Forget it. You need an apple what ain't got so many spots on it."

"But I like that apple. Most especially I like the spots."

"Enough talk."

"Dan."

I sighed as I slipped on my holster. "Yeah?"

"Who was that woman?"

"The Yoruba?"

"The one who used to wear the white shift."

"Woman, let me be."

MAY 1833
DOWNTOWN LEXINGTON
CAL FENTON

NOTHING SO SOOTHED CAL AS a thunderstorm with lightning ripping down the sky, the flashes showing the gnarled black clouds that lay thick on the face of the sky like the beard of God. At seminary, his roommate had thought him mad for wandering out into the charged electric air, to feel the first big, separate drops that became one single slur of water. The roommate excited himself by seeing the occasional woman. Each kept the other's secret.

Cal sat at the foggy window pretending to nurse a cup of cold tea. Dana was late. She'd gotten better at smuggling, but not more punctual. He shouldn't have gotten here ahead of time. It only meant waiting longer. The coach was ready, parked outside. Axles had been greased with beef tallow. The wheels had been trued for the bumpy Maysville Road. Inside, he'd stashed gentleman's clothes for the slave. Jacob was light-skinned enough that he could pass in some company. The main thing would be getting Jacob into the coach and through town without recognition. Outside town, unless someone knew the slave by name, they tended to see a darky as a darky. Cal had done this many times and never gotten caught. The first mile was the critical mile. They wouldn't be facing a tracker at the Maysville crossing, not likely. There were too many other attempted escapes happening for anyone to focus unduly on this one grizzled slave.

He and Dana had waited for one of the errand days. This meant that the slave could wander around the center of town unescorted, where citizens had grown used to seeing him, without attracting much attention. It was a simple matter of the slave walking into the blind alley where they waited with the coach.

Dana came through the entry, shaking drops from her hat as the door jangled. "Sorry I'm late. I had to wait for the rain to slack off so I could cross the street. You could float a paper boat between the paving stones."

"Don't worry. In ten minutes, the sun will be shining. Get ready for heat and mosquitoes."

"He said half an hour. At least when he walked past me under the canopy of the tobacconist, there was no one there to see us. I don't want anyone to think I smoke."

Cal laughed. "I'd say that's the least of our problems."

"You look handsome in that topcoat."

"Do I? I don't really think about such things."

"You should. You're attractive. With the right haircut, you would qualify as an eligible bachelor."

"Would I? I guess all I need is the feminine touch."

"Doesn't every man?"

"In addition to your school for ladies, you well might open a school for men. We're desperately in need of guidance, us bachelors."

"I don't think a school is needed. It's quite simply a tutorial from the right woman."

"And who would that woman be? Anyone in particular?"

"I am sure that many a female parishioner has barely suppressed the urge to leap to the Eucharist table and seize your person. You know that ladies love a man with authority. It makes us feel secure."

"I've thought about getting a fiancé. But these abolitionist forays in fact make me a dangerous prospect. That's why I remain unmarried: There's important work to be done."

"So it would have to be someone who shares your passion, your sense of danger. Someone who would put herself as much at risk as you."

Cal smiled and held her gaze. "And who would this person be?"

Dana looked away. "It's not for me to say. I'm a mere woman. The man gets the first say."

"And the woman the last. Tell me: at your Female Academy, do you instruct your charges in the art of seduction? Because you're quite good at it."

"If you call playing the piano, speaking French, and knowing that the man leads when dancing 'seduction,' then yes."

"I'll contemplate your advice. I do in fact feel that this smuggling of slaves must come to an end before long. It's gotten to the point where I hear barking dogs in my sleep, and just the other night I dreamt that you were taking pistol shots at a pursuer."

"I suggest, dear Cal, that you and I have a picnic soon, sans slaves. And I am going to spruce you up as your clothier, barber, and manicurist. As it is, you're a waste of a perfectly good man."

"Then that's settled. I will turn myself over to your friendly ministrations. And what about you, Dana? So beautiful, so elegant, so poised, so well turned out that you have other women biting their own tongues in envy. On the few occasions I attend social dos, in my capacity as a citizen or man of the cloth, you are on everyone's lips. Where is your beau? It's the mystery of Lexington."

She leaned across the table and smoothed Cal's collar. "That's kind of you to wonder, Reverend Fenton. But I only want to be on one's person lips, with my lips. In the meantime, let's take one more man to freedom."

May 1833
Larkspur Ridge
Dan Baskin

WHEN I SET FORTH TO Fontenot's house out Larkspur Ridge, my hair still wet from the faucet, there was only a midnight wind to keep company and somebody's loose cur that trotted alongside until it lost interest. That tailwind did follow me though, as if to urge me forward. It reminded me of the early days, before my knuckles ached so bad, when I would ride half the night just to feel a steed's spring beneath the saddle. A hundred whores ago. My luck was such that his place was toward Maysville, about an hour's ride, so's at least I'd be headed in the right direction.

I splashed through a crick or two, otherwise all dry ground, and my steed's feet held sure in the dark. The waxen moon showed its face here and there to help us along. I tried not to think much, rather to hear the soughs of air bothering the branches. Fontenot's place was on high ground. In the flood three years ago, they say he didn't even have to change his shoes. I'd been charged to deliver him a serving-woman once upon an afternoon, so I recalled where his land lay, as my memory is all too keen. I had never brought back a runaway slave for him. To hear folks tell it, they didn't run from him, and I wondered which was his secret, good treatment or cruelty. Once I stood upon the grounds, birch trees—I believed them such—was casting their night shadows every which way as the moon pressed from behind a cloud bank like fire through a charcoal smear. Leaves had grown so thick around the manse that even in fair daylight you wouldn't see the building until you was almost right up on it, not spread out but tall, a cliff of lumber and stone. A hound skulked behind, making no noise. It kept its distance as I dismounted. I paid it no mind. There was no need to tie my horse, as he knew better than to run off on me. I knocked, not overloud, and without haste. In time, a light showed in an upstairs window, zinc and stained glass. There was grumbling at the door as a lock was slid and a hasp was undone.

A coffee-dark woman with her hair unpinned answered. She looked none too happy to see me. I didn't give no explanation, only said I had to see Monsieur Fontenot. She seemed about to give me what for, but said she'd ask what the master could do. She didn't leave the words stuck in the roof of the mouth the way some do, just rolled them, and peppered her phrases with Creole—*mepri, sakrifis, troub.* I figured her here by way of the Caribbee.

I waited a spell without complaint. The girl didn't come back nor offer me so much as coffee. I expected Fontenot to descend in a silk robe and with his hair mussed, but as he appeared on the stair, he was already dressed for day, his hair just so. A little womanish, I had forgot that detail, but his hand was surprisingly strong as he took me in his grip. He had a forelock, like my horse. Didn't ask why I was there, only invited me back to a porch and instructed another girl, younger, to bring a pot of coffee. She was a good-looking, light-skinned girl what would have brought easily six hundred at market. Still in child-bearing years, with a fine turn to her shoulders and wrists. Tall as most men; Fontenot only had about an inch on her. Good breeding stock, sturdy yet delicate. She laid down the coffee and a basket of crusty bread and made herself scarce. From the way she pulled his sleeves back, I wondered whether that was his woman or only his chattel, but it was none of my business really. He gestured for me to sit and partake.

"So, how may I help you?"

"I didn't come for breakfast."

"Yet here it is. Suit yourself. You won't mind if I eat."

"I don't mean to waste your time."

"It's all right. It is still the middle of the night, so I'm not that busy."

"As best I can make out, you sent for me, roundabout."

"By way of the luscious Leora, you mean. Our common indulgence."

"It seems you had a message for me about Pingrim."

"If the message was delivered, what else do you want from me?"

"The slave in question has done run off, as I understand. That makes it hard to have a conversation with him."

"I suppose it does."

I took out my pistol. "My first impulse is to shoot you right in the forehead for riling me up for no good reason. You don't send a message like that through a whore without any warning. You could have at least summoned me here and said it yourself."

As he buttered his bread, flakes of crust fell onto the tablecloth. He took his time spreading marmalade over it, from a little glazed pot, not in no big hurry, and then returned his gaze to me. I'd never seen such a cool stare, and in my line of work, that is saying a lot. "I won't even bother to state that there are witnesses. You might reason that they're only slaves, and their word won't be worth much."

"I wouldn't venture that."

"If I had a pistol on my person, I think we might be at even money as to who would kill whom."

"I know you've killed men in duels. That's what they say."

"Be that as it may, I didn't bother to bring down a gun to breakfast. I know enough about you to feel sure you won't kill me in cold blood."

"As you wouldn't either. Is that right?"

"I'm not you. Your reputation is that of a fearsome tracker, and yet also of a man of honor. That's why your brethren hate you. It's called envy."

"Don't overestimate my morals." I slid into the chair and laid my gun on the table. I bit into the flaky bread and swallowed coffee. "I never spoke of her with anybody."

"All I know is what I told Leora. Pingrim passed it on, maybe accidentally, through a lady friend of mine. I don't know where the woman is. On her way to Maysville, that's my guess."

"I'll assume you guessed right, unless I hear otherwise. You're closer to the source than me. But if you was going to pass this tip along, why didn't you do so before?"

"I've only known a few days. Believe it or not, I don't base my life around you. I began to worry about my friend, and what she knows. She's special to me. Also, I thought you might want to be informed. So you can buy back the slave girl who got away."

"With what money?"

"You've earned well. I surmise that much. You've captured a lot of escapees, more than anyone else. Did you throw it all away?" I averted my eyes and didn't rightly answer. "I thought so. Well, there will be a reward, of course."

"If Brat pays it."

"If you can catch up to Pingrim before he gets across, I believe Brathwaite will pay what the slave would fetch on the open market."

"I'd say he'd bring four hundred for sure, maybe as high as five for them as understands what they're buying."

"As I don't have to tell you, slaves are not easy to bring back, once they've crossed. We've had a fugitive act for forty years now, but no one up there enforces it. They've got problems of their own. And if you're lucky enough to find and apprehend one, the tribunals are cumbersome, unless you just drag them back in the middle of the night. Abolitionist activity in Ohio is hot. Oberlin, Chillicothe. It's a nightmare. Several of my friends have lost slaves and never had them returned. I believe this is the worst year so far. The good trackers, like you, are few. Not everyone who calls himself a dentist can extract a tooth without mauling the mouth. I've heard that there are as many as thirty thousand escaped slaves living in the North."

"I never counted."

"Brathwaite may be mean, but he's not dumb. He'll want Pingrim back now, unharmed, and not have to send at his own expense half-wits into Ohio on the slight chance they'd find him, and if they did get so lucky, possibly kill him. Besides, he hates to pay any kind of expenses up front. The clerk at one of my stores told me once that Brathwaite came in to buy seeds, but didn't want to pay until he saw the plants actually sprout from the ground."

"And not pay for the ones that's dormant."

"You've got it. Bring the slave back intact, and he'll pay the commission without question. That's how the man works. Now, Pingrim is intelligent, and he'll know enough to lay low for a good, long time. He knows how his master thinks. But that slave is worth more to Brat than all the rest he owns lumped together. If you need a couple of hundred to get a stake started, I'll loan it to you. The rest is on you. So, go home, or go find Pingrim. Isn't that what you do? Run after escaped slaves on a moment's notice?"

"That's right. But help me. Who is smuggling him out? What's their plan?"

"I don't know the plan. I avoided those details. Then I really would be an accomplice. All I've done is give you a lead on how to bring a fugitive to justice. What else you find out in the line of duty is your affair."

"Fair enough. But what is your friend's name? I've got a hunch she's the one smuggling him out."

"Yes. I admit it. She got tipsy and was bragging about becoming an abolitionist, which I believe ought to be kept a secret, as it's a capital crime, but she felt compelled under oath of brandy to confide in me. I didn't press for details. I'm a slave owner."

"Don't trifle. Give me her name. If she keeps your company, she has to be someone easy to recognize. And I can ask along the way. A woman of society is a hell of a lot simpler to track than the slave she's hiding."

The mulatta came in to refresh our rolls and coffee, and her eyes met Fontenot's. I can't be sure of the meaning of the look that passed between them, for I have no proof. But the look was familiar to me. It stirred all the pangs I'd spent so much whiskey lulling to sleep. Fontenot twiddled a porcelain cup between his hands, looking out the window at the birch trees. Their profiles had begun to show in the daybreak as the jays hopped and squawked. Out of a folding wallet, he counted out two hundred dollars in bills of ten.

"The woman's name is Dana Curbstone. I have one condition. If you capture the slave, Pingrim, you let her and her travel companion go free."

"That's a big condition."

"Look at it this way. The very scare of being caught should make them go out of business. They'll understand that they're known abolitionists, if only by you. She's not fit for that kind of risk. And if he included her, that means he's slipping. He needs to take a hard practical look at his objective situation. My guess is that he's been active for years. She didn't mention his name, but it's clear to me that it's the Methodist minister Calvin Fenton."

"Yes, I am familiar with both them names. Persons of standing. You don't mind exposing them?"

"On the contrary, I'm quite sure they're going to get caught. For all I know, she shared the same news with someone else. I tried to talk Dana out of this misadventure, but she paid me no mind. Obviously, I'm not going to turn in a dear friend myself, even if she is misguided. If you get to them first, they're less likely to end up in prison. I'm sure you can stage things in a manner so that in the retelling, you found the slave, but not the liberators."

"I'll say nothing. That's my word. It goes to the grave."

"You'll have success, then?"

"I can't assure it. Depends if they stayed at a safe house or not, which gives me more time. I know where the best crossings are on the Ohio around Maysville. But I've never ventured acrost the Ohio to bring a slave back. I work on the near side only. Once he's free, as I see it, he's free."

"Well, good luck."

"How do you keep yours on the property?"

"How should I put it? I try to make them believe there's no other world besides this one."

Fontenot accompanied me to the door. The hound was nowhere in sight. My horse still stood in the same spot. Fontenot instructed me to go around back to the stable, where I would find water and hay. Then Stalker and I hied at a soft trot toward the Maysville Road. You can't break a steed into a dead gallop right away.

Pingrim shined my shoes once, at the Phoenix Hotel. As I understood it, Brat couldn't make a profit off his chattel just with seasonal work. He complained about the economics of the situation, how his property got sick and how much it cost to maintain it in the off-season. So he leased out Pingrim during the winter to wait table and black boots at the Phoenix. I remember him down on one knee scanning the paper while he shined. That's how I knew he could read. Wasn't the least bit deferential. Stuck up, more like. I had to tap him on the forehead, said "Mind what you're doing and don't stain my trouser cuffs." Though he really didn't need to look at me to perform menial work. That job was beneath him. I only said what I did to get a rise out of him. I wanted to hear him spout off, see the extent of his vocabulary. He was probably thinking about astronomy, for all I know.

The bootblack was in fact smarter than most, you could plain tell it, though he tried to pass himself off as middling. I wasn't having none of that *massah* nonsense off him. Rather tell it like it is and may the best man win. I tapped him on the forehead again. I said "It's a good thing your master has you apprenticed and secured and that he'll vouch for you and protect you. Because otherwise you'd be off agitating for an uprising. I don't doubt you could smooth-talk a bunch into your cause, even some white folk. Then you might end up dead." He didn't say nothing. I kept egging him on. "Yep. Your master is a thinker, giving you a little vacation in town. Restless son of a bitch like you, you'd be off and running to the homestretch if you didn't have room to stretch. Master ain't close by, you can pretty much do as you please and Persian carpet under your feet to boot so's you don't bruise your heels. If this was a flying carpet, you could sail on off across the Ohio and never look back."

He had the rag balled up in one fist and I wouldn't have put it past him to haul off and punch me. Cause he wasn't afraid, that I reckoned. He kept his head down and I swear I saw a smile cross his lips. I'd have give a nickel to know what thought come into his mind. If I could have right then, I would have invited him to sit at the bar with me for a drink, just to watch those moronic legislators wet their pants. I almost did. Only I didn't want the bootblack to get whipped on my account. He would surely get whipped on his own account soon enough. No wonder he could take my gibes, because he was probably planning his escape by then. In his imagining, he'd already lynched and hanged a hundred of us. A feisty bastard he was, a regular Zulu warrior. I don't care how humble he tried to make himself look. He was like one of them African kings who bows down and kisses your feet when you arrive in his village, because he knows he can slit your throat at any time. Royal courtesy, that's what he give me when he shined my shoes.

May 1833
Maysville Road
Cal Fenton

HERE IS A MAN SALUTING as he passes me on horseback. He tips his red hat. This traveler doesn't mind being spotted, in fact he wants to be looked at, admired, so he wears a red hat, yellow shirt, and glossy boots, and even his horse wears turquoise socks. Perhaps they're on their way to a jousting match. I, on the other hand, must keep a low profile until I retire from this dangerous business. I don't want him to recall later that he spied me at such-and-such a milepost, in a green cravat and wearing a fragrance of huckleberries among the motes of dung rising from the road. Everyone I lay eyes on during these trips is my mortal enemy. They may wish me well today, as they jangle along smiling, but how would they feel tomorrow, if they were stopped for questioning about a certain Cal Fenton, that respectable citizen who doesn't look bold enough even to smuggle a puppy from his cousin's house to his own? Yes, that's my reputation, and I prefer it that way. I assume that every trip will be my last. That boy with the pitchfork tossing hay in the distance, he'll launch it toward me at any moment and it will be my crucifixion. I'll die pinned to the coach, the vehicle of my sin.

MAY 1833
MAYSVILLE ROAD
DANA CURBSTONE

WHAT TREMENDOUS STRENGTH IT TOOK to be a woman. Heaven forbid she should seem put out under dust and relentless sun. Not even noon, and her mouth was no cleaner than the bottoms of the horses' hooves. Her hat, a parabola of sun and shade, masked her face. Mislaid, low-fired bricks tottered underfoot as the horses trudged forward, trying to get up speed. Out of the corner of her eye, Dana watched Cal sweat at the hairline, his gaze inward. She dabbed at his face with a kerchief.

Dana owned a pistol, no bigger than an éclair, one that fit perfectly inside her beaded purse. She'd taken it one night to a dance at the Phoenix Hotel, to feel the excitement of walking around knowing it was nestled between the fan and the vial of powder. Cal wasn't a believer in firearms, saying that if you had a gun, you'd only end up needing it.

She luxuriated in the memory of pistol practice a few days ago. Monsieur Fontenot was at ease with his ruthless effeminacy, and he expected no less from her. On a barn at the back of his land, he kept a soft copper target hung. After an hour of practice, she'd pierced the copper's center. Monsieur Fontenot had been raised on duels. Between gunpowder blasts of the flintlock pistol he favored, with floral carving and rubies embedded in the butt, they smoked perfumed cigarettes together, then sat on his wraparound porch, half-reclining on the wicker divan. She took her leave with hands scented and softened with lotion, the ghost of a kiss on her wrist.

But for the squawks of a jay making a run at Cal's head when he strayed too close to an overhanging branch, June birdsong was obliterated by hoof clops on brick and the clatter of axles and joints. Horses a-snortin, that's really how they said it in Kentucky. Even the more refined girls she taught had to throw in the extra syllable. It was hard to break the girls of their pronunciation, even after they had learned such genteel skills as Japanese painting. *I'm done a-paintin',* *Miss Curbstone.* As her ear had gradually grown used to it, she had developed a tender spot for the charms of her charges' misspeaking. Somehow she'd managed to make a reputation in the feminine arts, and now all the best families in Lexington coveted her services. She had made a lot of money in a very short time. Serving as an abolitionist with Cal, under guise of pastoral care, kept her from losing her mind.

When they stopped to eat at a tavern, Cal's cheek looked as smooth as she'd ever seen it. She ran her fingers across that naked skin as she removed a speck from his face. He pulled out her chair. A lock of his hair had strayed across his forehead. When he brushed her arm as she sat, her eyes smarted. Perhaps he had taken to heart their conversation of the morning. Was it too much to hope that she had shifted his attention away from his need to be the most principled man in town?

He came up with one knee of his worsted trousers flecked with sawdust. As he sat in the straight-backed chair, its unforgiving shape so right for a preacher, his face relaxed. The girl served up watery ale with sediment at the bottom of the glass. He drank one half as quickly as he could, as if he were thirsty but didn't want to taste it, then pushed the glass away. Warm, flat, syrupy, impure. She couldn't bear more than a sip or two. He started to stammer something, the shape of a word, she thought it might be *wed* or *wedding* or *will you.* In the end he asked her to pass the wheat rolls. A boy in breeches was fishing pickles from a barrel in the corner with his bare hands.

She hoped to lead Cal out of his mental labyrinth and into one of their own making. The women in his congregation saw him as a five-year-old in need of a mother's care—with all the physical advantages of a grown man, of course. It seemed implausible that he didn't understand how good-looking he was, but there were men like that, beautifully clueless, not stuck up. That was part of his appeal, that childlike side.

What she wanted to do was usher him into some of the physical refinements of men in stations above his and whisk him off to New

England to live in society. He would make a splash. He'd carry an air of mystery, a past he wouldn't speak of, because that's how he was, and she would keep their abolitionist secrets. Those secrets would be like a silver locket, split into two, yet fitting together perfectly.

Jacob waited outside, in the coach, under a shade tree, eating a lunch she had packed. The first time she'd laid eyes on Jacob was at the Phoenix, when he waited on her and three senators of the Commonwealth. He served so well and so silently, she had no idea he normally worked there as a bootblack, and that the proprietor would only press him into table-livery for certain private parties. She needed relief from the boredom of her three smug male dining companions on that day. Two had taken humanistic degrees at Vanderbilt before going on to read law, but even they could not bend their minds away, verbally, from the disposition of cemetery plots and the maintenance of sewage canals, of all things. They had that masculine habit of choosing arcane yet banal topics, far beyond their ken, then peppering one another with details on the matter they had all doubtless picked up from the pages of the same newspaper.

The pointless one-upmanship with weights and measures ended only when the bread pudding arrived (their invariable dessert choice, because it was heartiest, slab for slab), or when one of them hit upon another topic, ratios for steamship boilers or the chemical composition of moustache wax, equally lacking in interest. Thomas Jefferson had wrought far more carnage than he knew. Feminine company wilted her, and she came to groups of men each time with the fresh expectancy of curt, cutting, cathartic swagger and repartee, brilliant words wafted on the sharp aroma of cigar smoke, only to be disappointed on every new occasion. The swagger never lacked, but the repartee—well, it seldom materialized, unless she was lucky enough to snag a day-date with one of those handsome, ever-dueling Cantwell brothers, or unless Cal could free himself for a few hours from his sense of perpetual and aggravated ministry.

As her dinner companions slogged through the legalism of eternity as it pertained to burial practices and long-term leases, she ardently wished for the Rapture to come at that precise moment, exhuming all corpses from the newly broken ground and freeing her spirit likewise from its corporeal place at the table, so she could hover gleefully above the three bowed men tearing gravy-slathered venison into strips with their forks while holding the steaks in place with their knives. She began to watch Jacob who, without ever uttering a syllable, seemed to know precisely when to clear plates, offer the next course, touch up the tea, top off the whiskey, whisk crumbs into his cupped palm, never meeting any eye until she kept her gaze steadfastly on his. At last he returned that gaze, however briefly. On his lips lay the hint of a smile, as if he were thinking of a devastating quip. How she wanted to extract it from him. In his eye seemed to dance a twinkle, but that could have been the reflection of the water glasses. All at once she became cognizant of his lanky, sinuous height, the ease and assurance of his movements, the natural grandeur of his bearing.

As he bent to slide a hand under her plate, she half-crooned, "*Aidez moi,*" with a playful and discreet wink, just to see how he'd react. The three senators halted their analysis of the ideal dimensions of a sewage canal that would ensure optimal flow, in order to watch the exchange. "*J'ai besoin de toi.*"

Jacob spoke. "So then, Madame would like the truffle with raspberry sauce?" The men sat agog. When he had departed to fetch dessert, leaving their moustaches and eyebrows quivering in his wake, she said lightly, "He must have been born to a Creole owner." The men seemed to relax as they fumbled for cigars and started to argue about superior brandies. Patois. Gumbo. Po'boy language. Mercifully, she had deposited them back on the shores of the known and explicable world.

May 11, 1833
Maysville Road
Jacob Pingrim

THE HARDEST PART OF THE trip so far was being shut up in the crawl space above the sleeping porch. It was barely big enough to fit his frame. There in the dark, with no company except the sound of skittering on shingles above, probably a restless squirrel or a grounded starling with a broken wing, there was too much invitation to think. And into his spacious mind came Creech and Rye. He'd been able to hold off their specters this entire journey, but now they came unbidden.

In the quarters, Rye sometimes awakened Jacob right after dawn with a little song of her own improvisation. *I wake up early to do the wash, and you scoop me up like a butternut squash. Sugar, sugar, melts in your mouth. Take me with your fingers in my hair.* In the middle of their lovemaking, Creech would fuss from her corner and Rye would just pick her up in the swaddle, place her right in the bed alongside and go back to what she was doing. Rye knew what pleasure was. She always told him you didn't have to ask permission for pleasure. Tried to teach him that too. Shut the other part out of her mind for a spell; it was a gift she had. To be scooped up like a butternut squash and placed in his mouth, where she let herself dissolve. For her, that was the way things were. What is, is, and what was, was. That's about all the philosophy Rye would abide. Didn't want to hear about context. One tattered curtain, one she had sewn, half-hung from the window. They would watch it flutter for a moment or two before the day called them into many arduous hours, during which they might not see one another until nightfall, even if they stood only a few hundred yards apart. He never knew where the mate of that curtain ended up, whether it got pulled down for some other use, but even though she was an excellent seamstress, Rye never replaced the missing curtain or tried to repair the other one. Instead, it fluttered. A quality of light accumulated around its edges, and though they never spoke of the matter, the two of them watched the one tattered curtain dance for a short spell many mornings.

Creech had a little soft bump on her right temple just below the skin, was born with it. Though Rye declared it benign, he worried about the bump, thought it might be a tumor, and would stroke it gently with his thumb while he held Creech in his lap, but it didn't come to anything except an inconsequential distinguishing mark. Right at her nape, underneath the mass of hair, she had downy wisps, soft tendrils he would straighten out with his fingers and let spring back into place. His caresses made her sleepy; he would palpate her skull as if he was looking for ticks, but he wasn't looking for anything. He only wanted to feel the shape of her head.

One morning in December, a week or so before Christmas, he had gotten Creech to go to sleep like that, just as Rye finished building up a good fire, because Mistress Brathwaite, without saying anything to her husband, had an extra load of wood sent down to their cabin, good seasoned oak, perfectly dry, out of the mistress's woodshed. The oak aroma was soothing, punctuated with stout pops at closer intervals as the wood caught hold and the core heated up. It should have made him drowsy, the smell of Creech and the firewood intermingled, but he kept getting more and more alert, more and more wound tight, as his girl slumbered against one shoulder. A corn husk doll Rye had made for her daughter's holiday present lay next to the hearth, alongside a skein of rough wool, not perfectly carded, threads of chaff still stuck to it, out of which Rye was knitting something or other in the odd free moment. His wife, on her knees, turned to look at her husband with an indulgent smile, heartfelt, with no doubt to it, for she loved seeing the girl asleep in her daddy's arms.

That was when the sudden urge leapt up in Jacob to hurl Creech into the flames. His hands shook with the impulse. There would be the initial shrill cry, followed by the echoing shrill cry from the kneeling Rye, and he would have to hold his wife off, her flash of superhuman maternal strength, while the child burned. If Creech burned to ashes, nobody would ever get to her. It was a strong sensation; one Jacob had to fight down, that desire to pitch her into the flames.

His eyes watered. He shifted the child to his other shoulder and she murmured with contentment. Rye asked him if he wanted a mug of apple cider. She and the mistress had pressed apples earlier in the season; she'd stored away her portion in her tiny pantry like a good little housewife, and now she was showering the largesse at her disposal all on her family this one day, rather than saving it for Christmas day, simply because today was no special day and she felt like it. It was good to be able to give something when you wanted to. She scolded gently that Jacob just had to be careful holding the hot mug and the baby at the same time. She didn't mean to be a nag or suggest he wasn't careful, but accidents did happen. He promised he would be extra careful. Bringing the mug, Rye knelt before him with a grateful look of love she didn't always have the energy to muster. While he sipped the cider, as bittersweet and pungent as the oak, his wife nuzzled her forehead on his leg.

MAY 10, 1833
DEER LICK TAVERN
DAN BASKIN

I HAD RODE HALFWAY TO MAYSVILLE without pause, kicking up slag, to close the gap. Hugging Stalker's neck and crouched down low to keep out of the drag. I didn't get excited, we just moved fast. I cast nary a glance to the side. I wasn't going to waste time on the early miles, any more than they had. I figured they was going to make tracks to get Pingrim away from Lexington. His skin was light, so he might pass, if they made him up and dressed him right. On the other hand, he and they was all familiar faces. As such, they would stay in at least one safe house, maybe two, to be cautious, rather than try to get him there all in one day and risk capture, the more as so many had run off recently. The lady with him, Curbstone, would draw attention to herself and palaver with any curious souls. She was there to deflect. But nobody is careful all the time. They get to a certain point without trouble, and they start to relax. My instincts told me I was not far off their vicinity. I knew the lay of the land. Once I had caught up, I had a couple of days at most, I reckoned, to run them down. If I had to cross over into Ohio that was another matter. There, for me, is where the real wilderness begins. Almost all my captures had been on this side of the river.

The Deer Lick Tavern hove into view, with its familiar pitched roof. I was parched; so was Stalker. A runt set astride a crate, spinning a top. He jumped up when he saw me spring out of the saddle.

"Hey, lovely. Hey, mister. I'll take her over yonder for a drink and a rest. You can do the same inside." The boy was covered with dust, but he didn't seem to care as he run off with Stalker's bridle wrapped around his wrist like he was trying to lift a kite off the ground.

Inside, it was too dark to suit me. I don't know why you can't have any damn light in a tavern, except nobody wants to look at himself or at his friends real close, I guess. Half of them is waiting to pick each other's pockets. They was a table of loafers, the kind that had lingered since morn, and I decided to pull up a chair and keep company, to see if something of value might spill out their mouths.

A sport with a checkered hat squashed over his pate was holding forth to the rest as I signaled at the barman for a pint. "I ain't saying you purchased a bad mare, Andy. It's a mere fact she's been bought and sold at least five times. A frisky little tart, that'un. She's like my sister-in-law. If anybody ain't rid her, I want to know the reason why."

Everybody snorted and I thought the jokester was gonna choke on his own spit.

One of the no-counts, who owed me five dollars, recognized me after a minute.

"Dan Baskin. How the heck you been?"

"Hey, Teddy."

"You are *the* Dan Baskin?" asked the one who'd bought the frisky mare. I nodded. "Is it true you can hear mice skittering through the fields when you ride?"

The way a couple of them twitched at me, I could see they had been told the same thing.

"Only some of them." That brought another hearty laugh and initiated a round of swigs.

"But really," said Buford. "I heard tell that in the winter of twenty-seven, you and an Ojibwa hied ye to the deep poplar woods with knives and cut slits in each other's calves until one of you passed out. The man what informed me never explained who won, but said it was the scarifying ritual of that tribe. Then y'all went to the Phoenix and you drew that Ojibwa up to the bar. And the bar-keep was so skeert from the dried blood on your hands that he served the feller anyway, and free of charge."

"Don't believe everything you hear." Right then Teddy reached over with his cane, caught my right trouser cuff, and lifted it. They was a line of perfectly even scars on my calf, running side to side from below the knee to the ankle. That provoked a couple of low whistles.

"Then what in the hell is that?" asked Teddy.

"No comment."

The owner, Alt Fitzsimmons, brought me a pint of ale and I slaked off it. It was pure syrup, warm and flat. He stayed by with a napkin hanging from his hand. "Thanks, Alt."

"Like it? That's a new recipe I'm a-brewin'."

"Ain't never tasted anything like it, that I'll say."

"Why thanks, Baskin. You're the only gentlemen in this pack of dullards. They told me it tasted like pancake syrup."

"Rather, I was hoping you boys could help me out. There's a fine lady and a pastor what probably come along here in a coach yesterday or today. They might have stopped in for lunch."

"Nobody like that has been through this tavern," said Alt. "Don't get much clergy, excepting a Catholic priest now and then. Nothing but the usual scalawags. You know I keep a sharp eye out. You got business with them?"

"Are you on a jaunt, or looking for runaways, Dan?" asked the horse-buyer.

"Just searching for them two. We got a rendezvous. Nothing urgent. I was delayed, but I'll catch up directly."

"I figgered you'd be up this way on business. Heaven knows they has been a bunch of darkies took off this summer. Got everybody up in arms," said Teddy.

"I heard you had retired, Dan. All the other trackers have been gossiping about it. Said the market is now wide open, and they is going to make a lot more money than before," said the horse-buyer.

"I'm wore out from the spook stories," said Buford. "Let's call today a holiday and let all the niggers who wants run on acrost the river. What say ye?"

"No, I ain't a partisan of that logic," piped up the horse-buyer.

Buford leaned in to take exception. "Why? Got slaves of your own?"

"Can't afford any such. Don't like the idea of it, that's all. I might have a few someday, if my fortunes turn."

"They'll turn, all right. For the worser."

Teddy interrupted. "Who's got the bones to stay after these bucks? My lumbago has been acting up from the jolts on this damn road, that's why I had to take a rest. I sell spoke-tighteners, bridles, spurs, and whatnot, but I swear I need a tightener for my own ligaments. I keep waiting for the transportation authorities to make improvements, but they never do."

"It ain't their top priority, that's for shore." Alt chimed in, emphatic.

The horse-buyer had more to say. "Reckon they don't want to make it no easier for niggers to hightail it up to Maysville. River is mighty porous, from what I hear. Some say they's a tunnel underneath, that the niggers walks through, right under the Ohio and don't even get their ears wet. So they keep this road in bad shape on purpose, to slow 'em down. And in the process, they hold the rest of us back from progress. I was in Pittsburgh for a spell, back last winter, visiting my cousin, and I assure you that unlike this commonwealth, they done invested in their infrastructure."

Buford look piqued. "Yeah, well this ain't Pittsburgh. Why don't you live there instead?"

"Can't afford it, otherwise I would and no lie. More civilized. They done took the common man and raised him up into the principles of Jeffersonian democracy. In Pittsburgh, every man is a gentleman."

"Including yourself."

"Including myself."

Alt threw a dishtowel over his shoulder and scratched his head. "I did hear one bit of news this morning. A pilgrim come by all in a sweat from down Lexington way, not an hour ago, and said that Walter Brathwaite's best slave had escaped. The one they allus say is like a doctor of botany, only he ain't never learnt in a school."

Buford whistled. "Now that's news. I heared he is almost as smart as a white man."

Alt smiled. "Brathwaite is offering five hundred dollars for the capture."

"That tightwad? Are you sure it ain't five dollars?"

Teddy looked slowly around the table, as if he were at a high-stakes poker game. "Hell, it's a fortune. The old coon cain't be worth much more than that sum, don't care if he was a true doctor. If the reward is real, it's sheer cussedness. Walter cain't afford it."

The horse-buyer looked morose. "Wisht I was a nigger so somebody would pay half a thousand for my paltry skin. My wife wouldn't pay fifteen cents."

Alt held up his hand. "He ain't a businessman. Everything he owns come direct from his pappy. That Jehosephat was a wizard. He's the one figgered out the slave was a genius, let him get book-read in science and whatnot, and made a pile of money off crop improvements. Ain't that right, Dan?"

"Yeah, that's what I heard, too."

"Can ye imagine?" asked Alt. "Them was probably the first books Jehosephat ever bought. That scoundrel wouldn't even abide the Holy Bible on his night table."

"The pilgrim said they was combing Lexington, figured him hunkered in somebody's cider basement for the nonce, till the initial ruckus blows over." Teddy smiled and shook his head, and nobody knew whether he was making up that information on the spot.

"His name is Joshua, I believe," said Buford.

"No, I think it was Jacob," said Alt. "You heared about that, Dan?"

"No, I'll swear I heard nothing about no five hundred dollars. But if I was to get the right information, I might perk up. And I'd have to give ten percent to him as got me the right information. So that's fifty dollars."

The horse man said, "I heard there is a safe house two hours ride east of here, place called Gobbler's knob."

"If the house is safe, why would anybody know about it?"

"Hear tell, that's all. Said it has a red roof. Only one in that valley."

"Well that sounds inconspicuous."

"In all seriousness," said Alt, "I'll scour the customers what comes in, and see who knows what. If nothing else, even gossip sometimes turns out to be true."

"If I had any chance of catching them, I'd have to step lively. I wouldn't be back this way."

"Well, if you get on the track and then off the track, you're better off gathering your wits and seeing who know what. I leave that up to you."

"Well boys, don't go spreading it around that I'm after anybody, because I never said that. I'd hate to disappoint you. All the same, keep your ears open. Thanks, gentlemen." I laid a dime on the table.

Teddy leaned forward and gave me a hearty handshake. "See you, Baskin. If you run into any Ojibwas, send them on around and we'll buy 'em all the liquor they can hold!"

"Tell 'em about my new beer!"

MAY 11, 1833
CLOVER TRACE
DAN BASKIN

AS I EASED STALKER THROUGH the woodbine, a berry got squashed against my shirt and smeared it with a splotch of blue-black. The horse nibbled the bine-berries on the bush. A titmouse on a near branch eyed the bush too, but in the end, decided to rush by and settle on a sunflower at a distance. I pondered for the first time in a while that this was where I'd rather be. Wasn't nobody near but Stalker and that titmouse with his pale gray cap, as if he might doff it to greet me. Drops of sweat settled between my hat and brow, but I was not going to quit my hat, as otherways there'd be ticks a plenty to burn off my crown later.

I had wanted to press on last night, but I could see Stalker needed a rest and I couldn't have him drop dead on me right when I needed him most. Also, he sported a bruise on his hoof and needed a rest to let the tenderness die down. That was a tactical decision that might cost me my prey, but in this business, I'd learned to be patient when I must. I wouldn't find anything without Stalker as a partner. My judgment was to depart from the Maysville Road and follow the narrows of Clover Trace, half-overgrown, where you only make way atop a beast or on foot. It's seldom trafficked by journeyers, because it means the long way around and in many places ye can only go one abreast, like frontiersmen. In this wise, the fugitives would avoid several of the toll stops between Deer Lick and Maysville.

The gambit was one of two: They'd either ride in a coach on the open road, and hope for the best, or else bushwhack through the cover a-horseback. Fenton could ride with the woman behind, if the slave knew how to mount, which was not unlikely. I did not underestimate this preacher. He was a capable man, a physical one. Even a man of God in Kentucky must know how to throw a punch if necessary, set a fire with wet wood, and move in stealth and quiet, if he's to prosper in this line.

His other two main choices were to go by day or by night. I figured it for day. The vigilantes in particular was roving in bands after sundown, sometimes lynching the darkies for sport. They was running down whatever moved and asking questions after. Trackers, too, tend to assume you'll rest by day and run under cover of night. So, opt for day and stay off the turnpike. Not only was there toll-stiles to cross, but traffic all along. You'd either have to hide a man bodily in a false compartment, which, in this weather, could suffocate him, or else try to make him pass for white. I'd seen both in my time, including a mother and child dead on arrival.

A minister was not apt to do something so inhumane as nail Pingrim underneath the coach in a false bottom, not in this swelter. He might as well go on and nail up Almighty Christ. Fenton might try to make him pass. But it was a gamble.

If it had been me, I'd split off at this point and follow the trace, the first ingenious departure, which was actually a better road of packed earth than all them overturned stones of the pike, infamous for laming mares, and the source of many a busted wheel.

It had been rumored, several years before, that Cal Fenton was slipping slaves out. I first heard tell from a harness-maker, Bob Friendly. However, that ruckus lasted a short time because nobody could turn up a whit of proof. I knew a couple of men were watching Fenton's movements for a time, but if he had been active, he laid low for a year anyway, because nobody caught him out. The rumors died down and attention turned to other suspects, like the tan-yard owner Abel Jackson, who sure enough turned out to be an abolitionist, and they caught him and hanged him in a split. I never forgot about Fenton, though I never catched him at work neither.

Last night, I'd slept under the rare stars that showed through the scuds of bank, after I throwed down at the edge of a large acreage. A morning shower doused me and wet my blanket. I could still smell the wool a-drying saddleback. I parked myself under a stand of trees until the sky cleared off, bringing on the pink day. Then I plunged straight into the woods.

Rabbits drunk on desire and too fool to stay put darted back and forth, daring me to shoot. I was tempted to bag a tender morsel. That's all I needed, for the crack of rifle to give me away for a quarter mile all around. The poison oak lay a-plenty and must be avoided. The broken twigs I spied on bushes choking the narrow passages showed green, and wet leaves leftover from the gully storm had been trampled under hoof. That didn't prove nothing except that somebody had passed in the previous couple of hours. Could be a mere hunter athwart his eager mare, stag-bound, but they tended to bring their hounds along, and I hadn't seen nary a mound of dog-drop, only the stools of rabbits, foxes, and deer.

Five hundred dollars. With that and my two hundred, they was no way I couldn't fetch back that gal. It all come down to a simple idea, me and the Yoruba gal, and I don't care what after that. We'd work it out. She'd be free to go or stay, but I had to find out which. I'd overpay. I'd waste the money anyway, unless she was good at managing house. What I made after, as a wrangler, I'd turn over to her. She might like the West. What did we need, except a mess of beans, a hunk of pork fat, and a bottle of beer from time to time? A Choctaw blanket and to sew up the split in my boot, the one I've neglected for weeks.

I'd seldom seen a man who wouldn't part with his chattel for an exorbitant price. Even them as wants to bed them, they'll find another younger after a time, and when they want them to bear get, they have them pregnant with child right soon, and once a woman has produced one or two offspring, she can be parted with for the right dollar, unless she is one of them rare prize fertile ones who can wring an acre of squash out of a blackberry seed.

Once I found out where she is, I'd have to return Pingrim to Brathwaite, but Brat wasn't to touch so much as the slave's pate until I got full money right in my hand. I wouldn't care whether Pingrim stayed or goed, except that he was my coin. Brat was unpredictable, got a chip on his shoulder, and wanted everything for free. Felt he'd been abused, and somehow was owed by all and sundry. Now and again I'd see him at the Phoenix Hotel bar, when he rolled up his shirt-sleeves and hung about with the white Hottentots.

He put on their thick manner of speech, a downtown brogue, like maybe it wasn't exactly him talking, but some bad brother of his sprung from jail. He told them that the abolitionist movement was only a fancy, they didn't have to worry, how politics had trends and phases, he had inside and privileged information. He continued to guzzle, bragging to them about how he had got his Daddy to change the will a few years back after the old man done got crazy on religion and wrote up another will on a whim to free all the slaves upon his death, at least that's what Brat heard because nobody had actually seen the document, crafty old Jehosephat had it hid away in a wall somewhere.

You couldn't locate the will no matter how much you knocked your fist against the wall, because Walter had done already visited his Daddy's lawyer, who even under the threat of a tail-whupping or being fired and replaced, kept insisting that Jehosephat had not left the will in his keep, and nobody at the bank, not even his cousin the vice-president who would have told him no doubt, knew anything about a safe-deposit box under his Daddy's name. Why, they could barely get the old man to keep money in the bank, much less documents.

Jehosephat didn't believe in investments or anything you couldn't actually see with your eye, like a house, crops, fields, chattel. In fact, Walter joked, it was about all you could do to convince his Daddy that a corn plant would spring from a seed. That was just too abstract for Jehosephat, and now after the bastard had enjoyed slaves his whole livelong life to bring him his bakker and likker and cornbread and pick the ticks off his blueblood dogs and rub his gums with linseed oil, yes he made them actually stick their fingers in his mouth and wipe the selfsame mouth at table, and trim his nose hair because his wife wouldn't do it, she drew the line there, and probably the slaves washed his rump-crack after he got done in the crapper, because Jehosephat hisself shore wadn't gonna touch nobody's potty hole. Not even his own, and after his personal coachman, in the olden days, done sat outside keeping grizzled counsel in the broiling sun many an afternoon without so much as an umbrella to shade his freckled bald pate, while Jehosephat wallered with whores and sundry other'ns. And after Jehosephat threatened to thrash the coachman within an inch of his life if he ever breathed so much as a word about what Brat's daddy called his sportsman's hour, where he got to make his own rules by which to play, he'd then go back to the normal way of living. Go back, even though Walter's mother, God bless her, who was taken to the Upper Room long before Jehosephat, she took mighty sick just from the plain misery of abiding his reckless foolishness. She abode, even though she knew about all of her husband's many peccadilloes, too many to keep track of even if you had the presence of mind to write it down in a hard black ledger book. She all the same pretended it wasn't happening, what difference did it make, she just knew she wasn't going to wash his dirty crap-hole. She would do that for her children, but not for a grown man. And God alone surmised what he might be doing with Felicia. She didn't even want to have suchlike called to her attention. But if whosoever was touching his backside, they might as well touch the rest of his hurly burly as well. She herself wasn't going to touch anything except his church clothes to lay them out on the bed after Felicia put them through the wringer washer and ironed them. That was about as close to Jehosephat's body as she wanted to get. And after he enjoyed all that himself, with no thought whatsoever to the consequences, Walter couldn't understand how his Daddy could get laid up by a fit of terminal sanctimony and decide to free all his slaves when he died, just to increase the slight chance that his miserable soul, if he even had a soul, might end up somewhere in the vicinity of heaven. It wasn't right to eat fruit all your life and then tell your son he couldn't eat fruit.

One of the fellows at the bar had tried to slow down Walter's spewing, said, "Excuse me, uh, Brat, that is, Walter, Mister Brathwaite, I mean to say, maybe you oughtn't speak of your daddy and mommy like that among common laborers at a public house, especially after they is both dead and gone to their reward," and then Walter, in a slurry retort, offered to knock the man down off his feet. Drunk as he was, I don't think he could of done too much damage, but the fellow who had spoke, out of respect to the deceased, averted his gaze and walked away from the bar, shaking his head while several of the listeners made witticisms about Jehosephat's backside that they would be repeating for days on end to any rogues not lucky enough to be present on that occasion of the spew.

As the trace met with a crick, I detected a presence down the drop-off. In its wild meander, the trace at this point veered back close to the Maysville Road, within a quarter-mile, as close as it ever got from then on. I slid off Stalker, barely setting one leg to the ground, letting the other foller. Untying my rifle from atop the bedroll, and slipping it from its soft leather case, I did my best to float atop the branch-fall and stub-grass, the way the Ojibwa once taught me by example. They called him Feather Sole for every good reason.

At the overlook, I spied below a mere girl, her face mottled with big freckles like a quail egg. She was so lost in dangling a hook from a length of twine that had I rolled bodily to greet her, I don't believe she would have noticed. I slung the rifle over my back so as not to startle her. "Hey, yon pip," I called out. She jumped up anyway, tangling her torso in a bait line.

When she'd recovered, she set herself in a stance and glowered me down. "Who in hell's blazes are you?" she challenged, her red hair putting a punctuation point on the question.

"Baskin," I said. I don't know why I used only my last name, as if caught off-kilter.

She took me in, my draggled clothes and slouch hat. "I ain't doing nothing illegal. Catching blue gill is all."

"I'm not the law."

"Never said you was. But grown-ups do pester. They always think you're up to mischief. I only like a lonesome spot to catch fish in, though today I've had no luck."

"How old are you?"

"Big enough."

"You talk big, that's for sure. Where's your parents?"

"As if you cared."

I mused on that blank accusation. "All right, I do care."

"Prove it." Like an idiot, I took out my pocket-knife and tossed it at her feet. "You giving me that?"

"Can't afford to. I use it daily. Or else I would. It's just for you to look at."

She poked at it with her foot, picked it up. Running her fingers along the carved pearl, the girl whistled. "I'll bet it cost a thousand dollars." I didn't contradict her. She closed the knife, tossed it straight at me, and I caught it. "My daddy is dead. Got himself stabbed over some lollipop in a wayside inn. My mommy has got the morphine rickets and mostly lies in her bed."

"I'm not a doctor, but I do believe that rickets is got by young folk."

46

"Well, that's what Daddy used to call them. She got all twisty-looking and stumbles around. When I stick to home, I get mopey. I stay there enough so she won't send me to the orphan's home. So mostly I ramble in these woods. Mommy's gentleman callers don't mind if I make myself scarce. And she barely knows whether I'm home or gone. I made myself a lean-to, stole an animal skin off one of her suitors, and it's comfortable enough. I can trap small critters, and the fish are plenty, excepting right this minute. I never come but for two or three days at a time."

"Have you been alone in these woods for long on this trip?"

"I was here today and yesterday. I seen a few people. A man who thought he might catch a bear if he went far enough. I told him he was in the wrong woods. He kept on anyway. You know one time I spied a falcon? Right on a cliff peak. He sat there for the longest time, then flew almost straight up. I think he was on his way to heaven."

"How would you know what a falcon looks like?"

"Seen it in a pitcher book once."

"And from that far away you could tell what he was?"

"I suppose you think your eye is so keen. Could you spot one?"

"More likely than you."

"My eyes is younger. You probably suffer from moculism."

"Moculism? I don't believe that exists. You made it up. Or did you see that in a book too?"

"You can't prove otherwise."

"All right, you win. I've got moculism and you saw a peregrine falcon flying at a hundred miles an hour into the sun. Now, back to my question. Anybody else besides the man hunting bear?"

"Yes. Three people. A man in parson's clothes. A lady in a summer dress with beads on the bosom. Someday I want a dress like that. And another man, kind of fancy dress too, only he had pants rolled up and was wading in the stream barefoot."

"Black or white?"

"The man and lady was white. The third, I don't know. His face looked—blotchy. Like it was melting off. That sounds peculiar, but it's so. And he caught a blue gill in his bare hands. I never seen nobody do that before."

"About what time?"

"Did he catch the blue-gill?"

"What time of the day were they here?"

"How come? Are you looking for them? Are you really the sheriff after all? Did they do a crime? Did they steal money? Was it buried in the ground?"

"I am not the sheriff. But I am looking for them. Because— well, they're friends of mine. We had a quarrel and I want to set things to rights."

"That's a lie."

I was astounded. I scarce knew what to say. I had been caught flat out by a slip no more than twelve year old, though she sassed like twenty. "What's your name?"

"Rae."

"Like ray of sunshine?"

"Sometimes. It depends on the day. Other times, like ray of thunder."

"I think you mean ray of lightning."

"I say bolt of lightning. But have it your way. Only don't change the subject." She cheated forward and took my measure once again with that quail-egg face.

"All right, I lied. And I don't do it well, because I seldom have cause. I'm usually on the side of the law."

"You don't look too lawful to me. Kind of scruffy for a sheriff."

"Tell me, Rae. Did those three continue up the Maysville Road?"

"I ain't telling nothing more until you let me know why in hell's blazes you're after them."

I couldn't help but sigh. She made me feel like a schemer. This half-sack of turnips was outwitting me. It was easier to give straight answers, without going into names. "Them two are abolitionists. You know what that is?"

"Nigger-lovers. That's what Mommy calls them, when she gets in her fits."

"They is helping the third man escape to his freedom. And it's against the law. So I need to find them."

"And you'll get paid for it. Or are you just doing a good deed?"

"No, it's for pay."

"I thought so. It seems to me they ought to put them other two in jail and let the third one go. He's the most useful of the bunch. I didn't see them catching no blue-gill."

"Well, they will go to jail if he gets free."

"That slave will get whipped and maybe killed if you take him back. Ain't that so?"

"Not killed. But whipped, yes, probably. I have no control over what happens once I turn him over."

"Well, I been beat plenty, and it don't feel so good. My daddy used to whale on me all the time before he got stabbed. And once Mommy hit me in the middle of the back with a fireplace poker when she couldn't get no more poppy. It swole up my backbone where I couldn't get out of bed and move around for two days."

I gritted my teeth. I knew I couldn't tell her anything untrue. "I promise that if I return him, and if he's beat, I'll go and steal him back again. How about that?"

Rae squinched up her eyes and fell silent for a spell. "I suppose that's fair. But will you fail?"

"I admit that I have got no experience taking slaves out of their master's homes and setting them to freedom. I do the opposite. But I'm in the business. I feel confident I could work it out if I had to."

She came close to me, as if the birds might overhear. "They was here about noontide yesterday."

"Was they in a coach?"

"That I couldn't see."

"So you don't know whether they took the road or the trace? I've had to make my best guess, because I can't go both ways at the same time."

Rae scratched with her stick in a patch of dirt for a bit, sending fire ants scurrying. "Yes, I do know which."

"I thought you said you didn't know if they came in a coach or not."

"They had two horses. If they arrived in a wagon, maybe they unhitched the horses. One black, with a white forelock. The other one, the opposite. Maybe they unhitched the coach a couple miles back, and hid it. To throw you off the track. That's what I'd do."

"It's possible. That's a smart deduction, pip. You've got the mind of a tracker."

"They took off down the trace. The woman with the beaded dress had to hike it up to mount. She didn't look too happy about it, but the black man turned his eyes away, and he jumped on the white horse with the black forelock. Off they trotted. The lady didn't complain. I think she was holding her breath."

"I see. Well, Rae, I thank you for your information. I've got to get on with my search. I hope you prosper and catch a passel of fish today."

"They're quiet. Must have heard you coming." She dropped her pole in the dirt. "I want to go with you, Baskin."

"I don't think I heard you right."

"You heard me. Don't play deaf."

"I am not taking no little girl on an errand this serious. Besides which, you got a mother and it would be unlawful."

"Oh yeah, you're a real law-abiding citizen. I'm sure you are. And you know why? Because it's legal to screw whores, and bust heads, and get so drunk you fall off your animal, and hunt down Negroes who never did nothing to you, without caring what becomes of them. All that's in the law books. And it's legal, I reckon, for a mother to spend all her waking hours washing her tonsils with morphine while her daughter is out sleeping in the woods so she won't get hit again in the back with a fireplace poker. Or if it ain't legal, nobody does nothing about it anyway. Do you think she'd care if I run off? She don't even bathe her own body for days on end. In fact, you've helped me make up my mind. Soon as you're gone I'm going to hightail it up the trace anyway."

"What do you expect from me, Rae? I never had a child. I wouldn't know what to do with one."

"I'm not no child. I'm thirteen. Old enough to work as a whore. My own brother already put the stuff to me before he shot off to be a pickpocket, and landed in jail."

"You ain't going to work as no whore. That's final."

"You have no say in the matter, Baskin. You ain't my daddy."

I was walking back toward where I'd left Stalker, trying not to make eye contact as she trotted alongside me, that glower of hers all fired up.

"I'm not in Lexington, where I could mind you. I've got business to attend."

"You said I was a natural tracker. Or did I hear wrong? I know the trace better than you. My uncle and his mates used to let me ride back-saddle on their hunting trips. I seen bobcats, owls, and of course lots of game. I know all the crannies, and I'm not gonna slow you down. If we don't run 'em down, when we get to Maysville, you send me into the taverns and hotels and I'll ask around and I swear I'll catch their scent. I'm a regular hound. Wasn't it me who saw them? Without me, you'd just be pissing against a tree and splashing your own britches right now."

I jumped on Stalker so hard I almost overshot. He whinnied in complaint. I wheeled him around, trying to create space, but Rae had her hand on the saddle edge, and wouldn't part with it. Being near her was like getting stung by wasps, hornets, and nettles all at the same time. As I tapped my steed's flanks, I thought she was going to get trampled under, so I had to brake. Her red hair was all disarranged. She was probably fuller of ticks than a long-lost hound. Her pants drooped like they was about to fall straight off, and the knees couldn't have been more chewed up if you'd set a pack of rodents loose on them.

"Get the hell on the back of the saddle. You'll do everything I say exactly the way I want. We're going to be back here in two days. And that's the last I'm going to see of you, runt."

Without a stirrup, Rae climbed up the side of the saddle as if she was a prisoner scaling a wall.

A family of foxes was feasting on a milk snake at a clearing. From what I could see, the snake in its turn had choked down a robin's egg. As we approached, the foxes looked up at us with their slope eyes, but did not move aside, so I shied Stalker around them. "I love their fur," said Rae. "Sometimes I sneak up, hide behind a stump, and watch one groom itself. Even the males are ladylike."

"I never thought about that, but you're right. In Ojibwa language, fox is *waagosh*."

"What does that mean?"

"It means *fox*."

"I guess that was a stupid question."

"Not stupid." I smiled. "Knuckle-headed is all. *Waagosh* also mean that their tails flicker."

"Did you ever watch a candle, Baskin, on a blowy night when the wind is whistling through the cracks of your cabin where nobody chinked it? The flame dances around, and you keep thinking it's gonna go out. But then it don't. The wind seems to suck the flame right off the wick. And then, it comes back, like magic."

"I've spent plenty a late night watching a candle burn down."

"I guess you're a bad sleeper, like me. They call that *moonsack*."

"I don't think that's correct, Rae."

"Is too. It's like you try to put the moon in a sack, but it keeps shining through."

"Maybe. We ain't going to make no gain on this trace. I was hoping to catch them out, alone, camping in the deep wood. But they're gone. We'll have to wait until Maysville. Are you sure they came this way?"

"Sure I'm sure. Why the hell are you asking me again?"

"Don't get bristly on me. I don't see no sign of recent hoof among the animal tracks."

"What if they cut loose of the trace and stomped through the trees?"

"I would of noticed that."

"So are we going to ride hell for leather now?"

"Normally I would. But I ain't gonna bounce you off the saddle and give you a broke neck."

"I can hold on. I plan to be a circus acrobat one day, and I'll walk along the pony's back as she runs around the ring with a five-foot feather coming off her brow."

"Is that so?"

"You'll see, peckerwood."

"I've decided not to go in hot pursuit. Stalker is tired. I spurred him all the way up here. He can't travel no faster."

"I wanted to run at a dead gallop, and feel the air lift up my locks liken I was an Arabian princess."

"Riddle me this, pipsqueak. You ever handled a gun?"

"I seen plenty."

"But have you shot game?"

"Like I told you, I set traps I make out of sticks. Sturdy, too. Whatever small thing wanders in, I have as a meal."

"So you know how to skin?"

"Lickety. I'm hell with a knife, Baskin. My daddy taught me that much. I can bone a fish, when they's big enough."

"Don't you beat all, little slip. I'll teach you to bag a jackrabbit. I've got you figgered for a fair shot."

"All right! I allus wanted to handle a weapon. But after Daddy died, Mommy went and sold all his guns for the morphine."

I fotched the rifle down. It was a half-stock, lighter than most, nine pound. I don't need much weight or punch, as my aim is not to kill a person. It's more important to come out quick, exactly so that shots won't be fired. With them long spidery arms of hers, I reckoned she could handle the nine-pounder. I fed in the shot and give her the brass ramrod from the pouch to pack the barrel. She run her hand along the walnut stock like she was stroking a baby.

I instructed her in how to stalk a jackrabbit, where to stand in hiding, create a good sight line, gauge the distance. I motioned for her to stand between my legs, as I brought my arms around to show her how to hold the pistol. She nuzzled her cheek against my forearm and straightened her head, looking straight on. Them thirty-two inches fit in her arms better than a rag doll. Her first shot was at the trunk of a tree, and she missed. Her second, me still holding her arms steady as she sighted, hit the tree trunk. We searched for a rabbit, which were plentiful in these woods. When we spied one, we did the same as before, and her shot was just off.

"Damn it, Baskin, that's three shots for nothing. If you'd quit bothering me, I could aim for real."

"After you hit your first rabbit, you'll get a turn on your own."

With me guiding her again, she wounded the next one we saw. Not a clean kill, just blowed off its back legs, but I finished the rabbit off with a quick slit of the throat.

"Not a bad start, little girl. We'll make a sharpshooter out of you yet."

Nary a tear sprung at her eye. I handed her a hunting knife. "Can you handle that? Or will you cut your elbow off?"

"You're comical, Baskin. It's a wonder you ain't in the music hall, entertaining cowboys. I said I knowed how to bone fish."

"Then pretend the rabbit is a fish. And pry as much shot out of it as you can, nice and slow, while you're at it. Take it slow, unless you want me to do it. One nick of your own skin, and you're off duty."

Rae give my big knife a doleful look, as if she might be hearkening to her dead pappy. Then she took it in hand, turning the blade over a few times. She squatted over the rabbit and went to work. "That's sharp. Don't hack your finger off." She paid me no mind whatsoever. It wasn't the prettiest cuts I ever seen. Yet she gutted it somehow and trimmed the skin off. I didn't intervene. She turned to me with sticky hands and a frown. "Truth is, I usually hack off a piece of meat and leave the rest for the buzzards."

"That's a waste. Go on and wash your hands at the rivulet. I'll pull the bones off, pick shot and get a fire started. Bring back a couple of chunks of wood." She skipped down the watershed, crunching pinecones as she went.

MAY 1833
MAYSVILLE, KENTUCKY
DAN BASKIN

RAE AND I MEANDERED AMONG the stalls right off the main square. Scads of black-eyed Susans and daffodils, even yaller roses, gushed from cans set all around. A young chap, cowlick and spittle, scarcely higher than my waist, ladled beer from a bucket. The beer had no foam, in spite of all the sloshing. A girl was jumping rope, but just as her pigtails got into a rhythm and her pallid knees begun to fly, she had to stop to make a new space for herself as the crowd pressed in around her without taking the slightest notice. I bought Rae and me two cakes and slices of smoked pork wrapped in butcher paper.

"A woman won't take you seriously when you've got ragtag britches." A vendor was holding up a pair of pants, trying to persuade a feller to buy. He could have used the improvement, but he shook his head and walked on.

"Come on, Rae. We're gonna get you some trousers that fits." I studied her from top to toe. "On second thought, how about a dress? You said you was a-wanting one."

"With beads?"

"No, we'll stick to something practical." She sulked. "But pretty." That brightened her up a bit. We found a green dress that fit her clatter of bones. She put it on right over the clothes she was already wearing. I told her she looked like a proper girl, and she twirled around so I could see the whole number. I bought her shoes as well that buttoned up the side, and a straw hat with a green flower on it. "Now, don't lose that hat, because it's the only one you're gonna get."

"I won't, Baskin." She had the hat clutched between both hands so hard I swore she'd crush it.

"You can put it on your head. That's what it's for."

"What if the wind blows it away?"

"There ain't no wind. Fit it on your crown real snug and hope for the best. I ride like hell on my horse in rainstorms, and mine don't never fall off."

"Okay." She squashed the hat down on her noggin and let go, one hand at a time. She'd noticed that one of my boots was split, and tried to get me to repair it when we passed a leather-smith. I said I'd tend to it tomorrow or the day after.

"Right now we're going to find a hotel. I would normally sleep on my bedroll under the sky, but I'm making an exception."

"A hotel! I never slept in one. Is that where you take your women?"

"Never you mind. That is not matter for the mouth of a little lady what just put on a green dress."

"Is you and me going to sleep in the same bed?"

"Of course not. What a thing to say."

"I'll bet they'll only have rooms with one bed."

"In that case, we'll ask the proprietor for a cot. And if he don't have one, why, I'll sleep on the floor. The main reason I'm getting us a room is because I'm going to leave you indoors while I tend to my affairs at the riverside. And I don't want you running around on the streets like a damned waif. You ain't in the woods no more, and they is lots of bad people about."

"But I want to come with you!" I could see the fire coming up in that little swole-up face of hers. "I come all this way a-horseback. I want to see you kitch that slave. I'll help."

"I thought you said he ought to go free."

"I trust you, Baskin. I know you'll do what's right for everybody."

She got me flustered again. "You—listen—I don't even know if I'll capture anybody. They could be long gone by now, and you and me jest on holiday."

"They ain't gone. I know they're here. Maybe a few feet away from us, peeping around the corner."

"If I do sight them, it will be a dangerous moment. There might be guns going off."

"Guns!"

"And if they do, I do not want you to get hurt, young lady."

"Why not?"

"Because it ain't fittin'."

"And why else?"

"Because—well, you're somebody's treasure."

"Whose treasure am I, Baskin?"

I looked down at the split boot, to where my sock peeped through. "Lots of people's, Rae. I'm sure you're a treasure to all kinds of people."

"No, I'm not. Only to you, Baskin."

"That's enough of talk. Here's a boarding house. We'll query and maybe the woman what owns it can keep an eye on you so's you won't run amok raising an insurrection."

May 12, 1833
Northern Kentucky
Jacob Pingrim

W E HAVE ARRIVED AT ANOTHER safe house where we are to stay tonight, this one right at the edge of Maysville. There were words as to whether or not to try to cross in the dark, a change of plan for which I have no appetite, but I said nothing. Dana was a partisan of waiting until the morning, claiming that it is more cautious and better for me to be well rested. Cal is afraid that a possible search party might gain on us. It seems he likes to get it all done in one day, as a rule, and this is the longest he has ever dawdled. In the end, the standoff was settled in her favor, though she is the novice. He insisted we get going early enough to avoid any steamboats.

The idea is to be out before dawn, once the river patrols have died down and gone off to sleep the morning away. For the first time, I'm having doubts about whether I should cross at all. If I return to Lexington on my own, there will be a beating, perhaps, but I have received those before. And even that may not happen. Walter is tired; he has liver problems, ones that have laid him up for days at a time. The Mistress is likely to intercede. I can tell Walter I had to get off by myself for a couple of days, that I slept in the Negro cemetery next to my grandfather's grave, and the escapade may pass as nothing more than a darky's stubborn whim.

Walter can report abroad that I was "broody," claim to have given me three or four stripes as punishment, and that will be the end of the matter. He'll be able to say to his friends and associates that I can't live without his largesse; my return will stand as proof that I have been treated well, and that there is a kind of affection between us. He can continue proclaiming that there is nothing wrong with slavery itself, only with the "bad" masters. His associates will pretend to agree, and mock him to one another behind his back. I remember their saturnine faces at the parties he gave, when I was serving table. They let him go on with his political theories as long as the brandy held out.

Chances are, he'll simply nod and set me back to work, without tears on either side. If I do get caught, then of course, it's going to be terrible. Then there's no telling what Walter'll do. Kill me, perhaps, unless I kill him first. A task for which, after all, I have little appetite. My hatred should have been enough, by now, to bury a hoe in his neck some sunny morning as he came to inquire about the progress of the string beans. Why haven't I ever been able to do so? I have surely fantasized about his murder more than once.

And to what am I going? Does some improved state of affairs await me in Ohio and beyond? I've heard all kinds of stories, not all of them pleasant. The North is no paradise; of that I am well aware. I'm not one of those naïve souls who believe that if you follow the drinking gourd, all will be fine. Although Reverend Fenton has supplied me with a couple of names of persons in Boston, I will, if I make it, arrive alone, without wife and child.

Long since, Creech and Rye have reverted to their elemental form, their soft pine coffins, the ones I built with my own hands, rotted away, allowing my wife and child's merciful dissolution from pestilential flesh to something cleaner, baser, able to be absorbed into the water table. *Daddy, Daddy*, Creech would burble as I bathed her with a bucket. *Miss-a-siss-a-ssippi. Miss-a-siss-a-ssippi.* No knowledge of that dreadful word except beautiful sounds. Will a sentry pick me off as we row, and will I fall overboard and sink underwater? Will my submerged corpse flow westward along the Ohio, carried by floodtide and implacable currents? Will it sooner or later surface as it bloats to a fetid blackness my skin has never possessed, to get caught in the branches of a fallen sugar maple with exhausted roots? Will the men who find my body fish it out? And if so, will they at least dig a hole and throw me in it, in a perfunctory show of compassion, dispensing with the superfluous coffin? Or will they maul my corpse, throwing pinecones at it, gravel, peppering it with buckshot for the sport of releasing the hideous gases?

The couple hosting us could not be nicer. They keep asking whether I have blisters on my feet, as if I had run here the whole way. I assure them that I do not, only a slight callous from wearing a pair of new shoes. They are imagining me in manacles, bloodhounds bounding behind, baying at the moon, as I stumble, up to my knees in swamp-mud. Forget that there are no swamps here, only the occasional seasonal bog no larger than the room in which they serve me crumpets and cake. They are exceedingly polite, warm, and I admit that it feels good to be treated like a human being, to be served rather than to serve, only I wish our common discourse weren't surrounded by false gaiety.

I wasn't shut up in any closet upon arrival, and it seems I am simply going to be allowed to sleep in a guest room like everyone else. Apparently my anxiety about being cloistered was discussed among them, and the risk of not stashing me in the basement was deemed acceptable. I don't think I could make it through another suffocating night like the last one. I thought my heart would stop. I smile like hell, and make jokes about our mutual situation, its eccentric peril, raising my eyebrows, raising the world on the lever of my levity. I am trying very hard not to cast off on them the cocoon of gloom and torpor that enshrouds me at this moment. I'm supposed to be as happy and expectant as a pregnant mother, if a little nervous. Naturally, they want to experience this radical transaction as a good deed, and project my future success, imagine me as a tailor on Chesapeake Street. It's all they can do not to burst out in song that I am the most well-spoken Negro they have ever encountered. A light startle sparkles in their eyes. I have changed into the clothes they kindly provided, their fit approximate at best, after scrubbing myself down as if I had been in steerage for the past month. The host presented me with a wool coat, the dimensions approximately mine; it belonged to his grandfather.

Only we can't talk about anything of importance. I don't know their last names and don't want to. In case I am captured and tortured, I don't want enough information to implicate them. Cal and Dana have already put themselves in my hands, and that's enough guilt and stress to bear. So I ask about the sterling silver on the sideboard, admire its workmanship, and the lady exclaims that it hails from her deceased aunt, that the heirloom has been in the family for several generations, and she shows me the tiny, indelible scuff marks of its use, which polish will not remove, in order to prove to me its authenticity. This is no replica, she tells me. It's the real thing.

And I, base, wicked, insufficiently grateful, struggle against the desire to throw up my borrowed shirt, exposing my back and its profuse scars, shocking my generous and noble hosts, indulging in a childish perversity, telling them that polish won't remove those either. And adding, as they quake, that those scars have also been in my family for generations. Of course, I do no such thing. I ask quietly for another spot of tea, and the imperiled hostess scurries to the silver pot, all too happy to oblige.

I ask permission to go alone to the breakfast nook, with its large picture window overlooking a grassy dale. There's not a house in sight from that vantage. I know they are all worried, nonetheless, that someone with a telescope is perched in an oak tree, scouting, waiting for my appearance. That fear is not entirely unreasonable. But tacit nods are given all around. I can see that Dana, alive to the flux of my mood, wants to follow, but she stays herself among the porcelain cups. I am allowed a few moments of privacy to grapple with my melancholy, and the fact that unaccountably, at this moment, the one other person I am missing is Mistress Brathwaite. Me, homesick? How perverse.

I make myself comfortable in an armchair and stare out the picture window. This summer's afternoon is pregnant with shimmering, blue-silver swarms of gnats, live as sparks from a fire. And yes, I am thinking of the mistress, the only living woman in whom I truly have any real trust. Dana means the best, she is sincere, but I mostly know her through her dinner parties, where I ladled from a tureen into her bowl. And we will separate soon.

As for my former owner, I do not even evoke the word 'mistress' mockingly. I desired her not, though her looks, no doubt, entitle her to be desired by many and sundry. Why was her husband, Walter, so jealous of me? I never cast a single unchaste glance in her direction, during those months when she took me out of the fields and put me into house service, in spite of Master Brathwaite's objections. If I had a pang of sentiment toward Master Brathwaite it is because, by falling into unreasonable blind rages, ones whose real causes he never understood, he acknowledged my existence as a man. Yes, I had a lingam and testicles, ones he'd rather not think about at all unless they were being carved out of me as I swung from a tree branch.

As for those few half-beatings the mistress gave me, I grudgingly respect them, simply because she, barely six stone in weight, ludicrously meted them out with her own small hand. I counted that as a compliment. She might readily have broken one of the many fine bones located between her wrist and the tips of her fingers. She could easily have called on the burly Irish fellow, Slim or Slam or Slab or some such name, who came to replace broken panes in the intricate, handmade windows and perform a myriad of other small specialty labors. Such delicacy and nimbleness in those huge knotty hands and squat fingers of his and such thickness of expression in his lean face! Slab itched to give me a sound thumping, for no reason except that I kept her company indoors while he labored under the sun in the dooryard tapping out panes. Sometimes she'd send me out with a glass of water for him, which he regarded as if I had handed him a thimbleful of vinegar.

But she availed herself not of his stout smithy's arms, always at the ready. She spared herself no labor. The vapors would overtake her and some remark I had made, not the least bit controversial, would set her off. Then she'd fly at me as if we were in the midst of a lovers' quarrel. I thank her for that. Once, I was actually contemplating suicide on that day. She began to smack me with her open palm, over and over. Her slaps and tears ratified my existence, making me decide to prolong my then-miserable life. Mistress Brathwaite started me out of the worst of it. She gave a fright to my hiccup.

She confided in me many things that, had Master Brathwaite known were being shared, would have gotten me flogged at the least and murdered at the most. With his thin profit margins and poor business acumen, he was loath to lose any owning of value. But even he had his limits.

I knew about the loss, barely out of the womb, of her seventh child. A certain morning, she first had me drive her out to a remote parcel of land her side of the family owned, down past Garrett's Knob, where she had fashioned a grave for little deceased Selma, in secrecy, because her husband instructed her to get over that death once and for all. She had six other children to look after without moping over the seventh and he forbade her to place a headstone in the dooryard, as she had wanted.

Mistress and I made a later visit to the gravesite in the midst of one of the harshest winters we experienced together. That same winter, one of her other children contracted pneumonia and nearly died also while sweating out the fluid. When we arrived at Selma's grave, the headstone was entirely capped with snow. We two stood in silence revering its blankness, as if it could have been the grave of anyone; perhaps her grave, perhaps mine. This prospect, more than the searing, shearing February wind, made her shudder. Without her asking, I knelt on the ground, felt the moisture seep into my trousers at the knee and brushed the snow away, revealing the letters of Selma's name and the astounding dates. She'd had the stonemason chisel August 14, 1817 as the date of birth and August 14, 1817 as the date of death.

She approached me from behind, as I remained kneeling. As she came into my peripheral vision, I could tell she wanted to bend down and kiss me. Instead, she reached out absentmindedly and stroked my hair several times, as if petting a good dog. I didn't feel condescended to. I took those pats as the equivalent of a kiss, knowing that if she could have, she would have buried her face in my neck. It's better for her that she didn't. She only would have avoided my gaze the next day and the day after that. Not that I would have looked at her in any particular or different way, but she would have begun to imagine that I did and that is the same as my gazing on her with lust. Then she would have had to banish me from the house and she needed my company very badly at that time. Yet what a kiss there might have been. Three months later, winter had fully passed and both she and I had been riveted back into a more banal certitude. It was better for us simply to have Master Brathwaite remove me from the inner premises, claiming that he couldn't dispense with my botanical expertise. Actually, he never used the word "expertise," nor "botanical," but rather muttered into a glass that I was "uncommon good with plants and suchlike." It was the highest compliment he ever paid me.

Naturally, the next day, under the slightest of pretexts—I believe I had accidentally trampled some ears of corn while traversing the cornrows—he had me beaten again with the infamous plank, the blandest instrument of torture ever devised, yet as fearsome in my case as any of the iron screws of the Inquisition. Mistress forbade its use during my entire time as a house-servant. Now it returned to action. She stood by with quiet fatalism, finally turning to go into the house. At least she made herself watch me being beaten for a couple of moments. What it might have cost her to witness that spectacle I can't calculate. The blows hurt like hell, but I minded that beating less than almost any of the others I received over the years. On that day, I knew I was indispensable to both of them.

Now here is Dana, the swish of her skirt hem announcing her arrival in the breakfast nook. She is explaining to me that the others have repaired to the sitting porch so that monsieur can smoke. Cal, ever the gentleman, will suffer the stench of the host's motley Creole tobacco as the wife fans it away.

"What is it, Jacob?"

"I'm anxious. That's to be expected. Or not?"

"Of course. I'm sorry this episode is dragging on. At least the pea soup was good."

"I know all of you have made great sacrifices to bring about my liberation."

"It's our pleasure."

"Pleasure. I hardly think that word describes the experience on any side. It's all dreadful."

"Don't say that. You're not thinking of running off on us, are you? Like you did when you jumped from the coach?" I remained silent. "Because I'm getting that distinct feeling."

"Yes, I was thinking about it."

"That would be ironic, wouldn't you say? Us forming a search party to keep a slave from going back home."

"Don't worry. I won't leave you in the lurch. After what you've both done."

"We're not going to force you. I only say that were you to do escape in reverse, you might regret it later. I've known Walter Brathwaite for a fair amount of time, if only in society. If he ever gets his hands on you again, his full wrath is going to come down. He'll make an example of you to his other slaves. He's just that childish."

"I'll take that as a word of caution."

"So I can depend on going to sleep for a few hours tonight and knowing that you'll be here when I awaken?"

"Yes, madam. You may count on it."

She took an apple from the fruit basket and rolled it around on the tabletop, much as a small girl might. "You have beautiful eyes, Jacob."

"Don't say that."

"I meant that they're soulful. Smart. I'm paying a compliment. Maybe you don't get those often."

"Not any more, I don't."

"Well, I retract the statement. I don't mean to offend you."

"You want to know what's going on inside those soulful eyes?"

"Naturally."

"Nothing fascinating. The usual pain. My wife and child died, five years ago. And they're on my mind."

"Yes, I remember their deaths. It was horrible. We spoke about it, briefly, but you were in another world. Your eyes actually lost their color for a while."

"But it's not Rye and Creech as such who occupy my thoughts right now. It's me myself. After they died, I moped in my shack. I was obsessed by the fact that there were free blacks roaming around Lexington. One of them owned a tack shop over on Deweese Street, where Master Odrum sometimes conducted business. It didn't seem to bother him in the least to pay his money to a black man. 'Does good work,' I heard him comment. He sent me over to have saddles repaired one day and there stood the owner, in an apron, his head as smooth as burnished leather, humming some minstrel tune, quite pleased with himself. It was all I could do to keep from strangling him with one of the harnesses that hung from the wall."

"Is that when you first decided you wanted to escape?"

"No. That desire is recent. It welled up one day when I crushed a fistful of honeysuckle blossoms. The aroma was unbearable."

"Didn't you think about getting another mate? After the grief, I mean."

"After?"

"Surely you had opportunities."

"Oh, yes. The two available young females on our grounds got scared off by my dark looks and pithy phrases, when they tried to bring meals and console me. After a couple of barbs, they didn't speak to me much. One of them, Effronce, a sweet sad soul whose own husband had been sold off some years earlier in Louisiana, hoped that, as kindred spirits, we would make common cause, and perhaps work out a common-law arrangement. Effronce didn't expect much. More than anything, I believe she just needed a man in her bed from time to time. I probably should have gone to her, as she, more than anyone, could have understood. Somehow, she had extinguished the bitterness in her heart and learned to serve with a cheerful disposition. I held that against her as much as anything."

Dana stood and held out her hand. I took it, and she gave mine a squeeze. I allowed myself to return the squeeze briefly before letting it go. She held my gaze in hers an instant longer before releasing me. "Get some rest, Jacob. You need it."

MAY 1833
MAYSVILLE, KENTUCKY
DAN BASKIN

A FORK OF LIGHTNING CROSSED THE sky, followed by a roll of thunder, as Rae and I hurried down a side street. "Thar's your ray," I said. We checked into the hotel and I hauled my saddlebags up the stairs. The inn had a keep for horses, and the hay looked far from stale, so I knowed Stalker would be all right.

I was looking forward to sleeping in a hotel. My bones ached. Rae sat on the bed, testing the mattress, and bounced a hundred times, running her hands over the tassels on the spread, jabbering about this and that. They was a washstand, bowl and pitcher, straight back chair, and a picture of Andrew Jackson, looking like a carrion bird. I remembered that he'd killed a man in a duel.

I'd already made my guess that the trio would cross to the east of the burg's edge. Nine of ten are going to do the predictable thing. It's a big country, in theory, but in practice almost everybody has a version of the same idea. It's as much a matter of timing as of location. I know the best places to enter the water and leave in this weather.

A big thunderstorm was brewing, we had already caught its mineral scent, and it would hit sometime tonight. The current would be running swifter before the morrow. I had my choice narrowed to two crossings, each within a couple hundred yards of the other. In this weather, it almost had to be one of the two.

"Baskin, are you listening to me?" Rae stood up and twirled.

"No."

"I was saying that me and you ought to take a trip out to California. Is that more than a day from here?"

"Mhm."

"You're not paying me any mind!" Her voice went up a span, shredding the air.

"Rae, can't you throw yourself down and take a nap?"

"I can't, cause yer settin on the cot."

"That bed is yours tonight."

"For the both of us?"

"No, jest yourself. I'll take the cot."

"Well, I still can't lie a-bed, because my rump-bone is bruised from the ride. I wish I'd rode all the way here in a coach, like that one they was in on the trace. The lady set up high and coasted off like an Egyptian queen. And my belly still hurts from the half-cooked rabbit we et."

I caught a glimpse of her sly little eyes. "What did you say?"

"The rabbit wasn't cooked."

"Before that."

"That my rump—"

"You said 'rode here in a coach,' and 'set up high and coasted off like a queen.' Was you leading me on about them taking the trace on horseback?"

"As I remember, Baskin, you was the one said that."

"You know full well I did not. I ast you."

"I meant before the trace—I was—that is, I thought I saw 'em unhook the horses, but I can't be sure."

I flew to my feet and backed her toward the wall in two quick steps. "You made the whole tale up. Was they even there on the Clover Trace? Did you see the gentlefolk and the darky? Or did you not?"

"I swear I did. She had lace on the bottom of her dress."

"What else did you make up? Did your daddy really die? Is your mother on the laudanum? And did she beat you with a fireplace poker?"

Tears brimmed around her eyes. "They really did stab my daddy. He walks with a limp. And it was him beat me once, when I smashed the eggs in the hen coop."

"And your mommy?"

"She smokes cigarettes." I become aware of a smear around her mouth, like when a little girl tries to put on lipstick. In her hand she squoze a bar of chocolate, half-melted, and spots of cocoa was smeared on the front of her dress. "Whar in the hell did you get that confection?"

"I—I borried it."

"You borrowed a bar of chocolate? You mean you stole it."

"I was hongry." She held it up for me to inspect.

"Hungry? You ain't done nothing but eat since we got here. I thought you was gonna pop. Didn't I pay for every blamed geehaw you ast for? And don't you think I would have bought this too?"

"I wanted the chocolate, that's all."

I slapped the chunk out of her hand. "You little thieving bitch. You've played me for a fool. You made up hogwash against your own mammy to soften me up. God knows that woman must be out of her mind with worry. I don't know whether to saddle up and take you back tonight, in the dark, and you a-wailing the whole way because your tailbone hurts and you want more chocolate, or finish this mission. Either way, you'll cost me."

"I love you, Baskin."

"Shut your little slattern mouth. You're a child. But there's no differ between you and all them whores I lain with, as far as you'll say whatever works to a man to get your way." I raised my hand again, and Rae let out a wail. I found the door, and slammed it behind me, shaking the timber of the frame.

I almost tripped going down the stairs. Outside, pellets of rain had blowed up. People was a-running down the street, looking for an overhang. I let the gusts blow over me. A man plowed into my shoulder and fell into the gutter. As he righted himself out of the sop, I didn't offer a hand. I had left my hat on the straight-backed chair. My hair was drenched, as were my pants, shirt, and skivvies. I pulled my shirttail over the holster to keep the gun dry.

I banged open the door of an establishment. As I bungled in and flung myself down into a chair, I drew the looks of surprised diners. A short man sidled up to me, speaking in a language that must have been Italian or Polack. He was trying to hand me a menu. I didn't take it from his hand. Finally he came back and set down a bowl of stew, which I didn't touch. I threw a few coins on the table. He brought a mug of hot liquid and patted me on the shoulder.

How long I set there, I can't really say. Other customers came and went. The Polack replaced my mug with a new one. I took a sip to make him feel better. *Agbára.* I said the word out loud two or three times. He smiled and said, in English, "You're welcome."

I walked back the few blocks to the hotel. The rain had settled into a steady pour. Betwixt the cobbles, a crooked stream carried sundry trash downhill. There were no more light flashes. It was going to stay like this until morn, and I was just glad Rae had somewhere dry to pass the night. I would wash her dress out in the bowl so she wouldn't have to wear a blemished garment tomorrow.

In the lobby, a gent had took out his monocle and held it up to the light. As I bounded up the stairs, my drenched sock squelched. The door to our room stood wide open. Before I walked in, I knew Rae was gone. I called out twice.

I bounded down the stairs. The desk clerk was counting out bills. "You seen my little girl?" He shrugged and went back to his stack. Outdoors, the street was empty, save two roughnecks at the entryway of a tavern across the way. String music bounced from the door. When I went in, every last straggler had found a seat. A feller sat perched on the edge of a cane-bottom chair, plucking the banjo and crowing straight into the ear of his nearest neighbor.

> When you go to the boatman's ball,
> Dance with my wife, or don't dance at all;
> Sky blue jacket and tarpaulin hat,
> Look out my boys for the nine tailed cat.

I scanned the tables of laughing faces. On them lay booze and swill, pork rinds, pickles, and beer. Peanut shells crunched under my boot-soles.

I was about to withdraw, when I caught sight of Rae at the bar, atop a stool. She sat in profile, talking to a man. She had on the green dress, and it looked like she'd tried to wash out the stains, and instead spread them across the whole front of the garment. She'd tarted herself up with rouge. Who knows where she'd got it. Her hair was gathered up into a wretched knot that passed for womanly wiles. A tumbler set on the counter and she sipped on it through a straw, laughing like a coquette, above the banjo music, moving her head around like an epileptic fit was just a-coming on.

Next to her sat a big oaf in a stripy topcoat, his mess of hair mudded down with tonic. I don't even know how the stool could bear his weight. He had placed one hand on her shoulder and was patting it, squinching up his face to show how interesting her palaver was to his ears. His dull wits was trying hard to make his eyes shine bright. As I moved close, I could smell whatever taffy he'd splashed on his neck to disguise his pork stink. I caught the words "little one." I stepped right between them.

Rae didn't bat an eye. I'm shore she had shit her britches on the spot, but she wasn't going to let on. "Baskin," she cried out, as if she could not be more happier to see me.

"Shut up."

"Now that ain't no way to address the little lady."

"She ain't a little lady. She's a girl, in case you hadn't noticed."

"That's a matter of opinion. I find her enchantingly advanced in her mind-set."

"Baskin, this here is Duane. Baskin is a famous slave-tracker. He has seized upwards of four hundred slaves and was decorated by Andrew Jackson for bravery in the line of duty."

"Now ain't that something. I'm a textile mag-nape myself."

"Magnape? You mean jackanape?"

"There is no sense getting personal. What say I buy you a cider and you run along and relax to that banjer concert while Rae Jean and I continue our reverie?"

"How about you move along before I move you?"

The oaf stood up to his six and a half foot stature, and meant to surround me with his bulk. "I ain't afeart, sir. I consider myself a couth blade, but I have caused mayhem on the frontier as a cavalryman. I will cause mayhem now if the occasion calls for it."

I grabbed the idiot by the back of his neck and slammed his head on the bar four times. I could hear his nose break on the first contact. The bar had got real quiet on the sudden. I pushed back my wet shirttail, removed my pistol from the holster, put the barrel right on his broken nose, and held it there. "I consider myself uncouth. I don't like to blow people's faces off. I only done it the times I had to. But right now, yes, I would enjoy watching little shreds of your skull fly all over the bar-back. And if I don't explode your head apart this second, it will be because she's setting there, and for no other reason."

He tried not to weep. "I didn't give her alcohol, I swear. She was sipping on ginger-fizz. She told me her charms was for sale. Said she didn't have no daddy, that he died of the typhus in the Foreign League. If I'd knowed her pa was going to show up, I'd have give her more of a berth."

I let Duane the mag-nape go and he backed off to nurse his broke face. I stared down the barkeep. "You allow this truck to happen under your sight? Don't you know better than to let a grown man flirt with a child?"

The barkeep was not fazed. He dryly poured another man's drink before answering. He'd seen the like of me many times before. "Maybe if you took better care of your daughter, she wouldn't have got herself in this fix." He slid his hand under the bar, as if he might have placed it on his own firearm. I put my gun away, grabbed aholt of Rae, and rushed her out. She had been dead quiet, but she went right into action, hollering that I wasn't her daddy, that I was going to sell her into white slavery to my friends. No one so much as stood up from a chair.

In the hotel lobby I roughshod her toward the stairs. She'd turned into a hellcat, long arms trying to scratch my eyes, shrieking like a demon-girl in the hands of a tent-preacher. I had to pick her up bodily and press her to my chest to carry her across the carpet. Her yelling for help the whole time, that she had been kidnapped by a famous lady-rapist, for somebody to call a constable. The several guests in the lobby and the clerk paid her no mind whatsoever, except for sidelong glances. They assumed I was her father, that she was my disobedient daughter in a tantrum, and that I had every right to manhandle her. If I'd beat her half to death, nobody would have stepped in.

I carried her upstairs, where the door to the room still lay open, and kicked it shut. "Rae," I whispered to her ear full of bug bites. "Rae, I'm going to let you down. I'm sorry I said you was a tramp. No matter what, I shouldn't have walked out on you." I eased her down on the mattress, where she sobbed for a good long time. She kept telling me that I was a bastard, that I was a despicable person, that I would be the most horrible father in the world, that it was a blessing to the world I'd never had children of my own, but that who knew, maybe I had spawned some on them loose women I liked so much, that there were probably lots of little girls and boys running around the countryside with sky-blue eyes like mine, blue eyes so crazy and so quiet, lips so crooked but so pretty that women liked to kiss, swagger, rough broad shoulders, and that ridiculous boot that needed to be sewed up, and all them kids had horses with soft footfalls like Stalker. She kept ahold of my hand the whole time she was sending me to deepest hell, her freckled fist inside my palm. I closed my fist around hers until she fell fast asleep.

That night I dreamed of the Yoruba gal. She come floating out of the water, face up.

I woke at four a.m. The air in the room was a-prickle. I found the candle by stealth and lit it, then bent over the bed and shook Rae. I told her she had to dress in her pants and shirt. "I ain't going," she mumbled.

"And I ain't leaving you here by your lonely. You won't be out of my sight today."

She surprised me by rising up at the second call without complaint, washing her face, and putting on her old clothes. She smiled at me, freckles pale in the candlelight. "Hey, Baskin."

"Hey, pipsqueak."

"Can we get a pumpernickel roll on the way to the river?"

"Every place will be closed. All I got is hardtack and jerky in the saddle bags."

She rolled her eyes. "Mmm-boy. That's a tracker's breakfast, I reckon."

"It is today." She ate a ration, making faces the whole time. Down in the stall, we unhitched Stalker, who wouldn't stop nuzzling my shoulder. He looked like he had fed a-plenty. He nickered until I shushed him. The stones shone clean in lamplight as we crossed the square. It was still drizzling. I offered Rae my jacket and she said she'd rather cling to it than wear it. The clops of my lone horse rang along the lane until we reached the edge of town, where it gave way to packed earth. Soon the aroma of ferns closed in. Stalker picked up his pace without my bidding. A scatter of morning larks defied the wet branches with scant song.

The way Rae cheated up against me, I figured she had fell back asleep. But out of the dark she asked, "Baskin, how many men did you kill after all?"

"The ones I had to."

"Well was it three men, or seven hundred?"

"A handful."

"Would you have killed that man last night?"

"If I had to."

"Over me?"

"Don't exalt yourself."

"It's hard not to draw a lesson that I was the cause."

"You're lucky it wasn't your nose I broke instead of his." A stand of pines swayed in a low but steady breeze, shaking hard drops over us.

"Would you really break my nose, Baskin?"

"I'll break it right now if ye want."

She spread her arms around my back and held on tight. Stalker was in the mood to supply her with the dead gallop she'd wanted on the trace. I let him go apace a quarter mile before I checked his progress. The drizzle had become fog. It rolled off the river sheet and drifted past the banks.

"Why did we stop?"

"We're near the first crossing. I'm putting you to work. We'll dismount and search for a rowboat. If we find it, we bust a hole in the bottom with a crowbar. If we find a raft, we pry it apart with the same."

"With all this fog, it's like a treasure hunt."

"Okay, enough of talking. Our voices will carry far. It's silence from here out, and in case of need, a whisper at most. Them abolitionists could be anywhere about. Understood?"

"Yes," she whispered.

I led Stalker by the bridle. I didn't want to have to whistle for him should we get separated. He'd woke up good and sound with his morning run, and the cold had got him over his sleepy nicker. All I could hear was his long breath in my ear, with a whiff of oats behind.

"If you get lost from me, Rae, make a low hoot as if you was an owl."

"Hu-hoo! Hu-hoo!"

"Not so sparky. Just natural-like." We walked along the rushes, feeling at tree trunks. They was no way I could straddle a palisade and watch sentry unless the morning sun come and burned off the fog, which didn't seem likely. I could hear the hiss of the river before the moving air exposed patches of it. There was no foaming across rocks, like the narrows of the Elkhorn, only the long, steady pull of a big river's expanse.

"I found it!" Rae's voice hollered. "I found a damned row-boat!" From the sound, you'd think she was entering the gates of heaven.

"Remember to keep your voice down. If that's possible."

"Don't get ironical on me, Baskin. You said find a boat and didn't I find one?"

"Yes, you did. Would you like to do the honors?" I held out the crowbar I'd removed from the saddlebag. She took it and whaled on the planks, making three good-size holes in no time.

"I don't see what's the differ about me talking, when splintered boards make an awful racket." I didn't give her the lie. All the same, she hushed and we kept walking, up and down a stretch of several hundred yards. Other than a couple of loose boards, we found nothing else. At length I told her we would park and listen. It could be hours, so not to get impatient. I removed my jacket, set the rifle up against a tree, and handed the coat to her to use as a blanket. She shivered and settled into my coat, burying her face in the brittle leather and smelling it like it was a bouquet of daisies. The only sound was the lap of river-tide and spots of bird-song, mostly wrens and grackles. I spotted a single white-bellied wren asleep on the ground, a few feet away, his tail straight up. I could only imagine the grackles we'd left behind, peeping their blue heads out of the pine-thicket we had passed. Rae begun to sing snatches of a child's rhyme in a lowdown tone.

> Lavender, blue, rosemary green
> You air the king but I am queen
> Shuck the corn in the midst of storm

While my bosom keeps the bed warm.

A set of voices bled through the mist. I held up my hand and Rae quit her singsong. At first I thought the noise was coming from the north bank. It stopped and started, and the direction seemed to change as it bounced off the water. A woman, a man, the same woman again, the man again, then another man. I put one hand over Rae's mouth. Her big green eyes got wide, as her clammy breath pushed into my palm.

The day had broke. No sunshine; only light. The fog commenced to lift. Now I could locate a sole male voice. They had got to the boat, and the preacher cussed. That made me smile. I had cussed a-plenty; now it was his turn. Staying against the current in a boat would be difficult, but not all-fired daunting. With strong arms, the trip could be made and back in less than an hour. Now, without transport, Pingrim would have to swim on his own. And that was a different game altogether.

The journeyers had done fell still. A woodpecker clacked, worrying at a sap-tree. I motioned for Rae to crouch down and stay put while I advanced in the wet undergrowth where the katydids buzzed. Then I seen them. Clothes fresh; looked like they was headed to a prayer meeting. The conversation had turned to the fact that Jacob would have to disrobe to make the swim. That's what the preacher said. Then Pingrim, who had not yet dismounted from the mare, answered that he had been told he would not have to swim, and the preacher said, "I didn't promise anything, I hid this boat and now it's wrecked. The next one I can use is two miles up, and it's too dangerous to waste any more time. Someone is patrolling or lying in wait, otherwise the rowboat wouldn't be smashed. You can swim, or you can return. I don't have any minutes to waste."

I admired his practical streak. It was the right thing to say in the circumstance. The woman was turned away as if the slave had done got naked, but in fact he had on somebody's wool coat, much nicer than any one I'd ever owned.

Finally, he hoisted himself off the horse. And that's just when I run forward, grabbing the preacher by the neck, yanking a pistol out of his coat, and throwing him to the ground. I could feel the bite of the carved ivory ring against my finger as I squeezed the gun butt. I trained the guns, mine on the slave and the preacher's on himself. I figured he knew his own piece was loaded.

"If you've got a pistol, darky, lay it on the ground, and shoo that horse. You don't look like no shooter to me, but I been surprised before."

"I'm not armed."

"All the same, take off the coat and pitch it on the ground. The shoes, too. In fact, all of ye fetch off your shoes and throw them in the river. Miss, you come get comfortable right here alongside the gent. Now, first off, you're all catched. Accept that fact. Any heroical ideas that are bothering ye, put them clean out of your minds. Else your next home is a bier."

I could see that Jacob Pingrim remembered exactly who I was, though he might be loath to let on. He appraised me in the same stuck-up way as he had at the Phoenix, the day he shined my shoes.

The preacher spoke. "Are we being apprehended?"

"We'll get to all that. First, Pingrim—I want to know where she is."

"Who?"

"You know who."

"I'm afraid I don't."

"The Yoruba woman."

"Ah, her. Is that who you came for?"

"I came for you. But as long as we're both here, I might as well ask."

He studied me top to toe for quite some time. "You don't know the name of the love of your life? Did you travel all the way here to find out?"

"I traveled to pocket you."

"You've got us." The preacher had rose to his feet. "Why don't you let him go? What does one slave more or less matter?"

"To you or to me?"

"You can say he was on the far bank when you caught up with us. I can give you fifty dollars for your trouble."

"There is a five hundred dollar reward on this chattel. And I plan to use that money to buy back—"

"Who?" Pingrim smirked at me.

"Don't get sassy. I'm in no mood."

"Her name is Abejidé. It means 'born in winter.' Because she was birthed in the middle of a blizzard."

"Well, whar is she?"

"What makes you think I know?"

"Because you sent a message to me."

"I sent you no message." Now he shifted his gaze for a long look at Miss Curbstone. Fenton also appraised her with a skeptical humor, and she had nary a returning glance for neither.

"One way or another, I guess they's loose tongues about. Once one person knows, maybe the whole world knows. It's hard to keep all the secrets amongst the strange tribe of them who seeks freedom."

"And who is it told you that I knew anything?"

"Never you mind. A reliable source."

"I see. Meaning someone of your tribe. What makes you sure that whoever told you first heard it from me?"

"Only Rickman, my boss, was witness to our—time together. And I'll swear it wasn't him."

"Yes, Rickman, the gentle betrayer of chattel. Witness to your tryst. I remember his kindly smile as he took my own wife and child in hand. Almost like an uncle. Of course he wouldn't betray you. Did it ever occur to you that Abejidé herself told lots of people, after she was auctioned off, and just before she left Lexington, about her experience of being sequestered? Her own kin, the other slaves at the market. And later on, when she got to a bona-fide plantation in Virginia, the tale continued. Of all people, it seems that you, the one who, so they say, speaks some Yoruba, would realize that half of the people who go on the block at Cheapside are kin. Descended from the Kingdom of Benin. For a time, our rulers weren't willing to trade their men, but the women, yes, always. *Fun mi owo na.* Abejidé is a distant cousin of my dead wife. The traders liked to buy a whole school of darkies from the same group of villages, if possible. It's easier. You only had to pay off one or two *obas*, instead of several. Like casting a net and bringing up a school of cod. You don't ask the cod who their relations are, right? You drag them in and let them die in the hold of a boat before you chop off their heads. Did you ever ponder that?"

"No, I never did."

"We all knew about you. What you did to her."

"You don't know what passed between us. You wasn't there."

"No, I wasn't. I can only imagine it. *So o fe sun pelumi?* Her terror, her youth. Your superior physical strength. Your ability to explain things in your own way. I imagine her with urine running down her legs."

"She felt desire."

"Maybe she did. Who's to say? She was seventeen. Her body might have decided to take what it wanted at that moment. But what did you think she was going to say afterward? What a beautiful experience it was? What a gentleman you were, and how much she was looking forward to a return engagement? Or a real engagement, with a jeweled ring? How proud she would feel at the altar, and what gorgeous children you'd have? And how much you would enjoy their little victories, and clip their hair as souvenirs for a locket, knowing that eventually they'd be sold off?"

I wanted to tell him she'd gave me a ring of ivory, but it would only sound worse, as if I'd stole from her. "I'll admit that I never got that far in my mind. I wanted her. That's all. But not as chattel."

"The irony, Mister Baskin, is that if your children were born of a white mother and a black father, they would go free. Because the assumption is that a white woman would never voluntarily go to bed with a black man. Those are the laws of the Commonwealth of Kentucky. I learned because I myself had a white father and a black mother. That's why I'm a slave. I don't even know who my father is, or was. But I don't imagine he was as noble as you. He just had the usual lust. The other interesting fact I have often mused on is that the lighter your complexion, the more it angers your master, and the more he'll beat you to keep you in your place. Ask any light-skinned Negro and he'll tell you the same." He took off his shirt and turned around so I could see the scars that covered almost all of his back.

"Whatever my mistakes of the past, I will make them right. I will treat her like a wife. I'll live somewhere they don't have slavery. Up north, in South America, I don't care where. I'm giving up slave catching. I had done give it up already, until I got the news about her."

"So, you're going to let me go free if I tell you where she is?"

"I would. I swear I don't care nothing about you going back to Brathwaite or not. Only I need those dollars to buy her back."

"Well, that's not my problem. Today I'm looking out for myself. Maybe the reverend will take up a collection for you, if you don't turn him in, too." Jacob took off his socks and vest and walked to the bank. "If not, then what? You'll beat the truth out of me with your rifle butt? You won't get anything from my mouth. I've been whipped once too often to be afraid of that prospect. As for shooting me, go ahead. If the alternative is going back to massuh, I don't care whether I live or die. You'll be doing me a kindness, I think, to finish me."

He had begun to wade through loam into the river, his back to it. I raised the rifle, putting a bead on his forehead. I wanted real bad to hurt him. Not for pay. Only on account of what all he said. His mockery. What did I care of his travails? I had enough of my own. I heard a rustling at my back, like a buck about to spring. I whirled and thar was Rae, skidding to a stop.

"Don't hesitate, Baskin. Fire a shot, as if he was a jackrabbit about to bolt. I want to see you in action."

"Stand back, pip. I told you to stay put."

"Well, ain't that what you learnt me? Don't doubt, you said. True to the purpose, that was your schooling."

"I never said any such. That was all in your head."

She lunged toward the rifle, and all I did was move the butt aside and trip her up where she'd fall and not disturb me no further.

She clawed at the dirt. "You didn't plug that giant last night neither, when he wanted to screw me. When're you gonna act like a man?"

"You don't know what you're saying, Rae. You ain't seed no corpse, excepting rodents and such."

"What do you know? I seed a passel, and I'll see more still in my tender years."

I turned back to Pingrim. "I don't aim to kill, or wound ye either. If that was my purpose, I would have done it right at the start."

"Then do we have a bargain? You let me go, and I tell you where she is."

"Yes."

He was in the flow up to his knees, legs already a-straining to keep upright. Pingrim was strong enough, I reckoned. It was going to be one hell of a swim.

"Three weeks after you raped her, and let her get sold at Cheapside to a gentleman from Virginia, who very much liked the look of her, Abejidé drowned herself in a drainage ditch on his property. They found her face down, attended by a cloud of mosquitoes. As it was told to me, there was not even a pine box, and no funeral of any sort. The master ordered that another ditch be dug right away, next to the canal, and she be thrown in it. The plantation owner's name is William Chapin. I hope that helps. He shouldn't be hard to find. They say he's quite a prominent citizen in Charlottesville."

Pingrim turned and swam out into the torrent. For a while, he was making good progress, angling himself upstream, raising his head every few strokes, choppy and jerky and fighting for breath, but sure and steady, his figure growing smaller. He went under, resurfaced, went under again, come back up. None of us said a word; we just drew closer to the bank's edge. As Pingrim reached the middle, the thick of the current caught him and swept him downriver, clean out of our sight, in a matter of seconds. Simply put, he was gone. The woman uttered a sharp cry and moved as if to leap in after him. The preacher stayed her from any such.

I shouldered my rifle. "The two of you is free to go. Don't speak of me and I won't speak of you. From what I know, hence and forth, we never met. Let's go, Rae. We got a long road back to your home place."

May 13, 1833
Ohio River
Jacob Pingrim

THE WATER DRAGGED ME DOWN, down, down, and all of eternity ran through my nostrils. I cried out, hark ye angels, spare me your delicacy. Dredge this channel with my boisterous body, lest the ditch contain one stray carp. Together may we drag our bellies in the mud before the angels whisk me anew into the air, above where the trunks were scorched by men building illicit campfires or holding torches, that could be read from the air if God were so inclined. The angels set me down, scraped, choking, my throat made slime, on a shoal of shale on the north bank. I was as surprised as anyone to find myself alive. Then I entered into the wood, saw a hoofprint in the mud, a squashed fly in the hoofprint, chiggers in canebrakes, ships of cloud puffing in the airstream.

My left foot was bruised by stones. There were rushes, bulrushes, cows and dung. I slopped through terra infirma, mosquitos swarmed, wild geese screamed. Next thing I knew the starry sky and my tarry scarred skin had become one. Scuff the rind, wind the watch, watch the fireflies scotch the darkness with their dull green luminescence. My presence, even when I'm presumed dead, lost here among rafts of trees, boils up an abrupt belch in the cosmos.

The wound that pierces the black sky, making visible a breach of blue, will not heal. The firm fact of me cannot be forgotten. In Cheapside, and at the riverside, trackers hold flames aloft and call my name. Even if I were to wake up dead, my going off north of the Ohio requires that someone must pay. The score is tallied with a broken stick of chalk. As I fester in half-sleep, wearing someone else's shoes, a size too large, the crickets report to one another my meager condition. Somewhere along the way, I stole out of the woods long enough to steal a shirt, pants, socks, shoes, and an undergarment, from an unattended cart. Then back into the woods.

Dear Effronce, who wanted to be my beau, only remembers me as the transient wet streak between her legs. Slugs touch me through my pant legs while I slumber, as their slime tracks venture ever so slowly up my shirt toward the next millennium. The slash marks of brambles that decorate my calves are slapdash.

A toad hops as I traverse a farmer's night field, still afraid to show my civil face in this so-called free region. It lands with a thump on a sodden stump, then a slab of stone, then the stone-cold ground, and I feel the toad trying to bust from its blistered skin. Each time I poach a muskrat, its acrid entrails incinerate my sadness. No matter how much I spit, one word remains: survive. Rancid acid blackens my taste buds and turns the world's primeval flood into the weak water of my saliva. In the burnt branches starlings slap their wings against ash, urging me to inseminate the earth with my brackish sperm. I lick my own sticky hand, to remember where I came from.

PART TWO
THE CHARITY BALL

MAY 14, 1833
MAYSVILLE ROAD
DANA CURBSTONE

SOFT UNDULATIONS OF CLOUD SHAPED up. They looked like a woman's hair combed into a chignon. The river rushed below, receded as they fell inland. No burble now, only the soughing of grass-tops shaken by pockets of breeze. Patches of field riffled, and stood tall again. The first clusters of true sunlight burst through the branch overhangs, splashing dispersed leaves with sudden gloss, then shade supplanted it, then more sun. A sweet pestilence burst from the fringe of forest they skirted. Perhaps it was a tripped deer, gone to rot, or the collective shedding of the shells of bugs, overripe berries and pelts of woodland rodents expired from natural causes. The horse's rump under the saddle rolled beneath her legs, tickling her soft parts. Dana let go a deep sigh, emptying her being.

"Wistful?" He didn't turn around on the saddle, instead he spoke the words directly ahead.

"You could call it that."

"Well, what's done is done. Can't change a whit of it. Jacob is well along. It's his own struggle now, not ours."

"You're right. His struggle is his, and ours is ours."

Cal turned with a half-smile. "So, you understand that. I thought maybe you were going to swim across after him. To keep him safe and on track."

"Don't be ridiculous. I'm an even worse swimmer than Jacob."

This coaxed a laugh from Cal. "Then I'm glad I didn't have to send you in to rescue him."

They had to go back for the coach, then to Lexington. She wanted to tell him to take off for parts unknown. Fatigue stretched itself out within Dana as the horse fell into a rhythm on a rare smoother patch of the Maysville Road. On the way up, it had all seemed bumpy.

For a while, she fought the sleepy sensation, wanting to drink in the day, to decipher its sense of the possible. At last she gave in. Dana dozed against Cal's back, somehow cozy as a child in a featherbed, listening to the faint simmer of the summer fields as the warmth of the rising morning enveloped them. All at once she was jolted awake. Through the scrim of her gummy eyes she could see that three men on horseback blocked the road by an outcrop of rock. The first sported a mustache too large for his face. The skin of his neck was too ruddy for his jacket, the color of his eyes not a color at all, but rather a degree of hardness. Dana tried to cast off the sluggishness of her dream state. Something was indeed happening, and she would have to be a part of it.

"Dismount, please." The other two men hung slightly back, one haggard as if perpetual disappointment had wasted his body; the second, rotund and complacent as if he'd fed off the other man's being. All three had on uniforms—formal yet somehow threadbare.

Cal slid off the horse as easily as he had mounted it, his extremities limber. He extended his hand, which the man disdained to take. "Corporal, good morrow to you."

"I'm a sheriff, not a corporal, sir. An officer of the law."

"My mistake. How may I be of service to you gentlemen?"

"Are you Calvin Fenton, and is this Miss Dana Curbstone?"

"The same."

"You are being sought out for possible acts of sedition, treason, and the mongering of another person's chattel."

Cal stiffened, but his intonation betrayed nothing.

"I assure you that we have done nothing wrong."

"Can you explain your whereabouts for the past seventy-two hours, and the purpose of finding yourself on the Maysville Road in the company of this woman?"

"I ask you not to refer to her as 'this woman.'"

"Sir, are we not all of woman born?"

"Looks awful like a woman to me," said the rotund one.

"I could swear she was female," said the haggard one.

"I was called on an errand of mercy."

"I heard otherwise," said the sheriff.

"Oh?"

"That's right," chimed in the rotund one. "A fisherman in these parts, feller named Stan Cadwaller, said he seed y'all consorting with a big buck what wanted to take a swim in the river. Said there was another white man too, and a little redheaded girl. I wonder where they went. Cadwaller was too afraid to waylay y'all. Didn't know but what ye might be armed. Said he thought he seen a gun in the pip's hands. So he emptied his seines and went on along the bank upstream."

"You've got to be joking."

"Ain't joking, Reverend. Cadwaller is what he went by. It's a pickle of a name."

"I mean joking about us abetting an escapee, which is what you seem to be implying."

"You are about to be charged with seducing a slave into his freedom, as soon as I can get you back to Lexington."

"Cain't believe a woman like yourself been caught up in this-like," said the rotund one, speaking slowly to Dana's legs.

"And what am I like? I'm quite sure you don't know the first thing about me."

"Peace, Dana. These gentlemen will discover that we've done nothing except in direct service of the Lord."

"Are you going to stand by while they take possession of us?"

"We'll trust in God to open up our path, if that is His will."

"So we're to be traipsed to Lexington like slaves in a coffle, and do nothing about it?"

"Are you suggesting that I should overpower these three by force? I'll try if you want, but I don't like my odds."

"This preacher is talking some sense, little lady. You ought well foller his example."

"Wisht I had a woman like her. Sparky. Mine is a right-out bitch," said the haggard one, lending the final word a melancholy pitch. "If she was to roll over in bed by mistake it would flat-out kill you."

"Shut up, both of you," said the sheriff.

"I shall follow the Christian example," said Dana. She reached out and lightly brushed the hair of the haggard one. "No wonder this poor soul is so skinny, with a wife like that. I'm going to call you Jack Sprat."

"Madam," said the sheriff, "I'll thank you to keep your distance. Remount the horse you were riding so that we may escort you."

"Ah, well, escort me, then."

"Let her ride with me," said the rotund one with a hiccup resembling laughter. "I'd like it if she mounted my horse."

Dana smiled, as if charmed. "How gallant."

"I don't believe that arrangement is called for," said the sheriff.

"Ah hell, Marcus, you is always dragging us around on account of nothing, fotching us out of our beds before daybreak to finger the entrails of some raccoon what got squashed by a rock and you think it's a capital case of murder, because ain't nothing much ever happen down this way, and everybody done catched a nigger except you. Let us try to enjoy ourselves on this longacre ride that's gonna shake our tailbones to pieces. It's only a minister and a schoolmarm, for pity's sake. Don't bust a gut over it. And we is deputies who don't get paid nothing for our labor unless it occurs to you to buy us a stick of beef jerky once in a harvest moon."

"Very well. The lady may ride behind you. And that's as far as that matter will go."

"How far it goes is betwixt her and me," the rotund one muttered. "Two dollars says she gets paroled in three months, after she shakes a tail-feather at the right people. I know her kind."

"You seem to understand women well," said Dana.

Cal shifted his feet. "I prefer that she remain on my saddle."

"Yeah, Reverend, well you ain't got no preferences in the case. If you'd of lived by the Good Book, you'd not be in this spot."

"A lawsuit will come from this maladroit seizure of our persons."

"I don't even know what he just said," the haggard one confessed aloud. "Talks and talks, and don't say a got-damned thing I can cipher."

"Preacher, you was doing better when you was more compliant. Remember that the meek shall inherit the earth. My pappy done told me that a bunch of times after my mammy took a stick to him."

The two men burst out laughing. The sheriff didn't try to quiet them, just let the laughter spend itself before he spoke. There was a hint of pity in his tone.

"Sir, I am handing you off to the authorities, and how they dispose of you is their business."

His eyes searched Cal's slumped frame, as if he really wanted to know the answer. But Cal gave him no sign, instead stared into the nag's choppy mane. Dana turned away and the rotund deputy, suddenly all flourish and manners, helped her mount, even looking away briefly as her skirt left the ground. As they got underway, he made conversation in a voice as bouncy as his horse's gait. "This ride won't be so unpleasant, ma'am. Chesapeake, once we get her up to speed, she'll canter rather than trot. As if you was atop a gig rather than a-horseback. You only got to know how to speak to her right. She won't let nobody ride her but me." Dana didn't try to slow down his discourse. She simply kept one finger hooked in his belt loop, and let him wrap himself in two-bit gallantry as a hawk silently glided overhead, keeping perfect time with the horses' progress. The clouds had puffed up; they were going to be mammoth by midday, but no rain would fall until much later. The ever-moving air, though sticky, kept the bugs off. If someone had seen the group from afar, they might look like a picnic procession, or a damsel and four musketeers.

Then Dana yanked the rotund one's revolver from his waistband and slid to the ground. At first the men seemed to think she had fainted and lost her grip. They wheeled back to come to her aid. That's when they could see the revolver raised, her holding it with both hands. She stood dead still. The sheriff drew at once, challenging her. The haggard one's hand went for his gun, but he left his fingers at rest on the butt without drawing, not seeming to know what he should do under the circumstances.

"Madam, drop the gun."

"I won't."

"Give me the gun, Dana."

"I don't want to kill anybody. All I ask is that you let us ride on by. We've done nothing against you. I'll do what I must."

The rotund one had developed a smirk. He looked more amused than afraid. "Now ain't it a fair sight. Done got a bit of Kentucky sod under her nails and likes the feel of it. This strumpet thinks she's a frontierswoman."

"I might turn out to be one."

"Christ-o-hell, this is about the most entertainment we's had in a fair stretch."

"Shut up, Dwayne," said the sheriff. "It's your mouth that got us in this fix in the first place."

"Why, Marcus, we ain't in no fix. Little lady, have you ever shot a gun?"

"No." She half-lied. Not at a person, she hadn't. Only with Monsieur Fontenot.

"Didn't think so."

"How do you know the firearm ain't half-cocked, like you?"

"It stands to reason. And I know at the least that a revolver contains multiple rounds. I'll take my chances."

"Don't try to outthink her, Dwayne," said Marcus. "You haven't got that much brain."

"I've got the gift of gab, and that has to come from somewheres in my noggin. Hell, you is just worried that if she aims for me and pulls the trigger, she might hit you."

"So it is fully loaded and cocked," said Dana.

"I told you to keep your mouth shut, Dwayne."

"Loaded and fully cocked, exactly like me."

"I understand how you feel," said the haggard one. "I only laugh to keep Dwayne company in his mockery, but my heart ain't in it. Truth be, I wish I had the get up to do what y'all done. I never can make up my mind about what's right, that's a fact."

"Nobody cares about your politics, crack-pot. You're probably half-nigger yourself."

"Madam, I must ask that you relieve yourself of the pistol at once, or I will be forced to wound you."

"I won't."

"You'll only end up injuring yourself. As you can see, my firearm is well-drawn."

"Bejeezus, Marcus, you ain't gonna clip her. I know better and so does she."

"Dwayne, I will thank you to shut your trap right now, or you yourself will end up on the receiving end of my shot."

Dwayne gave all and sundry a slow regard, a shred of sweat-wet leaf stuck to his upper eyelid. "Fuck all, this is downright comical."

"Somebody's got to end this standoff." Dwayne walked straight for her, pistol at his side. "Give me that now, little lady, and let's end this charade."

Dana shot him in the foot. He yelled out, a mixture of surprise and pan. "You bitch! Oh vinegar Jesus!" he hollered from where he sprawled, covering his foot with both hands like a beloved pet.

The sheriff took advantage of the distraction to lunge forward and hit Dana in the face with the butt of his gun. She too went down, and as she tussled with the sheriff for her pistol, she shot him in the head. Blood flew against her blouse and she felt Cal drag her away from the sheriff's limp body.

She lay against the earth, dirt in her mouth, trembling, Cal's heft atop her, pressing her down. No more percussion shook the air. About their persons lay a rare quietude.

"Get off me," she whispered at last.

Cal offered his hand. She shook it off, got to her own feet as casually as she could. The haggard one had his gun drawn still. He said, "Missus, I may look to you like a sliver of a man, but it falls to me to take charge of this situation. I'm on your side, in a way, but I'm a crack shot, learned in the Black Hawk War. I killed five or six Indians. Don't trifle with me, please. I'll have that pistol, sir, and any other in your possession." Marcus, meanwhile, continued to curse and holler.

Cal took the pistol from her and handed it over. The haggard one emptied it of its cartridges with an unexpected efficiency "Damn, but I've got a headache like as a rock slab cracked my crown." The haggard one had delicate fingers. She hadn't noticed before. Nice hands, ones you'd expect to see playing a piano in someone's parlor at eventide, as the crepuscular glow suffused the taffeta curtains. He removed a rope from one of the sheriff's saddlebags and began to bind her wrists behind her.

"Begging your pardon, Marcus, but you're gonna have to get up and step lively on the one foot. We have two prisoners and a corpse to get back to Lexington, and you to a surgeon."

A bird chirruped. She could view it clearly where it perched on a nearby branch. It was a tanager. Adult female, yellow under-parts, olive back, dark cheek, gray wings, and greenish feathered edges of the tail. She observed it closely as she felt a thick knot of rope form between her pinned wrists.

JULY 1833
FAYETTE COUNTY COURTHOUSE
DANA CURBSTONE

S HE HADN'T WANTED TO TAKE the stand, but her chief attorney had advised her that it would doubtless go better both for her and Reverend Fenton if she were to answer direct questions to the best of her conscience and knowledge, and simply to exude her natural feminine charm and educate the jurors about how delightful she could be. She wore calico, flattering her figure yet not accentuating it. Her lips were dabbed with a hint of beeswax, which made them glisten without adding color. Makeup, carefully applied, covered most of what remained of her facial bruise, leaving only enough to remind the jurors that she'd been mistreated. Upswept hair made her face and neck open to inspection without flaunting. He said in the end they would vote on a feeling, an impression, rather than the facts of the case. The prosecutor called her "Mademoiselle Curbstone," or "the distinguished lady," and referred to her directly in the third person.

Cal refused to take the stand in his own defense, even when his attorney advised that his refusal to do so, albeit correct and constitutional, would only make him appear stubborn.

"Do you understand, Reverend Fenton, that your silence is not your ally?" asked the judge. "The more we know about the circumstances of this affair, the better we can determine the necessary justice to the case?"

"I do understand, your honor, but I also know I have the right to remain silent. And that is my wish. I've done nothing I am ashamed of before God, and that is enough for me. Whatever I say will be twisted."

"That remains to be seen. Have you so little faith in democracy, Reverend? Do you have contempt for its institutions?"

"I have no opinion about that, your honor. I do not make the laws of this republic."

He wore the same suit every day, even when she sent a proxy to waylay him in the corridor, as they were led out, between the second and third days in court, to urge him to wear the new suit she had helped him pick out and had insisted he purchase only a month before. He'd never put it on. It hung lifeless in his bedroom, like a man dangling from a rope. Perhaps he thought the simplicity of his person would carry the day. She listened to one character witness after another, even members of his congregation to whom she knew he had given solace in the midst of their quiet drinking binges and adulteries, their gaming habits and land thefts, turn against him, slander him in the most malign little ways, as if to pre-emptively cancel out his knowledge of their own sins, their expressions puffed with the smug piety that can only be summoned by the knowledge of immunity from reprisal. She wanted to leap from her seat, seize a brush from her purse, and rush over to straighten Cal's hair. She wanted people to see that he was refined, that he simply had been lacking a woman to attend to his needs.

"The reverend had many a queer notion," said one woman whose face bore too much powder and whose strategically tailored dress could not disguise her girth. "He often talked about how we are all equal in the sight of the Lord. And thinking back on it, I think he might have liked to see Negroes filling those back pews."

A man who nervously kept putting on the hat in his lap and kept being reminded by the bailiff to remove it, until the bailiff at last asked for it, allowed that he'd seen the Reverend coming and going at odd hours of the night. "I first assumed he'd got himself a woman. We all kind of hoped he would, truth told, and maybe he did get a woman, maybe Miss Curbstone was his woman."

"Please limit your remarks to matters relevant to the case."

"Yes, Your Honor. I only mean that I'd seen him be overly friendly to free Negroes in the town, as he thought they was like him."

"And what has that to do with comings and goings?" asked the defense attorney.

"Maybe nothing. But it's putting two and two together. If it ain't a woman keeping you up half the night, then why would he be a-coming and a-going like that? He ain't got no sick mother that I knowed about. And again, why was he so keen on those Negroes?"

"Because he's friendly?"

"Well, they's friendly and they's friendly. That's all I got to say. I leave it in the hands of the State and the Almighty."

If the charges against him were dismissed, some pillar of nourishment—not her, because she fully expected a conviction given the severity and obvious nature of her crime—but one of those ladies from the church who had forever thronged around him clacking peppermint in their teeth, the fleshpot Miss Postlewaite or the widow Culkin, would take care of him, affording him the quiet little life of a married preacher who ended the day pushing back the leftover plate of bones from the roast chicken, to leaf through his breviary and dust up his Greek while his wife, in the next room, plunged her hands into the sheen of scalding soapy water, welling up with gratitude that soon she would be lying abed with six feet of still-firm man.

A couple of times, as they awaited trial, she'd persuaded the jailer to take around a basket of leftover foodstuffs from the visits of the legislators, blackberry jam, a loaf of bread, a chunk of country ham, but the basket had been sent back, untouched, and she ended up telling the jailer to keep the victuals for himself and his wife of seventeen years, Sally, for the trouble he had taken on her behalf.

She wanted to know whether Cal blamed her for the turn things had taken. On the stand, she hadn't uttered a single word against him. If she'd thought that sleeping with the warden, whose salacious bent was becoming clear enough, would have helped secure Cal's release, she would have consented to the arrangement. What was her body to her now, except an encumbrance, the site of pointless if fastidious ablutions? Every day they brought her lavender water, at the warden's own behest, because "a lady needs and deserves to stay fresh." Fresh for what? The warden had kept popping in before and during the trial to see how she was holding up, always preceded by a harsh whiff of aftershave that seemed to be manufactured from overripe fruit. His admittedly fit legs, ensconced in trousers pressed and starched to a texture stout as hardtack, led to a determined potbelly, so round and firm beneath his chambray shirt that it looked carved from wood.

It revolted her that he'd taken to dressing up since the first day she was brought in, dandifying himself as if for a date, peppering her with pleasantries in his well-spoken but upcountry "courting" patois, which provided a grotesque contrast to the actual state of affairs. Things were already absurd enough due to the constant presence of the heavy-breathing legislators whom she felt compelled to receive in her cell as a political calculation, knowing that both Cal's fate and hers might in the end derive from whatever fantastical impression these men took to their bedsheets after they fondled the puppy, dandled the daughter, knocked the ash from the pipe, picked their teeth, patted their wives good night on the rump, extinguished the wicks of the lamps, and turned away on the mattress to indulge in their private nocturnal counsels. As much as she didn't want to think about it, countless men throughout the Commonwealth of Kentucky were flogging themselves on account of her. She had become the biggest free peep show north of Memphis. They were coming in by boatloads on the paddle-wheels to get a gander, and she didn't begrudge them, only hoped that this ostentation of her female figure might lead to some practical result that would redound to Cal's favor.

She often imagined herself sneaking to Cal's cell at night, having cozened a key from the jailer, unlocking the door with a soft click, and a groan coming from Cal's cot in the darkness. She would hold a lamp over his face, one she'd filched from somewhere. She would wipe the sweat from his face with her own linen dress, and its clean smell would revive him, as if she had offered mineral salts. Their lips would touch, and in that instant, she'd remove the savor of guilt from him, and return to her own cell to tremble.

Cal. He maintained his resolve to the end. Was he being strategic, or did he want to be a martyr? It was hard to tell. Dana had never imagined that killing would be easier than standing trial for murder. The killing had only taken a moment. Even now she didn't regret doing it; she only regretted that it had to happen.

For some reason Dwayne was not present, as though he'd been instructed or allowed or forced to stay away. She wasn't so naïve as to think that Monsieur Fontenot, who did not attend the trial, hadn't played a role; his invisible hand was felt in many places. Dwayne might not even be in Kentucky at the moment.

"Mister Lamont. You are the only material witness to this killing. Why this is the case, I don't know, but the only other witness has vanished. So we are all relying on you. Did you see the gun go off?"

"Well it's an interesting, question, sir. I heard it, that I can say without exaggerating."

"No one is accusing you of exaggeration."

"I seen the sheriff and Miss Curbstone wallowing on the ground together." There were titters from the gallery.

"Are you trying to entertain us?"

"I don't know how to do that. I've never been accused of entertaining anyone."

The attorney was clearly exasperated. "Are you an abolitionist?"

"Sir, not that long again I returned from the Black Hawk War, where I was decorated. If I killed Indians, why would I not kill Negroes?"

"What does that have to do with anything?" the prosecuting attorney practically shouted.

"Well the way I see it, if I was loath to kill Negroes, you might accuse me of being on the side of these abolitionists."

"You are not the one on trial!"

This time hearty laughter came from the gallery.

"For God's sake," thundered the attorney, "I want to know one simple thing—did or did not this woman kill the sheriff and wound his deputy!"

"I don't know, sir, you'd have to ask her."

The state's prosecutor stunned the court after three days of ambiguous testimony by announcing that the murder charge was to be dropped summarily on a technicality having to do with a second examination of the corpse. The death was ruled a suicide on account of the brutal nature of the gunpowder burns, which could not likely have been inflicted by a female unused to handling firearms, certainly not at almost point-blank range, without severely burning her own hand in the process. Not likely, repeated the prosecutor, looking hard at Dana as if for a contradictory sign, but she gave none. The wound to Dana's head insisted that if anything, she had nearly been knocked unconscious, perhaps while resisting arrest, making it less likely still that she was in a position to do harm to anyone.

No one subpoenaed Monsieur Fontenot. Few knew of their relation, and no one knew how they spent their time together. It appeared the prosecution would only go forward with the charge of sedition, which was quite serious, rather than split focus and risk losing the case against Miss Curbstone altogether. The point was that a slave had been allowed to escape. "She hightailed it with another man's property," the attorney thundered. "Let's not forget that. It's what brought us here in the first place."

The prosecutor had made a good gambit. The very next day, one could feel the atmosphere of the courtroom change, once the conversation shifted to Jacob Pingrim, and how Dana had "consorted" with him until at last she coaxed him into an illegal and successful run for his freedom. A senator, a former friend of Dana, remembered having lunch with her in the Phoenix when Pingrim waited table on them, how she had flirted and spoken with the servant in French. At the time he'd thought little of the exchange, but it all made sense to him now.

Cal's case looked to be so wrapped up by then that the prosecutor scarcely mentioned him, focusing with a combination of moderation and wrath on the person of Dana, and how she played the townspeople for fools, receiving their young daughters into her school to teach them manners, all the while degrading the Academy, its feminine ideals, by her wanton trysts with a local preacher. They stayed overnight together! Who knew what they might have done at some undisclosed stopping-place on the road, in some copse or barn? Beneath what arbor-branches had they spoken what words? What was worse, the prosecutor elicited testimony from a stable groom possessed of a pronounced stutter that a lit cigarette had passed from the slave's lips to Dana's own. The Lord only knew, and in eternity would perhaps forgive, the obscure and illicit motives that had put these three in league, leading Reverend Fenton to forsake his duty as a minister, and Miss Dana to guide an ignorant slave, with no wits to resist a woman's wiles, into temptation. She had seduced him into freedom.

OCTOBER 1833
FRANKFORT STATE PENITENTIARY
CAL FENTON

E WAS, AT THE LAST, making shoes. He'd gotten a break from the fields, at least. It was not that hard except that his hands were calloused beyond belief, making them less sensitive to the leather's spring. He cut the leather, sewed it tight, put glue on the soles, punched the lace-holes, and hoped they fit. If not, he'd call them moccasins. He liked the smell of the tannin as it bled from the treated hide. Acrid, pungent, and left stains on his hands. It ate the blistered skin away if he didn't remember to wash.

During the trial, Dana looked more beautiful still than when they'd escorted Jacob. Her eyes had turned positively Persian. Her waist looked trimmer than ever, as if cinched. Good skin, and she even found occasion to smile in the midst of the horror, to chafe her chief attorney during a recess. A different dress each day, also different silk-ribbon hats which she wouldn't wear indoors, but remove and hand to some man in the galley to hold for her during the session. The men looked surprised but they never said no, in spite of the stares of their wives or lady friends. It offered another way for Dana to receive the right kind of attention; easy for her. Cal didn't know why he ever thought they could pass undetected in a coach together. Everyone in Christendom, down to the crickets, had surely been watching them. But her fate and his were single, not joint.

Had they succeeded, she would have said yes to marrying him in a half-sigh, as if merely resigning herself to the inevitable, as if she didn't care because she hadn't a care, and they wouldn't be in this prison now. They would have proceeded northward, just like Jacob, leaving detractors behind to gnash their teeth. But things did not fall out in that way, and he could only blame himself. He really did commend himself into the hands of Almighty God. He knew he wouldn't be convincing in denying his role in carrying Jacob to the river. In some way it seemed to him shameful to deny it. If anything, he should have gone further than silence, instead declaring himself a prisoner of conscience. He did not regret what he did and that had been the chance to try to make people understand the importance of his work. But to do that, he would have had to go against Dana by also implicating her.

In some fashion, she seemed to have actually enjoyed the trial, the attention it garnered. The way every head turned as she proceeded up the aisle, as if in nuptials, and she, in her turn, swerved her head to look behind, as if a groom should follow from among those many would-be suitors. When she inclined to confer in a hushed tone with either of her attractive lawyers, every one of the assembled company wanted to know what she was saying, assumed each syllable was of the greatest consequence, when she might merely have been reminding one of the lawyers to send along later a poultice for her aching shoulders, or send a note of thanks on handcrafted paper to a well-wisher. He had never seen her more vibrant. It would have suited her best if the trial were to go on for years, whereas he felt each day of the intolerable spectacle was bringing him closer to his end. He wouldn't give them the pleasure of dandifying himself, as if he might implicitly have been begging their approval through draping himself in finery. He was a dirty little procurer of slaves. His showing up in a new suit would leave no one thunderstruck except Dana.

JANUARY 1834
FRANKFORT STATE PENITENTIARY
DANA CURBSTONE

ANA SMEARED THE ROUGE TO make its border less obvious. She couldn't quite get it to disappear into her skin. When had the skin of her face gotten rough spots? She saw pores where there had never been pores before. Five months in prison, even with regular milk baths, could do that to a woman. She'd gained ten pounds, but she could tell it was becoming, and that in truth, she'd always been underweight. She'd never felt she could afford to lose her starved look. But these pounds had come unbidden.

They'd let her use the lavatory off the warden's office. She was allowed to leave a variety of makeup and lotions in a basket, and was escorted there each morning. Frank—the warden—made sure not to arrive in his adjacent office until she had finished her ablutions. Usually their paths didn't cross, at the beginning anyway, but on occasion, he'd be there settling in with a sheaf of work right as she emerged, her face still moist with a residue of buttery slather. He'd abandoned his hearty manner long since, his upcountry accent mysteriously disappeared. For the most part, he would just give her a brief word or sometimes only a glance, neither friendly nor unfriendly. He was doing all this for her, making sure towels were left, setting this toilette up at an early hour before the other prisoners had stirred. His pace was leisurely as he settled into his creaking swivel chair, as if he had all the time in the world.

She never would have guessed he'd have come in so early to work, but apparently he kept regular hours. He had the complexion of a man who drank to excess, a hard protuberance of belly that presumably came from a bottle, but the truth was, she'd never seen him touch a drink, nor smelled liquor on his breath, only the awful aftershave, which she'd grown used to in any case, so his being a lush was all hearsay. No tippling from a flask in the office. He set a cup of sliced carrots on his desk each morning, which he ate as a parsimonious breakfast. One of his little quirks was that he'd often check the wooden buttons on his jacket, as if he feared one might come loose, spoiling the effect. At least she'd come to understand something of how he could have endured what must have been a difficult job. The job itself actually seemed rather boring from the outside, but it must have had its hidden intensity, given its nature. She found herself wishing she could hang about the office on any pretext for the length of an entire day, to see how he interacted with the rest of the staff and with other prisoners who were called in for a meeting with the warden.

Then she mustered herself to ask to be assigned to clerical duties, as a condition of her incarceration. They hadn't really given her anything to do in all this time, no hard labor, and if she had to knit one more item, it would be a rope to hang from. She kept hearing that she was going to be pardoned; occasional unsigned letters from Monsieur Fontenot hinted at it in the most innocuous and cryptic manner, in French, naturally. The warden let these letters pass to her uncensored, probably assuming that their perfume and the effeminate hand portended the rarefied chattiness of some inconsequential female of her former circle, rather than the penmanship of Dana's shooting master.

Some of the prisoners spread the rumor of Dana's impending pardon as gossip, whether through resentment at her preferential treatment, or else because they'd really heard it from the outside. She couldn't tell. It could all be a rumor only, but then she heard that the warden was locked in some struggle with the governor to keep her there, though he didn't appear to be holding any grudge regarding her initial rebuff, before the trial, of his courtly attentions. He simply didn't seem to think that much about her, after his initial burst of enthusiasm.

She didn't specify that her clerical duties be in Frank's office, but she made her request *to be used*, as she put it, directly to him, as she was leaving the lavatory one morning. That was the word that came spontaneously to her lips, *used*. He seemed neither surprised nor put out. He said he would think about it. Indignant but not letting it show, she asked what there was to think about. He replied no, nothing, just whether there were any duties fit for her. He was well aware she'd been a brilliantly successful headmistress of one of the region's most prominent finishing schools, everyone knew that—despite the fact that the school had closed its doors altogether and the building was up for sale—and he didn't want to assign her labors beneath her station. He had that much respect for her.

Without any touch of theatricality whatsoever, she replied that she no longer had a station. This was her station, and she wanted to make the best of her situation for as long as she remained here. She had, after all, been sentenced to ten years. He made no comment whatsoever about the ten years of her sentence, or whether he had knowledge to the contrary. The next morning he sent word, when the woman came to escort her to the lavatory, that if it were okay with Dana, she'd be staying afterward in the warden's office to help him sort through a backlog of handwritten files. They were attempting to create a history of incarceration at the institution, and spotty though the documents were, the warden had no close idea of how many prisoners had passed through these portals, much less how long the average stay was. The convicted came and went, sometimes multiple times, with nobody the wiser. Headcounts were not enough anymore. Besides, he was planning to run for political office, give the governor a run for his money, and it needed to be shown that there was a more humane way to deal with prisoners than had been the case.

It was enlightening to watch him interact with those who visited his office. The wives of prisoners had a way of flirting with Frank. They'd come in their sorrow, and he would explain to them in an unexpectedly quiet voice the ins and outs and probabilities that they'd ever see their husbands again. He had a fresh stack of handkerchiefs in the right-hand drawer of his desk, and he'd peel one off for the distraught woman, always keeping his head as she lost hers. He gave these women, some of them quite young, no visible encouragement beyond the handkerchief and the low-pitched voice and, on occasion, pulling his chair around to sit next to them at their critical moment, but the combination seemed to excite two or three of them, and they would pull their chairs closer to his, as if expecting him to lay an arm across their shoulders, or enclose them with the girth of a fatherly hug, but he never did, at least that she witnessed. Over a period of several weeks of Dana's observation, some would come for several days in a row, then less frequently, then they stopped coming. Dana didn't know whether it was because their petitions to get their husbands released were successful, or because they had decided to abandon them, or for some other reason. But then new ones came to take their place.

The orders he gave to guards were crisp but not brutal or impetuous. He always seemed to have a plan. She'd heard that Cal was being beaten regularly with a rattan cane, that he was made to build walls in the cold, and always, as she walked from place to place, within her limited discretion, she tried to catch sight of him, or hear a report of his condition, but to no avail. He was in another part of the penitentiary, and probably outside many days on one of the work gangs.

The one time Dana mentioned Cal to the warden, he stopped what he was doing, listened to her carefully, though he produced no handkerchief nor moved his chair to her side of the desk, perhaps because she wasn't crying. He said he would check into the allegations. The next morning he reported back that Cal did indeed have a rigorous job task, mostly making shoes and building furniture, which he was apparently good at. She asked if she could see Cal, and the warden, again without getting excited, said that wasn't permitted, she'd been given liberties enough, more than she could have ever expected. She asked if she could give up one or more of those liberties in exchange for seeing Cal just once, for a few minutes. The warden drew himself up over his elbows, exposing his full heft, stared her down, and with the first edge of flint in his voice that she'd heard since the beginning, he coolly reminded her that prison was not a bargaining system. It was, to be blunt, a lot like slavery, where privileges were few and one who had committed a crime and been convicted of it just had to bear up under the system. As with slavery, some inmates got better assignments than others simply because they were more tolerable to have around.

She didn't ask about Cal after that, nor address the question of his release and how it might be obtained, though she continued to think about him. It was hard to believe, from the vantage point of the warden's office, that anything unduly cruel was happening to Cal, as the warden looked to operate out of a rational set of concerns, and even if something horrible were indeed occurring, she simply had to try not to think about it, for now anyway. If an opening presented itself, at least she was in the best place to do something about it.

In truth, she thought about Cal a lot less than she would have liked. And when she did, she couldn't forget the image of his final confusion on the witness stand. He'd looked like a broken old man. She pitied him. All she wanted now was the opportunity to exercise charity on his behalf. But as she walked the line each day, she couldn't allow her mind to stray too far in any one direction. She knew where that would lead. Thus far she'd kept her self-control, her dignity, and she wanted it to remain that way. Matters could always get ugly in a hurry.

She smeared more rouge across her skin. Not quite enough yet. Frank would be arriving soon. He insisted on picking her up in person. The warden's wife had come down with a dire bronchial complaint, which she was prone to, in this unusually hard winter. The cells were freezing, and if it hadn't been for the quilt Dana wrapped herself in each night, she wasn't sure how she would have survived, because she was cold-natured, and quite easily she could have become one of the numerous casualties of pneumonia she'd been hearing about in this season of extreme weather. They said the Ohio River was frozen in places. Her nipples grew hard at night beneath her blouse, but not in the way she would have liked. It had been a long time since true relief had come her way, almost three years. As for a substitute, well, in a prison cell, she didn't dare touch herself as she had each night when she'd lived on the outside. Even in the dead of midnight, a cell offered no privacy, as you couldn't be sure some guard wouldn't come lumbering through for a surprise bed-check, deliberately done at irregular intervals, sometimes several a night, sometimes none for a week. Though she was given one of the few individual cells, even she wasn't exempted from the bed checks.

She wasn't really going to the winter ball as a stand-in for Frank's wife. He'd explained that carefully. It was a last minute, flat-footed invitation. She was under no pressure to go. But, he allowed, with a brief smile, her notoriety would surely render this ball the event of the season. It was for charity, and important for him to attend, to remind the constituency that he wanted deaf-mutes to live a better life.

It was mercenary, he knew (a word she never would have credited him with knowing in the early going, although he was exactly that) and yet mercenary in a fine cause. He knew she had done a lot of society work in her day, and wouldn't it be nice to get back to that? From what he'd heard, she was quite good at it. Her presence would easily double the take, if she appeared as a surprise guest, astounding the assembly, and then he could have the hosts auction off a dance with her and later in the evening, auction off her gorgeous evening dress, obviously to be taken possession of at a later date, he quipped almost shyly. She replied that she didn't have any such dress on hand, and Frank—the warden—informed her that was the business of tomorrow, for him to take the day off, and escort her, as a security measure, to dress shops and milliners to select the right clothing, to get it tailored at once, as time was short, and ensure she'd turn out in something that would cause a sensation.

So, she asked him, I shan't get to keep the dress? He replied that if she wished, he'd buy it back later from the highest bidder. He'd bid on it if that was what she preferred.

She liked his recklessness, but she said no, nor did she think it was most appropriate, nor decorous, for him to be seen about town, much less at the season's most important ball, in the company of a woman convicted of sedition, especially if he had political ambitions. He blithely let her know that he didn't give a damn about any of that; on the contrary, it would please him to singe the brows of some of these tight-trousered Kentuckians who considered him, despite all his success, to be little more than a glorified hick. He was willing to weather their disapproval, because he'd be able to feel their excitement right behind it. Sometimes it's good to let things happen right out in the open, and deal with the consequences. If the governor fired him as a result, all right, he'd find another job. He wouldn't die of hunger either way. But if she didn't want to go, that was okay; she'd get no further pressure from him. He'd just have to find another stand-in, someone lesser than her, on the outside—some young girl of a decent family who wished to make a splash, if only for one night.

She asked him who would be home taking care of his wife, and he said there are servants aplenty for that sort of thing.

Then she said yes. She couldn't believe he was so eager to be seen with her in that way, that he was even eager to take a big gamble. She was the only person to whom he'd let drop his political desires, even his own wife didn't know about those. The sheer theatricality of the two of them together would, in fact, astound the assembly. She hadn't experienced a thrill like that since the trial. Now, five months in, almost no one came to visit her anymore. Her curiosity value had worn off. In spite of her little privileges, she was close to becoming just another prisoner. And she was bored.

This evening also would be the perfect time to advocate for Cal's release. In spite of the warden's careful demeanor, Dana remembered enough of his boisterous side to know that something in him was indeed impulsive, and that if she caught him at the right moment, in the right mood, she'd be able to extract a promise, and then it would only be a matter of keeping him to the promise. Creating a sensation, a successful impression, at the gala, filling the charity coffers, electrifying the attendees, burnishing Frank's standing as a daring yet practical man, would give her exactly the right leverage to make him obey her wishes.

She knew she could pull it off. Everything in her training, in the way she'd lived her life, conspired to make this charity ball the exact occasion for Dana to wield her full power, to flaunt her prowess to the warden the way she'd done to other men always. Wasn't the trial proof of that, as if that proof were even needed? He could be the ultimate challenge. Though he was no match for her, when it came to that. Hadn't every man in Kentucky been worshipping at her feet? Hadn't she lorded it over them during the proceedings—the gallery, the judge, even the witnesses to the death of the man she'd killed in cold blood, the other two she had intended to kill also, and would have killed if Cal hadn't knocked the gun away, and then she and he might have fled northward, never to be captured, and would be at large, hunted perhaps, having to endure in hiding under assumed names, notorious, living out an alternate existence?

The ball was made for her presence, a historical drama only waiting for her to step in and claim it. All it had required was the providential aspect of Frank's wife getting severe bronchitis at the right moment, as if ordained. Dana herself was blameless. She hadn't tried to produce this occasion. It had simply come to her, and she would be utterly, willfully foolish to reject it. She'd been tried for her crimes, literally tried, it wasn't just a saying, the way it would be for most women who felt put upon, and wasn't she serving out a sentence, decreed by others, with whatever strictness or leniency the state and its representatives decreed and enforced? Pardon or no pardon, her own case was beyond her control, and it almost exhilarated her to know that. She couldn't afford to be headstrong just now, for it was in exactly this way that she would secure Cal's release.

He had gone to prison because of her, that's what she believed, what she knew, he'd broken down on the stand because of her, he was perhaps being treated harshly because of a sequence of events she'd initiated, first by asking to come along on the trip to Maysville with Jacob, and then murdering a man in Cal's presence. He was suffering for her sake. She wanted to be blameless again. It was within her reach. It was enough to hope for, without trying to imagine what kind of life she might reconstruct for herself outside, if she ever got that opportunity.

She owed him his freedom. Even if she stayed in jail for a while longer, awaiting her eventual release, a release that was inevitable, at least she hoped it was, she prayed for it every night, but even if she stayed in the penitentiary, Cal would be gone. They wouldn't have to co-exist under the same roof, not the domestic roof she'd always thought they'd share, but rather a maddening combination of proximity and anonymity, never seeing him, never knowing if she'd see him, nebulous, never knowing whether he had become a broken-down version of the solid man she'd first gotten to know. She'd be rid of all that, they'd be even, she wouldn't have to go through the rest of her life owing him.

One of the reasons she couldn't touch herself in her cell at night to relieve the burden, besides the bed-checks, was that the image of him that had so reliably brought her to climax in solitude day after day, for months, without them ever consummating the act for real, that image no longer worked for her. The image became about his emaciation, disease, arthritis, him skeletal and bowlegged, eyeballs protruding, lying naked on the stone floor of a prison cell with infected stripe-marks from a rattan cane across his back and legs. Him shivering, his scrotum contracted, his scalp shedding hair and a bald spot forming at his crown.

She painted her lips a medium red with a small Japanese brush that Frank, she assumed, had left in the basket without comment. The effect she sought was neither whorish nor discreet—or better, both.

She had to admit, he looked good dressed up. Frank actually owned a tuxedo, and it had been tailored to flatter his stout build. As they ascended the staircase together into the upstairs ballroom, their effect was visible on those braving the gusts of wind to observe this unprecedented entrance, as word of her arrival had passed a few yards ahead of her steps and his. She could hear the hubbub rising in the cavernous space with its high rafters. Dana couldn't make out the exact words, but she knew they were all talking about her, that they could scarcely believe it was happening. She hadn't heard that much passion arrayed around her person since the days of her arrival at court each morning for her trial, as onlookers jockeyed to catch a glimpse of her. So it was now, the crowd actually dividing to receive them. The society ladies in their crimson crepe and satin—so many of them had worn the same color!—pretended not to be particularly interested, but Dana could feel their eyes lingering as she passed each one by. Every woman had planned on stealing the show, had made copious provision for it, had laid out garments months before, and all for nothing.

If one didn't know better, she and Frank could have been mistaken for a handsome society couple; his florid skin went well with the season. His cheeks with their broken veins passed as the index of excellent health. Frank wasn't good-looking, she was well aware of that, but he had obviously enlisted the sympathies of a brilliant tailor, the kind of willing servant Cal would never have even known existed. Frank was the kind of man who presumably looked better in clothes than out of them. Not that she wanted to be able to provide the definitive opinion on that. Yet the tuxedo did become him, transforming his heft into solidity and giving him a patriarchal air befitting his station.

She guessed his weight at eighteen stone, half again as heavy as Cal. Now he was probably twice as heavy. How did it feel to his wife to be crushed beneath his belly? Was it pleasant? Did it make her feel more secure, or simply out of breath? Or did they still have relations? The wife didn't look all that sturdy, if the truth were known. Dana had seen her once on the corridor, bringing a group of benevolent ladies in for some sort of inspection. They'd passed her cell by without so much as a glance, apparently under strict instruction from the matriarch to make no fuss. Her walk was brisk, but her skeleton looked brittle. She was prone to colds and fevers, so Frank had remarked, like the one she was at home nursing this evening. What was it like to live that way?

On the way over in the carriage, as Dana experienced the newly familiar rustle of a silk dress, this one emerald green and *soigné*, soft cloth embracing her limbs for the first time in months, Frank seemed keen on bringing up the subject of his wife, making her present in her absence. She wasn't a loving mother but a competent one. Sentimentality was not in her nature. He described how, in the early days, when they first moved to town, he'd once gotten out of bed before daybreak in a snowstorm to fetch his young wife a half-pan of hot rolls from the baker's a quarter-mile away. On foot he'd brought the rolls back, bundled in a cloth beneath his shirt, against his chest, like a baby chick one might take it upon oneself to revive, moist and still palpitating. As he unbundled the rolls in the young wife's presence, shaking the snow off his jacket and hair, the yeast had exhaled a fragrance into the room, as if it had come from his own skin.

After rebuking him for tracking snow all over the floor, and enjoining him to wipe the boards with a rag, the wife began to eat the rolls, alone in the bed, without offering one to him, and she remarked, as she chewed, that if Frank had always smelled like that, she might have chosen to eat him instead. Dana couldn't tell whether he'd rehearsed that story beforehand, and she wondered whether he'd told it before, and if so, in what company and under what circumstances. It came out effortlessly, yet she had the sensation that it was spontaneous, leaked from the heart. Something in her had dislodged it, and he was telling it for the first time ever, after long living with it suppressed beneath the thick rind of his soul.

Frank wasted no time in announcing her, which by then was superfluous. There were a couple of hecklers somewhere far off, but their half-heard insults about Dana's person didn't seem to get much of a reception, and so they let them drop. Without letting the moment dissipate, and Dana close beside him, Frank at once closed the silence and went into auction mode, not mentioning her dress but promising a dance to whatever gentleman offered the most money for the deaf-mutes in exchange for that privilege. Caught off guard, the men in attendance, with their very wives and mistresses on their arms, began to shout out sums that soon ran into the realm of the fanciful. For the first time ever, Dana was able to calculate her exact worth at two thousand three hundred sixty dollars, and that was only for a single dance with her. What might the rest of her have brought?

As he kissed Dana's hand before handing her off to the winner, who took her in arms at once, possessive and close, near the trombone at the far end of the military brass band playing a familiar sentimental waltz with incongruously high-stepping whole notes, she caught a last whiff of Frank's fruit-scented cologne, remembering that the scent had become so familiar to her in his office that she barely noticed it anymore. Now she smelled it anew, and she asked herself, if he were ever to wash it off or forget to put it on, if he were ever to trust in his natural scent, whether he would indeed smell like bread.

So much of a man's appeal came from his smell. That's exactly what she'd liked about Cal, and the one thing she missed about him, and had let herself ache for in those early days. Monsieur Fontenot smelled like juniper berries, and if he'd ever let himself make a play for her affections, she might have taken a true fancy to him, and that might have been rewarded. But despite his occasional surreptitious ogling of her figure, all he wanted to do was shoot his gun, as it turned out, and regale her with tales of his many mistresses abroad. She'd wanted to believe Cal was the man for her. Someone had to be that man. She'd wanted to believe that his scent trumped all the other potential ones, that one solitary smell in the universe was meant to attract her, unique, a butterfly no less voracious because she fed on flowers, but that man had never stepped forward, not when he should have, not when she was intoxicated by the cloud of him and could put up no resistance, and not ask herself of nor begin to examine his potential liabilities, the many defects she knew she'd find there, inevitable, perhaps intolerable in the aggregate if she ever let herself count them up, all men had such qualities, but that was the art of coexistence, wasn't it, to remain blind to different parts at different times and only be guided by one's olfactory sense? Otherwise, how could you endure them for long? There was a moment, brief but real, when any man walking could have had her if he only knew the right words to say in the exact sequence. That wasn't too much to ask, that he divine her secret.

The winner of the dance was so close to her she couldn't even see his face. And the only odors coming from him were tobacco and sweat, not repugnantly strong but not appealing either. Such a pity it was. The last man who'd handled her, a full three years ago, was that young barrister who was just getting started in Lexington, whom she knew wouldn't amount to anything and with whom she'd never intended to stay. She remembered the velvety texture of his most intimate places, especially when they brushed her cheek, and his almost literally unspeakable gratitude when she performed a certain act on him. Wasn't that how they put it? Performing acts, as if that most private act were a public spectacle; everything that meant something always ended up as a public transaction, on the town's main square or in the courthouse, or at a winter ball.

She couldn't completely fathom the trembling depth of the young barrister's gratitude, the look of surprise he sported on the single occasion she'd had to provoke that expression in him. As for her relations with men, in truth their number had been few, three of them only in a lifetime because she was picky. It could have been more, many more, but it hadn't been. One thing she'd learned based on scant experience, you had to go to bed with the whole person, that was the trick. What unified the men was her consciousness that however things might have looked to a casual observer, it was she who held the power. Men thought they were strong, but in the end they were unutterably weak, down to the last of them. Power had a way of migrating from one person to another when least expected. If only the power she wielded on those occasions could have pertained to all areas of life, she'd probably be the Governor of the Commonwealth, rather than a subversive headmistress awaiting the pardon of that same Governor.

She was twenty-eight. The desire in her might only last a couple more years, and then would she become a sexless husk, like these exquisite hags who surrounded her now? That's what she'd been told by others, to the extent they'd ever brought up the subject, that a woman's desire died off all of the sudden at some point, and she never got it back afterward. What she'd treated as a luxury, from one day to the next became a necessity, then an impossibility. And that's what she'd observed around her, especially among decent women. They only wanted to be looked at, admired, appreciated, nothing more. Certainly she wouldn't make it to thirty-three, the soonest she might receive parole, with her carnal ability intact. She could count up the number of times she'd enjoyed a man, eight only, four plus one plus three, spread among three well-intentioned men who hadn't wanted to prevail too much on her good nature, on her feminine generosity, taking up all of about two hours of her life *in toto*, not counting the preliminaries such as dinner and hooks and buttons and moving the candle lest it get tipped over.

There had been a moment of clarity earlier on, when she'd gone back to Vermont for a season to help tend to her sick Aunt Ellie, who knew she was going to die. From under the heap of comforters that ill-disguised imminent death, Ellie, in whose mouth butter famously wouldn't melt, said "Try as many as you can, my dear, if you've got the bollocks! I never did." Ellie didn't say further what she meant; instead an expression of pain occluded the fading light in her eyes, but she most certainly hadn't been referring to peanut brittle.

"...how you've bounced back. You don't even look penitent!"

A woman in wool was touching Dana's chignon in passing, as if she were a delightful savage with unaccountably soft hair where one had expected kinks. She'd spent the previous evening with her smashed locks wrapped in an apricot paste, lying in her cell with nothing to do except feel the paste harden against her scalp. She didn't even have a new note in French peppered with literary references from Monsieur Fontenot as a distraction. In fact, she hadn't received a missive from him in more than three weeks. He must have been on one of his buying trips and too busy to write, but no matter, as she'd grown tired of using him as a conduit for yet another spurned legal entreaty. She was tired of remembering his chaste flirtations, always ending with her hitting the broad side of a barn, then a narrower one, then a single plank, then a spot in the grain of the plan.

That was a practice in diminishing returns. It had only supplied her with the ability to commit a murder, when if he'd whisked her away to France, to live among the scattered mistresses if nothing else, it would never have come to this pass. She wouldn't have to exercise a dubious gratitude toward Fontenot for having given her the wherewithal to slay the sheriff. She would never have given deliverance to Jacob Pingrim. The band ended a schottische, and the winning gentleman, not much taller than her, had brought his face off her shoulder long enough for Dana to descry his countenance. He was of indeterminate age, somewhere upwards of sixty however, and in desperate need of a fresh application of moustache wax. Now he was complimenting her clavicle, yes, *her clavicle*, while putting a whiskey with crushed mint leaves in her right hand, winking as if to imply that branch water by itself was for ladies, but he knew she was no lady.

She wondered whether she'd be called upon to deliver a speech, given that the auctioned dance was over, and she began to compose the words by mouthing silently a litany that would spark the human spirit without inflaming it, that would begin her rehabilitation while also setting the tone for Frank's remarks, why not? That's what the wife would have done had her bronchial complaint allowed; that's what a wife did. She only knew that whatever she ended up saying, the words wouldn't get stuck in her throat.

Dana was now in her second dance with the old man smearing his whiskers upon her clavicle, which had brought her value down to only one hundred eighty dollars per dance, and if this were allowed to continue, there was no telling what her ultimate value might turn out to be. There was the governor, at the far end of the room, holding that same radiant wife at arm's length, fending off her virtuosity while holding close her virtue. The warden was interposed, near the center of the room, between Dana and the governor. He seemed to be making a point for himself and Dana not to associate with one another too closely in the early going; he was working the room in his own way.

If she could just get to the governor, from whom no communiqué, despite the rumors, had ever come through, it would be possible at least to ascertain his opinion on the topical subject of her, the illicit ball and chain of the ball, and second, on the subject of Cal Fenton, whom she wished would get up his pride and make a jailbreak, there had to be a way for someone so seasoned in escapes, so why hadn't he tried? Why not tonight, in fact? It was the perfect time for it, with most of the staff diverted to preparations for the ball and guarding these premises. With so many important persons in attendance, a phalanx of police was here, as well as a number of the prison guards, ill-disguised in ill-fitting formal wear gotten up at the last possible moment. Such was their level of organization, as far as she could see.

Snifters clinked somewhere within the domed rotunda, with its painted splendor of foxes and foxhounds on the chase distorted into an aerial diorama of bodies elongating into wisps of cloud, their eyes stars, a heaven you could almost float straight up into, and the echo of glass magnified itself and sailed across the spinning couples into the oboe in two-four time.

The man was telling her he was a colonel, and in truth, once he got his face off her, he stepped lively and gamely if stiffly, and he appeared to know her, because he now made continuous reference to personages they'd held in common, to dinner parties she and he had separately enlivened on the same nights, though she couldn't place him, despite the fact that he spoke of three young women he had recommended into her charge. She thanked him for his patronage. He told her he'd never danced with a criminal before, and she replied that neither had she, which got him laughing. He said it was a luxury worth having, and that life might never again present him with this unique set of circumstances. He'd determined at once to make sure he availed himself of it, no matter the cost. He didn't care a fig about money, always had it and never knew what to do with it.

She steered him ever closer to the governor, leading him into leading her in the direction she wanted to go. Everyone was watching her, but she denied knowledge of every last one of them, even the ones she used to know, by squeezing her eyelids shut, as if to obliterate them by triggering blasts of gunpowder with sparks from her eyelashes. But when she opened her eyes again, the onlookers all looked pretty much the same to her, individuated only by accidents of physiognomy or quirks of costume.

"Mistreatment is relative ... "

The governor's wife, clothing and hair so sleek and shiny she looked to have been doused with water, would probably slap Dana if she ventured too close; she gestured in the relaxed manner of someone who can grasp the governor's hand anytime she wants.

"Made of *wax*, can you believe it? They'll last forever, unless ... "

But there was no chance to test the wife's reaction, for Frank, yes, now he was Frank again, not gearing up for a speech, that much she could tell, his eyes said as much, nor requiring one of her, relieved the colonel of his duty to escort her a certain number of yards, not as the crow flies, but as the woman moves, that is, in circles, and Frank took over the next dance himself. Her value stabilized; now she was just dancing, the first auction was over, and the auction of her emerald green dress so far loomed nowhere in sight. Then again, the evening might turn out to be long, and the longer the better, before she had to give up the dress and return to jail.

Frank looked a little drunk; well, he always looked a little drunk on account of his high color, but for once he acted a little drunk, yet when had he had time to imbibe that much? Enough to bring eighteen stone off balance.

" ... in England, they've got this all figured out, servants simply want to obey, they consider it their duty ... "

So it could be that he simply wanted to be a little drunk and thus was anticipating the necessary attitude, prior to the actual cups, of doing something before you actually get down to doing it, premeditating, everything about him had the tang of premeditation, the sly crouch of an ungainly man, for in fact when he grasped her in his arms he wasn't off balance at all. On the contrary, Frank brought Dana straight to his midsection in perfect rhythm, to a point of tangency with his tumescence, his load, his rock, his sentence, whatever pet name a warden would have for his own one, there it was, and he made her focus on it through the movements of his more-than-adequate dancing, yet another of his surprises. He wasn't exactly light on his feet, that would be overstating the case, but he got from one place to the next more swiftly than you ever could have imagined, and what's more, he took you there with him. Wasn't that all that could be expected of any man?

When the dance was over, they went to seek refreshment. The restrained gaiety of those standing by, combined with a humor seething in them, produced a sort of brisk yipping which he either ignored deliberately, or was oblivious to. She scanned the room for the governor, but he was nowhere in sight. Perhaps he'd left for the evening, on his way to another political engagement. She'd missed her chance. Frank handed her a lukewarm wine punch and served himself straight liquor. The rotting fruit scent was beginning to assert itself again, and her arm made an unpremeditated lurch, managing to slosh most of her punch onto the shirtfront of his tuxedo. Maybe that would kill the smell. One who didn't know might have assumed she'd thrown it at him in anticipation of misbehavior. Frank didn't seem to take it personally. He let the stain soak in, pinker on the cloth than it had been in the cup, and in answer he drained his own cup into his mouth and said, "Let's go downstairs."

"Are we leaving, then, so soon?"

"Only temporarily. We'll be back."

"And the auction of my dress?"

"I'm sure we'll get to it in time. I said we're coming back after a bit. I'll need to find a fresh shirt."

"Need I go? Am I going to hold your cufflinks?"

"You're in my care. You shouldn't complain. It wasn't me who threw the first punch." She couldn't help smiling. "You see, you're not the only one who can make a dreadful pun."

On the way out, there were gibing remarks from partygoers just this side of friendly, as Frank dutifully took a ribbing about the fact that the warden appeared to be in his cups and couldn't keep a handle on his handle. He didn't contradict anyone, just led Dana by the arm, almost occasioning a tender bruise above her elbow in the process. One young fop questioned whether the warden mightn't leave Miss Curbstone behind for a few dances while he went to change his shirt. With an incisive stare, the warden let the young man know that he would take her along for safekeeping.

The air outside made her wince. A gelid bell of cold had fallen upon the grounds. She could scarcely breathe. A compact carriage was brought round and the single horse pulling it had teary eyes. Dana didn't ask where they were going, as a fold of her dress caught in the door. She heard a slight rip as she extracted it.

Their destination turned out to be on another part of the grounds, less than ten minutes away. They alighted at a coach house with an apartment to which Frank had a key, one of many on his steel key ring. It had jangled merrily against the seat on the way over. The interior of the apartment was almost as small as one of the paddocks, but furnished with a bed, a dresser, a small table, and two chairs. No fireplace, however. There was a bottle of brandy as well, half full, and he poured two glasses straight off and handed one to her before removing his jacket. The walls of the apartment must have been thick, plank upon plank, for she could hear nothing outside, but it was still cold, just shy of biting.

"Do you have an extra shirt here?"

"I might. I'll look in a moment. Drink it." She took a sip. "No, I mean drink it down. You'll need it for the cold."

"I've had quite enough for one evening."

"No you haven't. Drink it down, Miss Curbstone."

She drank it down and held out the glass for another draught. He poured it fuller this time. "You're right, warden. I'm not even close to drinking what I'll need to get through this evening."

"Why do you say so?"

"Because I know so. I thought I was supposed to be the naïve one."

"I have some good news for you. Something that will no doubt make you happy. I've been saving it for the right moment."

"Something about Reverend Fenton?"

"No, I wasn't even thinking about him. Odd you bringing him up just now."

"Can anything be odd at this point? So, what is the good news?"

"I'll tell you later. It can wait."

"Then it mustn't be that good. You won't forget?"

"Depend on my remembering. Do you care for him?"

"I used to, but no longer. I only want his well-being." Blurting Cal's name at the outset wasn't the strategy of wooing she'd planned, but she couldn't seem to help herself. "This little room is cozy, if only it were warmer."

"I'm glad you think so."

"How many women have been in here before?"

"I'm not sure."

"Because you weren't here with them? Or because you don't keep count?"

"Something like that, yes."

"Well, thank you for your honesty. Such as it is. And what do you expect from me?"

"I expect nothing."

"What am I to give you?"

He leaned back in his chair and stroked his belly. It was the most ruminative look she'd ever seen on his face. "Everything."

"You're not attractive, do you know that?"

"Yes, I'm quite aware of it. That is, when I think about my looks, which isn't much."

"You're ugly. Though you do dress nicely, I'll give you that much. Most men don't. I should have opened a school for men instead of women. They're the ones who need finishing off."

"You would have done handsomely."

"And yet, you wear the most horrible cologne imaginable. It stinks. Do you realize?"

"No, I wasn't aware. Though now that you mention it, I don't like it much myself. If you'd asked me sooner, I would have exchanged that cologne for another. My wife bought it for me. When I run out, she purchases another bottle."

"Your wife?"

"Yes. No doubt she knew that its odor was repugnant. She has a keen sense of smell, so I'm told. That is, when her nose isn't stopped up. I suppose it's a clever little punishment she devised. I have to say I admire her for it. In the early days, she had the upper hand entirely, but I've taken away so many of her weapons over time. This may be the only one left to her. And me too much of an idiot to realize her mean trick."

"So, now what? I'm half-drunken, your coachman or henchman awaits outside—as if you even needed him."

"He's more superfluous than even you realize."

"You hold all the cards, so you can paw at will. Does that mean you'll force yourself on me? You probably imagine you can do so with impunity."

"Hardly. If it's coercion, it wouldn't be pleasant for me. I wouldn't enjoy myself nearly as much. The need has to come from you."

"Well, it isn't going to come from me. I don't have any need." She ran her fingers over the silk dress. "How much do you suppose I'll fetch for this dress when it's auctioned?"

"That old gentleman who overbid the dance would probably give you at least fifteen hundred. He's profligate with his money, in case you hadn't noticed. A sucker, really. And it only cost two, so that would be a boon indeed for the less fortunate who are to be recipients of our charity."

"Then shouldn't we get back and sell it off before the evening loses its luster? Before the sucker leaves?"

"I'll give you ten dollars for the dress right now. But you have to take it off straightaway."

She could hear her breath inside the glass as she gave herself another draught of brandy. "You bought it, warden. Therefore it belongs to you. I assume you'll remove it when you see fit."

"I said it has to come from you."

"I'll strike you a bargain. Isn't that what this winter ball has been all about—striking bargains? If you really aren't going to assault me, then let's negotiate. You promise me that you'll release Reverend Fenton from his bondage, and then you may have me. I'll accept nothing less. And if you promise, you must keep your word."

The warden examined the bright berry stain on his shirt at length. He began to unlace the shirt ties one by one, exposing flashes of his pasty belly, the thickness of his fingers making the job difficult in the frigid air. He had tied the laces into knots earlier and now he had to work each one free. Then he looked back up at her. "No."

"What?"

"I won't release Cal Fenton under any circumstances. His fate doesn't interest me, so I'll abide by the laws that put him there."

She could hear herself wheedling. "Promise at least that you'll consider it. We'll talk more about it later."

"I won't make any such promise. I'd be lying if I did, because I have no intention of giving the matter any further thought. You said you admired my honesty. Yet you want me to give you a pretext, an alibi, a noble sacrifice for what you're going to do anyway."

"You're cruel. You're a boor. An utter pig."

"Yes, probably I am. Take off your dress."

Dana's hands felt limp. They tingled from the cold. She began to undo the pearl buttons she had watched the tailor sew on with care, so that they wouldn't pop loose. She half-expected the warden to lunge forward and rip the front, but he made no such move. He waited for her execution of his demand.

Frank removed his own shirt at last, revealing an unsuspected thicket of hair just at the middle of his chest, incongruous with the nakedness of the rest of his torso. The belly was there beneath, hanging over his breeches. She reached out with both hands and rubbed it, to watch it sway in the lamplight. Soon it would be crushing her. He pulled the dress down, not violently, but to the place where her arms were caught inside it, and pressed against her. "Unbuckle my breeches."

Working her arms free, she did. He sat on the edge of the bed meanwhile in a practiced, exaggerated posture and pushed her down so that her knees touched the cold, unadorned floor. There was not even the remotest tenderness in his touch. She knew he'd enjoyed this same favor many times before, and that she was just one more, neither more nor less valuable than the one who preceded her, or the one who would come after. "You know what to do," he said.

"I don't."

"You may not know well, but you do know. Okay, you want to hear me say it? Take it in your mouth."

She did. As she worked on him, tears flowing, he began to talk about Cal. He said that Cal was regularly beaten, at his orders, by the warden's inferiors, with a rattan cane, just as she had heard. Probably worse than what she'd heard. Cal had taken sick and been sent to the infirmary for almost a month; everyone thought he would die but then he didn't. They revived him enough to be sent back to hard labor picking stones from untillable fields, down near the Kentucky River.

He'd gotten frostbite and lost the tips of two fingers. It was too bad that Reverend Fenton had to exhaust himself giving everyone fire sermons inside the cell, which only served to infuriate staff and inmates alike. He should have said those things while he was still on the outside, where they might have done some good. It was a waste of time to temporize about the injustice of the human condition after you were already locked up and could no longer do anything about it.

From the pulsations, she thought he was going to finish into her mouth, but he didn't, he only stopped talking and stood up. He made her stand, pushed her down on the bed, climbed on, and began to labor atop her, without finesse of any sort, just brutish, boorish thrusts without any regard for her. She was so excited by the unendurable weight of him, the surety that he would rupture her spleen and kidneys and bladder, so sure she'd hemorrhage, that a flash went over her entire body at once, and she cried out as if on a killing floor.

Once Frank had ascertained the job was done, he pushed himself off her with a small grunt and pulled up his pants without climaxing.

"What about you?" she blurted out, almost angry.

"What about me? I'll satisfy myself when I'm ready. I gave you what you needed, didn't I?"

Dana didn't answer. She turned her face to the wall and began to sob. "Now, now." Frank gave her the first tender strokes of their acquaintance, along her back. No doubt this was the way he'd stroked his wife during the time he went out in the snow to buy her the rolls. "Let's not cry over it, Miss Curbstone. There's nothing to be done. We'll get back to the ball and sell off that lovely dress. It's all in a good cause. I'll wait for you inside the coach. Take your time." He didn't have his jacket on, but didn't seem to care.

She sat up, catching his hand before he could open the door, hardly able to speak for the phlegm in her throat. "I know there can't be any deals. You've made that clear from the beginning. But I'll make you a suggestion. A petition."

"A petition?"

"Yes, as a supplicant makes to a king."

"Let's hear it, then."

"You've never touched Reverend Fenton by your own hand?"

"No, I haven't bothered. I have other men available for that work. I'm a practical sort."

"Beat him with your own hand. It will give you more satisfaction than you've ever felt from any man, or any woman. Beat him within a speck of his life. Hurt him as much as you want. Roll all the future beatings you have planned for him into one. Leave him practically dead. Then set him free."

"And if he should die afterward?"

"He'll endure. I'm sure of it, as long as you know when to stop. You of all people should be able to calibrate exactly when you need to quit. I'm sure your inferiors will back you up if his subsequent condition should ever come into question after his release."

The warden gave out a long sigh, as if he had the entire weight of the world on his shoulders. He sighed like a politician in the making, aware of his responsibility to civil society, and the burdens it would impose upon him and his private life. Then he gave Dana a faint smile. "All right," he said. "I'll do it this week, the Reverend's health permitting."

"You won't go back on your word."

He thought for a long moment before answering. "No," he finally declared. "In this case, I don't believe I will." The warden was buttoning up his tuxedo jacket. He wore the same shirt as before, still sporting the berry stain of the punch.

"Haven't you another shirt besides that in the dresser?"

"It will have to do. I don't keep any tuxedo shirts here. And there's no time for my man to fetch me another." He slowly retied his tie. "By the way, as for that good news I mentioned earlier—the Governor has decided to pardon you. I got word of it yesterday, upon my return from our shopping expedition. He sent a courier to my residence. He plans to announce it tomorrow. He made up his mind to overrule me, and take the consequences of that decision, whatever they are. You'll be released in a few days' time, I suspect. So tonight is a celebration, really, in your honor." He offered his hand so that she could rise from the bed, dress herself, and go.

October 1834
Frankfort State Penitentiary
Cal Fenton

THERE WAS NO END OF slaves to be smuggled. The transactions would never cease. Cal had to get free to tend to his work. That was the only hard thing. But if he managed, if he could breach these walls, what else could they do to him? They'd striped his skin, given him more lashes than Jacob Pingrim had ever endured; gnarled bark grew back in its place. Even without a mirror, he knew he already looked twice as old as when he'd entered. It took no time to go from young to old, only a stretch of days. He had become a shell. Little sensation left in his body. Less flesh. God was reclaiming him piece by piece, taking him home. How long would it take: months or years? It was harder to die than people imagined. A bit thinner and he'd simply be able to slip through the bars. The less of him, the more concentrated his spirit. Why had he ever doubted the Lord? God was good. God understood every travail and by and by, he would explain it all to Cal. He'd been unfair to his Creator. No more looking over his shoulder. No more doubt. The blow he'd waited for all his life had finally fallen, praise be. Let the other blows rain down, many and many. Some days he felt he could will the walls of his cell to fall with the mere strength of his mind. He was getting there. A trumpet, sleek, hard, and in tune. More concentration, less food. The meals were so vile it was easy to fast. He had no appetite, therefore he wasn't depriving himself of anything. He took his twice-daily meal and gave it to one of his cellmates, a man who had stabbed his own mother. The man said he'd never had any sense of taste, all food was the same to him, he just wanted more. There was no sacrifice involved, no charity on Cal's part. Handing off a wooden bowl. Too simple, really.

No supper for Cal, only suppurating wounds. Ugly pus. Green and dispiriting, yet somehow it didn't kill him. Nor had he lost an arm or leg. No gangrene as yet. Lucky. Blessed. If he did lose a limb, eventually, the Lord was nonetheless preserving him for a renewed assignment. As long as he had one arm to wave, so that he could preach, that's all he asked. That's all he allowed himself to ask for. Lying on his pallet, with the three other convicts in his cell nearby, he'd hoard his strength until the guards came by, and would jump up and thunder the Holy Word. The first time they thought him a lunatic, but he'd never been more articulate, more sure that he was teaching the inspired Word straight out of the furnace of first creation. Behind their bravado, they were awestruck, he knew. He was testifying, not even about himself, because his self no longer mattered, he didn't have one. Who was he? An instrument. A vessel of certainty. Mighty. It surprised him how many Bible verses he could retrieve from memory. Hundreds of them came rushing out of his throat far into the night. They'd been there all the time. How many mornings had he stood in the pulpit, thumbing scripture, trying to remember which of the books held the message he wanted to convey? Not being able to decide. A couple of times when he hopped to his feet to signify, the guards dragged him out into the yard and beat him to shut him up. Ranting, that's what they called his inspiration. But one of them, only one, yet it was enough, had a look in his eyes that boded repentance. He knew the man was ashamed, a seeker, a centurion on the threshold of a change. That alone was worth the thrashings. Two of his cellmates would have beaten Cal too, to shut him up, except that the third one, the one who'd knifed his own mother, the one eating his rations, put a stop to any such violence, and those other two were afraid of him. Afraid they'd awaken with their throats slit. They couldn't positively say the mother-killer had a weapon, but they couldn't be sure he didn't either. Best not to find out.

Cal wondered what Dana was doing tonight. Perhaps knitting a sweater. A lovely occupation that was at least marginally worthy of her talents. He never heard much about her, only that she did a lot of knitting for the orphans. She used to call him Ostrich. It still made him smile. Now what would she call him? Ghoul? Beast? Grandpa? So good, his Dana. She didn't deserve what had happened to her. It was his fault for letting her go along in the first place. Sedition was not for amateurs. He'd sacrificed her to his vanity. Now she had to live the rest of her life knowing she'd killed a man. What must that feel like? Somehow or another, he'd never been called upon to commit that act. The Lord had spared him. Poor Dana. She must be lonely. A woman like her was used to a lot of society. Keeping company, that's what she excelled at. Just depriving her of company alone might kill her. The trial had been her last bash. He imagined her lying in the corner of her cell, curled up on her side, with a vacant look. Utterly lost. Wistful and downhearted. Her cheek dimpling. Why didn't the other cheek dimple? No matter, it made her look prettier, that tiny imperfection. Had he ever told her so? One of the guards had tried to cheer Cal up by informing him that Dana had free run of the prison, that she still dressed in finery, that she'd been allowed to attend soirées in other parts of town, mixing again with the highest society, but he knew these tales of the guards to be fairy stories, like Cinderella going to the ball in a coach-and-four. Cruelty if she herself should get wind of it. She'd think they were mocking her. He hoped they didn't taunt Dana with such false prospects.

Blood seeped into a crack in his tooth. It almost felt good, tasting it. He couldn't explain why. A phoenix from the ashes, that bromide had always sounded ridiculous to him, but now he understood it. The simplest of platitudes, but it happened to be true. Someday very soon, he would stand in Cheapside, in the exact spot where auctioneers conducted their business, where they fondled the legs of female slaves with their fat, greasy fingers, and he'd use that platform as his pulpit. They would try to bullwhip him, to drive him out of the market, but the Lord would give him the extraordinary strength he needed for the occasion, and he'd yank the bullwhip from a trader's hand. He wouldn't whip his enemies, he wouldn't repay in kind, no, yet they would back away cowering, because they'd feel the power exuded from him.

No, no, he didn't need to be Jesus; that was pride, he only wanted to fulfill this providential destiny, to be a servant, a slave to the Lord's will. But yes, the auctioneers would back away and Cal would find the exact phrases on his lips to change their hateful minds. The buyers and the sellers alike would bow down, not to him, but to Jehovah, and would cry out in their iniquity to be redeemed. And

Cal would bless them with a beautiful benediction, the poetry flowing spontaneously from his mouth. He couldn't find those words even now, he couldn't penetrate their mystery, their sounds swirled around him, murky, elusive, confusing his mind, but he knew with the utmost certainty that the words would be there exactly when the occasion demanded. Only for this reason had he been humiliated, broken, spat upon, mocked, jeered with the name Preacher as if it were a curse. All that had happened to him was logical and in some fashion deserved; though beyond his ken, he trusted that it made perfect sense to one much wiser than he. Now all he had to do, as he watched his breath hang before his mouth in a small expostulation, as he listened to the bricks and mortar crepitate beside his pallet, was to focus his mind to blast through the wall on this winter's night so that he could become free to pursue his life's work. Then he would walk calmly among the guards, as slow as molasses, as slow as Moses after he parted the Red Sea, for then he would have all the time he needed to rescue tenfold as many slaves as he had already brought to salvation.

February 1838
New Albany, Indiana
Dana Curbstone

DANA HAD BEGUN A LETTER to Jacob, but she didn't know how to end it, nor where to send it. First she would have to know what city he was in. Or whether he was even alive. With all that was going on, now more than ever seemed a good season to get back into the abolition business. She'd purchased a house in New Albany, on the Indiana side of the river. That had been one of the conditions of her release and probation, the main condition, that she not venture back to Kentucky ever, under any circumstances. It was forbidden. There was no clientele left for her, in any case. She knew she was a lot more popular in jail than she ever would have been outside of it again. There would be beady stares and strained smiles, the kind you'd give a whore into whose care you had temporarily and mistakenly commended your daughter for safekeeping. Only the manners Dana had taught them would keep her former charges from insulting her right in the street. So it was better this way.

Her new house, right on the river bank, with a big window, even a sort of widow's walk upstairs, good for seeing far, would make a perfect refuge. It took a chunk of her remaining fortune to secure this land, but it was worth it. Even then, it would have been more difficult, except that the owners of the house didn't like the idea of all those darkies walking across the river at will. Too fearful a prospect, so they let go a prime spot. Dana had to take an oath in the governor's office never again to engage in subversion, sedition, treachery, treason, and she forgot what else. Half the words weren't even charges at the trial. They were trying to cover all contingencies. But she had no intention of keeping that oath. Oaths were for breaking. She would have liked to ask Jacob to join forces with her, him from an outpost up north, which could be the endpoint of a slave's journey, hers the very first house they would encounter. Symmetry. She'd see each escapee for a short time, enough to bathe their feet in warm water, stitch their small wounds, feed them a biscuit and a slice of pork, and send them on their way, with directions to the next safe haven.

Cal was somewhere. All she'd heard was that he'd escaped.

She couldn't let herself wonder too much about it. She'd have to lie on the bed face down for an entire day, surrendering before the blinding pressure, until the heavy eyelids, the dry tongue, went away and she could walk about again. An abolitionist could never give way to such weaknesses. She had to be more like Cal. He would have resurface one day. Not to her, not likely, but to someone. He was keeping a low profile. Possibly he had guided another few slaves. That's what people said, anyway. Yet no one had actually seen him. He wasn't going to go rumbling in a wagon over the misshapen bricks of the Maysville Road anymore; that was for sure. Not that the road was passable in any case until the spring melt, and then there would be so much mud, who knew how long until coaches could traverse it again?

Cal's journeys would have to be by stealth, possibly by foot, through the woods and vales, walking the beds of streams, avoiding all roads. It would take longer and the risks would be greater. But she knew he was out there doing his ordained or self-appointed duty, unless someone had killed him. Word of that would have reached her, surely. Her only chance of getting news of him would be to receive escapees into her house. They'd be likely to hear such gossip. So she would go it alone. She didn't know how to get started. She had no network of her own, outside Cal and Jacob. Everyone who used to respect her would repudiate her, the murderess, the privileged parolee, the warden's strumpet, the mad Frenchman's pet, the lover of smart niggers, or whatever other names her old admirers had thought up to describe her.

No matter. She deserved them all. Even apart from their contempt, who in their right mind would take a chance on sending slaves to such a notorious celebrity? Anonymity was what was sought. She was a liability. She ought to retire to live the quiet life of a beautiful leper, take up quilting, and sit at the sidelines of New Albany cotillions, if they even had those. She knew no one in the place, only the man who carried the post, the greengrocer, and a few other tradesmen who cared more about getting paid than about upholding a social reputation.

If she bundled up, she could stroll the woods of her property during the less harsh hours of the day, scanning the river for any Negroes running across. Maybe that way she could hear news of Cal, to stand at the bank like a simpleton and wave someone across the ice, someone who would probably start with fear and run in another direction, then slip and break an ankle in the attempt to get away from her. She'd spent some hours already at the widow's walk and at the window facing the river, trying to spot any lone figure, but despite the rumors of dozens or hundreds of slaves crossing, she hadn't spied a single one. Maybe they knew Dana Curbstone lived here. Maybe that's precisely why they avoided this stretch of river.

She bundled in wool, wrapped her throat in a scarf, and put on a fur hat and muff, then her best leather boots, ones she used to wear to the orchestra. On the way out the door, she glanced at the empty basket on the marble table. No one wrote her; even Monsieur Fontenot had ceased to correspond.

That is, with a single exception. She received letters from the warden approximately twice per week. She tried not to open each envelope, and then she would, slitting it open with her fingernail, usually after jerking awake at odd hours with the taste of brandy in her mouth. In the letters he called her Lovely, Loveliest, Dearest, Most Beloved, greetings as hyperbolic as they were interchangeable. Frank had two daughters, each of school age, one thirteen and one fifteen, each coming into her womanhood. He adored them. He probably called them Lovely and Loveliest when he greeted them each evening with open arms. Did they call him Father or Daddy?

Frank wanted Dana to be their nanny. Actually, *governess* was the word he used. His wife had gotten progressively sicker. She would never return to her previous state of health, that much was clear. She was far too delicate. There was pulmonary distress, lots of distress. This winter might kill her outright; then again, she might survive. But her days as a mother were numbered. The girls needed more. He'd heard New Albany was nice, one of the most cultured of the newer places. Forward-looking. Its future seemed assured. He was wanting to make a visit himself. Since he had decided against running for political office in the wake of the escape fiasco, which in its own way was a blessing really, he had more freedom to pursue his private life. The penitentiary practically ran itself after the reforms he'd begun to institute, except for the one nasty incident of the section of wall being blown out with gunpowder, and after the initial accusations, his superiors, including the re-elected Governor, seemed happy to treat the season as an aberration. Now that the prison had no famous occupants in residence, there wasn't much to quibble about. They were rebuilding sections with sounder bricks. The old ones hadn't been fired in a hot enough furnace; that's why they'd toppled so easily. It was a matter of construction. The Commonwealth was resolved to seek a better contractor this time around. While they were at it, they'd look into improving the toll roads, so that they in turn would become a better and more predictable source of revenue.

Frank was a practical man, as he'd told her before. He knew he'd never find someone as competent as her, as brilliant, as worldly, as evolved, as accomplished, as beautiful, as charming, as endearing, and especially someone who had no other employment prospects. It would be a good bargain for her. He could come to visit the girls every third or fourth week. Money was not an object. He'd pay her what she was worth. His wife had an excellent family income. He didn't mean to condescend. He wasn't assuming Dana needed his money, but he wasn't assuming that she didn't, either. They could discuss the matter in person if she'd consent to his coming for a prospective visit. They could get re-acquainted under more favorable circumstances. They'd treat each other as equals.

She'd written him one letter back, a short one, also unsent so far, saying she'd think about it.

Dana walked out into the air, only to realize she hadn't been outdoors in two days, and she had overdressed. The break in weather had arrived overnight. The breeze was mild and scented with wintergreen. Droplets of water were beginning to splash from the rime-sheathed twigs onto the disk of ice in the stone fountain. The wholesale melt couldn't be far off. Soon the river would begin to go soft in places, of its own accord, making it too treacherous; afterward, the exodus would slow. The water would be too cold to swim for weeks, and the spring floods would follow, carrying trees downriver, rendering boat crossing as well unpredictable for a time.

A cuckoo sang lazily from the nearest tree. At first she couldn't spot it, she was so out of practice, but then she caught sight of its drab gray feathers and down-curved bill. Trudging down the slope, through drifts still high enough to dislodge small cakes of frost onto the tops of her boots, which she didn't bother to remove, Dana crashed through the accreted brush, thinking she'd need a man soon to remove the winter's accumulation. She skirted an improvised marsh and arrived at the bank. Water stood at the bare edges, with the first whiff of flotsam underneath. Before long, it would all be moving downstream, slowly and then faster. If she'd shaken off her lethargy and come outdoors even a day sooner, she still might have been able to walk straight across to the Kentucky side. Now it was too late.

PART THREE
STRAWBERRY FARM

JUNE 1833
SOUTHERN OHIO
JACOB PINGRIM

OLD, COLD WATER. THAT'S WHAT the woman brought me, in a misshapen gourd with a crack in the side, from a spring she said was nearby. I had to drink fast before the water leaked out. She put her right hand under the cracked place, trying to catch the rivulet of drops as they escaped and then she fed me that too. I liked the scent of her skin mingled with the water, so I drank slowly, even though I was terrible parched. I know I looked a sight from the stretch of days escaping and hiding in the wild woods, yet she didn't object, only let my blistered lips graze her palm, as I sucked up the last bit of moisture. She said she knew I had slept last night in this old hay barn, in the dried-out bales of hay she was sure would catch fire one of these times, since nobody used it anymore. You could smell the mold. Mice had kept me half-awake scurrying from bale to broken bale throughout the damp night. She'd seen me when I went out briefly to trap a squirrel, which I hadn't yet eaten because I was afraid to make smoke, even under nightfall. The missus who owned this place was sick, she said, her children had done spent all the invalid's money, such as it was, and run off to God knows where, to pursue their vices on the few pennies left. Baduns, them. Poor old woman had the rickets and lung spells, and those little crumbled crackers she called kindred just didn't care.

I had been in a sound sleep. When she woke me of a sudden at dawn by shaking my shoulder, after climbing into the loft, somehow with the gourd still half-full, I almost grabbed her by the throat in my suspicious daze. But she managed to shush me before I cried out, giving me time to gather my cloudy wits.

I asked her if she was a slave. She rolled her eyes, said, "Don't you know where you is? Ain't no slaves this far up." I laughed in a giddy burst. For some reason the thought of being 'up' struck me funny, as if she had referred to us in the loft as a relative geographical location. Then she got a little frown on her face, said, "What?" because she thought maybe I was making sport of her.

And that's the moment she reminded me of Rye. It's exactly how Rye would have reacted. She could get real serious on you, in a flash, and she didn't take to a lot of funning, as she called it. Didn't have a stitch of irony in her whole being. Once in a while, when Rye didn't like the sardonic tone of what I was saying, she'd tell me I was too damn smart for my own good, and that was all she was going to say about the matter. If you'd hung her from the ceiling and whipped her with a broom, you wouldn't get her to elaborate on the remark. Also, this young woman was probably about the same age Rye had been when we first came together. It's strange to say, but I no longer remember what Rye looked like, only how she felt. I don't have any sort of picture of her, never did because I didn't know I'd be needing one, and for some reason, though I have been trying hard these last days, I can't summon her exact features to my mind, only an impression. But I think she may have looked like this woman. I should have had a cameo made to place inside the wheat-sheaf locket, but now I have given that locket away in any case, so in the end, it doesn't matter. I couldn't say if someone else would describe the figure crouching before me as beautiful, but I knew her face was kind, though she held it in a no-nonsense scowl.

"What?" she repeated, putting the gourd on the ground. "What's so comical?"

"Nothing. I'm just—awful glad to see you and to drink your water. I'm agog at your hospitality."

"Agog? What that mean?"

"You never heard agog?"

"Sound like one of them bad bible names."

I laughed again, and she couldn't help smiling, though she tried not to. "Yes, a bad bible name. I agree."

"You a runaway?"

"Well, that doesn't sound too noble, but technically—you know, I shouldn't say anything, really. The less you be knowing, the better for you."

"How come you say them words?" The frown was back.

"I'm trying to protect you, that's all. In case someone comes asking after me."

"No, I mean why you said, 'be knowing.' Them words ain't belongen to you."

"That's how I talk sometimes."

"Not for real. You putting on a show, that's what, city boy. Just talk the way God fashioned you to talk, let me talk how I talk, and everything else will be fine. If I don't understand the words you says, I'll ask you what each one means."

"To do otherwise would be anathema to my soul, I assure you."

"Okay, don't get too damn smart. I only said talk normal. And stop smiling!"

"You remind me of someone who was very dear to me."

"Don't get fresh. You can stay here for a few more days, maybe a week, without missus or anybody finding out. You ain't the first one who stayed here. Don't think you was. It seem to be the only abandoned barn for miles around, because there been a couple others. One got caught later, I heard, further up. Last year."

"I had thought to move on right away. I simply haven't had a full night's sleep in several days."

"You too weak to go anywhere now. Wouldn't get to the next property over before you collapsed. Then I'd have to fotch you back, and you half-dead. I'm gonna get you set up with grub. We don't eat too great around here, only fatback and such, but we has got beans and collards coming in, corn for hoe cakes, flour for gravy, so don't you worry none. I can make your belly bulge anyway. I does all the cooking, and ain't nobody here except me and the missus, watching this farm go to rack and ruin, since the other hands drifted off to see if another farm might feed them. We ain't slaves, like what you was, but it's about the same thing when you get down to it. Except nobody whip us. Anybody done that to me, and it would have done got ugly."

"On that score, let me assure you I had no intention of getting fresh with you."

"First off, you too damn weak to get fresh with anybody, even your own self."

"You made a joke. I'm starting to realize that you're a bit saucy."

"Yeah, and you need sauce. I seen how you been licking my hand like a mangy dog who ain't had no petting in a while, and expects a kick in the head instead. Get some food in you, and then we'll see who gets fresh with who, city boy." She bent down over me and rubbed her much softer lips against mine. Not a kiss, exactly, but something like. "Now, go wash up at the creek while I cook."

"Is that safe?"

"You been safe lately? So why you gonna worry now that you is? Do like I say. Ain't nobody standing by right at the moment, so you ought to be safe enough to get clean. Which you need in the worst way, believe you me. Ain't no females gonna come flocking to you unless they is way hard up. Got sweat on top of your sweat. I'll meet you back at this here same loft. If I spies anything, I'll just whistle real sharp like a whip-poor-will. I'm good at that."

"I'll bet you are."

"What that mean?"

"It simply means that I'll bet you are."

"Well, okay, then." As she descended the rickety ladder, she craned her neck upward. "My name's Esmerelda." She didn't ask mine. I heard her heels hit the hay with a soft plop.

Esmerelda called it poor man's lunch. But the hoe cakes, shucky beans, fatback, thin peppery gravy, collard greens, and especially the pickled tomatoes she had no doubt set back for some bleak winter's day were in truth the finest meal I'd eaten in many years. I realized how carelessly I had cooked for myself since Rye's death, and more, how wantonly I had refused the nourishment that others brought around to me. I had lived haphazardly. Like a slave. Once upon a time, I had really liked food. You might have even called me a gourmand. I reflected on what tender care the cooks at Master Odrum's place must have brought to preparing those steaming biscuits I disdained. On the occasions when I waited table at the Phoenix Hotel, I suppose I could have squirreled away rich man's morsels, as some of the other waiters did, while the cook turned a blind eye. He was gruff but not altogether mean. But naturally, I was too proud for that. He never offered me a meal, and I never asked. Thus, I ate badly in the finest establishment in Lexington, where even governors came to sup betimes.

Esmerelda insisted on holding the plate in her own lap while I ate. I was, in truth, trembling, and I believe she expected me to upend the plate, a turn of events she wouldn't abide after her labor of preparation. So, she fed me from her own hand. I had to make an effort not to gobble down the food, as a powerful hunger, one years in the making, was beginning to assert itself. I could see her pacing the spoon's progress, bringing it to my lips only at intervals, as if I were a mere baby. I would never have suffered this treatment at anyone else's hands, but I knew better than to argue. I wasn't about to try to explain the meaning of the word 'patronizing' to her. She'd probably only end up slapping me upside the head and telling me to shut up and eat my victuals. Esmerelda, I suspected, was quite capable of taking the plate away altogether without explanation if she felt I had transgressed one of her house rules. Thus, I tried to eat like a gentleman and to keep what remained of my threadbare dignity—no mean feat when eating from the hand of another—to prove that I was not, in fact, a baby.

Then I began to cry. To cry like a baby, one might say. The beatings with the plank had never produced a sound from me. But I was certainly sobbing now. I wanted ardently to stop my blubbering, but I didn't know how. In truth, I created quite an immediate spectacle, complete with racking chest heaves and slobbery gusts of bawling, which I was sure could be heard for miles in every direction. Soon crashing branches and the whimper of blue-tick hounds, catching my skin scent comingled with a whiff of fatback, would follow.

But no such posse appeared. Instead, Esmerelda set the metal plate on a bale beside herself, told me to hush my little mouth, and took my now-fluid face and clotted nostrils to her bosom, where she held me fast, nearly smothering me. She gave off a prickly smell of bitter wintergreen. I don't know whether she rubbed crushed leaves on herself each morning as a mock perfume, or whether that fragrance bubbled up from within her.

She was removing my shirt, still businesslike, as in all things, as if I had spilt milk on it and she would have to wash it. Likewise, my pants, which she fussed into a folded shape. "City boy," she said, "I swear, you need loving worse than you need gravy." Removing her undergarment, and without otherwise disrobing, Esmerelda wrapped her hard hands around my now-naked body and pulled it to her clothed one, forcing me to enter her with the erection she knew beforehand to be there.

With jaw firmly set, she began to buck against me as hard as she could with her bony hips, her movements almost brutal, screeching and keening. Her rhythm was so vigorous I was afraid she would topple us from the loft, and we'd end on the barn floor, with one of our backs broken. The screeches had quickly evolved into deep sobs, every bit as loud and urgent as mine. A boisterous racket is what we made. A passionate climax came upon her just as fast, also urging one from me. As so many others doubtless do, we invoked God in that instant of simultaneity. I felt a grass fire had spread over me, then just as quickly subsided. We lay in one another's arms, her clothing twisted, my naked skin dank with splotches of sweat, heaving as if we'd just engaged in a nasty fistfight based on a longstanding grudge.

My eyes remained closed, and I enjoyed the sensation of her fingers running through my hair, still stiff from the lye soap I'd used to wash it. The silky strokes of her fingertips made my scrubby thatch feel softer than it actually was.

"Your hair is turning mighty gray."

"Well, at least I still have plenty." I opened my eyes. Her expression had become relaxed and amused. The flinty undertone was gone, at least for the moment.

"You mighty good-looking for an ugly man."

"Thank you."

"You ain't laid with a woman in a long time. Am I right?"

"You're right. And what about you?"

"Many and many a month since I had a man."

"Why is that? You're fetching."

"Lots of bucks round here would have me, for a space anyway. They ain't got so many choices."

"Then?"

"I don't like 'em, that's all."

"And me? You pity me?"

"If only that was all, city boy. It ain't that simple."

"Explain it to me."

"I like you, that's all. Nothing to explain, really. Knew it as soon as I seen that raggedy butt of yours stretched out in the hayloft, and your face all swole up with bug bites. I knew it was gonna be trouble for me. Just my luck to get a sweet tooth for a beat-up, pappy-looking escaped nigger what ain't got no prospects whatsoever and might get me killed or at least whipped real bad for lodging him. And on top of that, soon as he opens his mouth, the city boy turns out to be an egg-head."

"You really have a talent for flattery."

"So, how long was you with your wife?"

"I never said I had a wife."

"You didn't have to. You got that look about you."

"And what does 'that look' consist of?"

Esmerelda remained silent for a moment, shifting her weight as if her legs were getting numb. But when I tried to pull away, she insisted on pulling me back to her.

"Sad. What was her name?"

"Whose name?"

"You know whose name."

"Rye."

"Awful short name. Mine got four parts to it. *Ez. Muh. Rel. Dah.*" She counted the syllables out on the fingers of her left hand, with a childish ostentation.

"We had a child together. Her name was—"

Esmerelda put her hand to my mouth to shush me. "Don't say another word. I don't want to know that baby's name. I know they both came to a bad end."

"You know because I said 'was.'"

"I knowed it before then. Just believe me."

"And why shan't I tell you the particulars, even if you know what happened in a general way?"

"If she was alive today, you'd be right by her side." She gave me a moment to contradict her. I didn't. "Let me explain something to you, egg-head. A woman don't want to hear much about another one, even if she's dead. That's too much woman in one place, and not enough man. I care about the sad look on your face. I want to take it away. Ain't that enough? Only don't tell me no stories. I wasn't there."

"Okay."

"Now get off me." The flinty look returned, imbuing her voice as well. "I got to see about the rickety old granny. You never laid eyes on a human being so white as her. I mean, you think you seen white and all down south, but you ain't seen no white. No doubt she's tinkling the little pewter bell I hate so much. Wish she had enough voice left to yell down the stairs, like a normal person."

An afternoon breeze played through the loft, bringing welcome relief from the stultifying air. The branches of a red maple scratched the edge of the window. I could hear a whip-poor-will, and I remembered how Esmerelda had boasted of her ability to imitate one. She answered the outdoor cries, her tone almost exact, except for the melancholy undertone she added by blowing through her cupped hands. She and the birds played back and forth for a couple of moments. Out of the corner of her eye, she could see she was amusing me, which is probably why she'd kept it up so long.

I reached for her naked torso, above the burlap skirt, and she thrust out her hands to stay mine. "City boy, you gonna bone me to death. Even when the dew lays fresh on the grass, it got a way of chafing."

"You just spoke poetry."

"No, I didn't. I is making a point. They is only so much rubbing my poor skin can take in a solitary day."

"I got your allusion. I understand."

"What I want you to do is roll over on your stomach."

"Why is that?"

"I been feeling raised ridges of skin on your back when I holds you. But each time I try to get me a look, you make sure I don't."

"There's nothing to see."

"There's plenty to see."

I did as she asked. Prone, I could feel her fingers tracing the outlines, as if trying to decipher the content of those strange letters. I had never let Rye do any such. Even though she liked looking at my chest, I seldom let myself be caught without a shirt in her presence. And her my own wedded wife. But I had no power to say no to Esmerelda. She took her sweet time, making sure she touched each and every scar.

"Whatever you done, it weren't enough to earn this."

"Who says I did anything?"

"We all done something. Hurt somebody. It comes back on us."

"And what did you do?"

"I know what I done, and I ain't gonna say. But I also know how I paid for it. I met you." I didn't ask her to elaborate. Esmerelda began to kiss the scars on my back. Her rough lips, bitter in the kissing, felt soft by comparison to the marks on me. I felt sure I had lost all sensation in those Godforsaken places, yet I could feel the ridges tingle beneath each touch of her lips. "City boy, I'm getting close to a place in myself where you could use me right up if that's what you was minded to do. Sap me until I ain't nothing but a dry husk."

"I don't think that's true. A moment ago you thrust me away."

"Only because you didn't push on."

"We've only known one another for three days."

"Don't make no difference."

"I don't believe you. You're one of the strongest women I've ever laid eyes on. Could anyone be more self-sufficient than you?"

Esmerelda rolled away to pick off a length of straw that had stuck to her leg. "I was married to a man for almost a year. Don't know why. All I ever did was make his life hard. I showed you more sweetness in a couple days than I let him see in a calendar year."

"I thought we weren't going to talk about our spouses."

"I let him have his due, as much as I could endure. But I never give him nothing, truly. And him a lot better looking than you."

"Where is he now?"

"Got his arm caught in a thresher. Bleeded to death in less than the time I can roll out a pie crust. And I think he was glad to go."

"That's gruesome."

"Not as gruesome as living with a sack of stone."

"Why did you marry him?"

"I was bored."

"When was all this?"

"Three year ago."

"And you haven't been with any man since?"

"Yes. I have. One man."

"What was his name?"

"I don't know his name. I wouldn't let him give it to me."

"It was that anonymous?"

"I call him *city boy*." She gave me a long stern look, stood up in the loft and began to dress herself. "I'm afraid that if I hear his name outright, I'll never escape him."

Esmerelda had a sister, one who lived in Pennsylvania, and she asked me to write the sister a letter from dictation. It was important enough to her that she took the risk, for the first time, of sneaking me into the main house, saying that the mistress had "took her serum" and would be snoring most of the morning away. I entered with more trepidation than I had felt entering the Ohio River. What harm a puny, half-dead white crone might possibly do to me, I couldn't imagine; nonetheless, every creaking floorboard in that old house unnerved me. The journey to the study was accompanied by the quarter-hour *bong* of a clock, a housecat rubbing at my leg, the promised snores, which could be heard even from below, and the pop of a loose floorboard that might as well have been a rifle report that shot through my chest. A hideous tickle formed at the back of my throat, and it was all I could do to keep from whooping up a cough.

Somehow we made it to the roll-top desk without incident and I looked around. It was the first time I'd been inside a study in quite some time. All at once I wasn't worried about my presence inside the house. The familiar smell of half-decayed paper was a comfort to me. I lingered among the mostly empty bookshelves, fondling someone's medical texts, perhaps those of the old woman's dead husband, or possibly ones she had secured in the vain search to restore her own life. There lay also, alone on a shelf, a tome of the writings of Cincinnatus, its pages uncut. I considered ripping a few of them apart, to let the words breathe, to let daylight touch them and bring their meaning back into existence. But I left them alone to molder, and a few stray words from some page of Cincinnatus I'd once read, no doubt, when Mistress Brathwaite gave me access to the study, came unbidden into my mind. "I issue from such burning blackness, I spin like a top, with such propelling force, such tongues of flame, that to this day I occasionally feel that primordial palpitation of mine, that first branding contact, the mainspring of my 'I'. I have lived an agonizing life, and I would like to describe that agony to you ... "

I couldn't remember what he'd written after that.

In the desk, I found a bottle of ink, somewhat thickened, yet still serviceable, a stylus, and sufficient paper. I asked Esmerelda whether her sister could read, and she said no, and then I asked who might read the sister the letter aloud, and Esmerelda said she wasn't sure. I asked if the sister had a mailing address, and she said she only knew what town the sister lived in. Then I asked who would carry the letter to the sister, and she said, her eyes now burning, that she would figure that out later. Could we just get on with the damn letter?

While I was getting set up to write, from the kitchen she had procured a bowl of strawberries, at their perfect pitch of ripeness, sweet and juicy as her tongue, and she popped one in my mouth to get me started, holding the others back as a bribe. I wrote out the first words she spoke: "Dear Malika, Everything here been fine. Dis been a specially hot summer. I barely got a time to bathe befo what I get up and another day done come down de sky." After only these few short utterances, Esmerelda asked me to read the words back to her, a strawberry poised between her thumb and finger. When I read aloud the words she had dictated, she squashed the strawberry decisively back into the bowl and grabbed the paper into her hands, staining it red with her thumb in the process.

"That ain't what I said."

"Yes, verbatim. Those are your exact words."

"You jus makin fun wid me."

"I assure you I would never make fun of you. Your speech is delightful. There's poetry in you."

"Not no poem I wanna hear. I sound stupid. Nobody ever said 'another day done come down de sky.'"

"You did."

"No I did not, and don't you be writing any such."

"This is the way you talk, and there's nothing wrong with it."

"Maybe when I say what I said, it been fine, but when you write it, it became stupid. You got to make it better."

"And how do you propose I do that?"

"You got to write the words like what I talk. Not the exact sounds, maybe, but some words that mean what I said."

I told her I didn't mind being her amanuensis, but that I did not want to take it upon myself to improve a manner of speech that I found perfectly expressive already.

"I'm gonna *manuens* you if you don't stop this nonsense."

"Amanuensis means 'scribe.' Actually, etymologically, it means 'handwriting-slave.'"

"You ain't my slave, you damn egg-head. You *used* to be a slave, city boy, but now you belongen to nobody. I'm yours, more like."

"If you say so. So then, I don't have to write the letter unless I want to."

"You ain't getting no more strawberries until you write a pretty letter to Malika."

"When you say 'strawberries,' what exactly do you mean?"

"I think you knows what a strawberry is. And I mean you ain't getting no more strawberries from me."

So, while Esmerelda talked in my ear about this and that, I wrote a pretty letter to Malika from Esmerelda, a letter I knew would never make it into the sister's hands, much less be read to her. She seemed fascinated just to watch me form the loops and sticks of the words with such speed. Eventually, however, she became bored with my repetitive strokes, so she curled up in an armchair and drifted off to sleep at my elbow in the middle of the morning, mumbling that she would finish later. I kept writing all the same, with the housecat as my sole witness. This is what the letter said:

Dearest Malika,

I am in love with an escaped slave named Jacob Pingrim. Actually, I don't know what his name is, because I won't let him tell me, and I only let him say his wife's name once, but this is the name I have chosen for him, Jacob Pingrim, out of all the names possible in the universe, simply because I like the sound. Sometimes I feel it came to me in a dream. I have uttered those syllables from my bitter yet still delectable mouth each night while I drift off, sometimes in the hayloft with him, when I could slip away, and other times in my own hard little cot on the second floor of the house, lying less than equidistant between the old woman's deep pulmonary snores, and Jacob's lighter ones. I imagine the day when Jacob and I may share a marriage bed. I have a quilt my grandmother began making before she fell ill with some poorly diagnosed disease, what we call an ague, though I'm not even sure what that means, and then I finished the quilt myself against a day I might have occasion to use it. I never brought it out from the cloth bundle where I kept it when I married Roscoe. He only would have lain upon it bleeding into the fabric when he fainted after his hand got mangled, and we would have wrapped him in it like a shroud when we had to drag his body from the room for the last time for burial. By now it would have disintegrated under the soil, alongside him. It is strange, Malika, often I miss Roscoe, even though I never loved him. I wouldn't tell Jacob, but his eyes are a lot like Roscoe's. Jacob might be jealous of another man's pretty eyes, even a dead one's.

Jacob says he doesn't like people. I find this hard to believe, as he is very kind to me, but then again it's only the two of us, and maybe Jacob is only capable of living in a world where two people exist. Maybe this hayloft is the closest thing to happiness he will ever know. I watch him sleep, and he has a look of suffering on his face, as if he had issued from a burning blackness and is trying to return to it. It's as if he goes deep down into a solitary place crowded with unbearable memories. I know he wants to tell me about these things, and I'm sure the confession would do him a lot of good, but I can't bear to hear it right now. I want him as he is given to me in this moment. There will be time for the rest later. I'd much rather have him try to tear me limb from limb when we couple, inflicting bruises on one another, and knowing through our mutual physical reality a fact solid and undeniable that doesn't flow from the past, has nothing to do with anyone else who entered our lives by happenstance or design. I was impassive when faced with my husband's grotesque death, yet I would shriek like a wretched ghost if someone were to come unbidden and snip a single lock from Jacob's head. I can shear his half-gray hair to the nub for no reason whatsoever if the mood takes me, but only my hands may do it.

I hope that Jacob has managed to make a baby on me in this short time. I don't know how long we will be together. I didn't want Roscoe inside me because I had a deathly fear that he might inseminate me, and though I loved his beautiful eyes, otherwise I did not wish to procreate his like into the world. Forgive me, Malika, that my misbegotten tenderness can only now come forth and show itself. We do what we can with the foul, confused little hearts God gives us.

I hope that you are well. Someone told me you had married and were with child. When the old woman finishes clinging to life and finally gives up, I will come to see you. Or perhaps it will be sooner. I am giving serious thought to accompanying Jacob Pingrim. I'm not sure exactly where he is headed, but it has to be northward, and perhaps I can persuade him to make your town, the name of which I have not forgotten, as part of his itinerary.

Your sometimes loving sister,

Esmerelda

I sealed Esmerelda's letter with wax and emblazoned it with her mistress's stamp.

The old woman was spending so much time sleeping that Esmerelda saw fit to move me into the house. I resisted, on account of a visitor might stop by unannounced, putting us both at risk, but she said no one ever came by anymore. A story had got back to her, she said, on one of her trips into town, that two ghosts lived on the place. The last thing anybody knew for certain was that a man had bled to death after getting his hand mangled. Taking her solid flesh in my arms, I asked whether the story about ghosts was true, and she just laughed and spun out of my grasp, her apron lifting up from her dress as she whirled. I don't know whether she was simply getting careless, in her self-assurance that we wouldn't be disturbed, but I decided to take her statement at face value, as indeed I had not seen one soul in the entire time make its way to this admittedly remote area. Esmerelda tended the truck garden herself, enough for sustenance, swatting gnats and flies and bees, and since the hands had traipsed off, she'd let the buildings go to ramshackle.

The place almost looked deserted, in fact. She wasn't going to repair anything. Soon as the old woman died, somebody would take possession of the place; she didn't seem to care who it turned out to be, whoever had a lien, or whatever brazen relative took it upon himself to come forward and claim the land. Nobody ever wrote the woman or came to visit or give her aid. Esmerelda herself didn't know why she stayed, the woman had been mean to her when she had more vitality, and didn't deserve attention, if you stopped to think about it, but you couldn't just go off and leave somebody to die what didn't have any kin worth having. So she tried not to think about it.

I wondered why I couldn't have been staying in the house the whole time, but I guess Esmerelda had to get used to the idea. Surprisingly, by the time she dressed a pallet in the study for the two of us to sleep on, near the door, where she could listen up the stairwell and descend and ascend throughout the night as necessary, I was more than ready to move in. If someone discovered us, I would deal with it. I even enjoyed the lumps in the mattress, knowing that she and I had put some of them there, and that the old woman's coughing wasn't the only thing keeping Esmerelda up half the night so that in the mornings she would sleepwalk through breakfast preparations with a sensuous, hip-rolling gait that pleased me no end.

When she got loose-limbed and slap happy, she lost the wary edge she carried before her like a cocktail tray at a tense dinner party. She lolled and lollygagged through the morning chores. I enjoyed those hypnotic ways, when she didn't try to be so blamed efficient about everything. She said she'd never touched liquor before, couldn't afford to, and I believed her.

I tried to help her with the cleaning and meal preparations, to compensate for my lazy ogling of her form, but she was too used to doing chores in her own particular way, and found my attempts a nuisance. Her only concession was to let me tend the garden in the early morning hours when not a soul was apt to pass by on the chopped-up country road that ran nearby the house. I had lots of ideas about what I would plant the following spring—turnips, beets, hominy, rosemary, zinnias, radishes, as if we held deed to the place, as if I'd always lived as a freedman, and as if there weren't an outstanding warrant for me.

I realized that in spite of my expertise, never in my life had I so much as contemplated having my own personal garden. Rye used to keep a small one, on a sharecrop basis, against my wishes. I had generally refused to lend a hand because I knew it wasn't ours, and my obstinate self could experience no joy in its maintenance. Nonetheless, with chagrin, I'd eat Rye's canned beans in mid-winter, sheepish but satisfied.

After a few nights of watching Esmerelda hop up and down from the pallet, as the old woman's coughing grew ever harsher, I offered to administer her narcotic in the middle of the night, and to go and mop her withered body. First Esmerelda said it wasn't right, a man could not do such acts, the old lady had her pride, then she said it wasn't safe, the woman might recognize me as an escaped slave. I told her this was preposterous, the woman had to be well-nigh delusional by this point; she probably didn't even know who Esmerelda was anymore. I could take care of her well enough. Esmerelda got real quiet and turned away from me on the pallet. I put my arms around her, told her I was sorry. I could feel her shaking in a way she'd hadn't done before. Then she said no, I was right, the medicine was on the kitchen table in a tin cup, and she wouldn't mind if I took a turn.

So up the stairs I went, into a room I could smell well before I arrived at its threshold. Its odor made me gag. I'd not experienced anything so foul during my stretch of days in the woods. No carcass I'd trod upon by accident could compare. I tried to suppress my retching. The woman must have had some infected limb, or internal organ that was shutting down. The window had been wedged open with a stick and a wind blew strongly enough to push back the heavy curtains into a flowing tent, but that didn't dissipate the odor any, only stirred it up. I could barely discern the woman's face in the guttering blue flame of the lamp I'd placed at her bedside. I hadn't known she was that far gone. Her face had collapsed on itself, seemingly without structure. Truly I could believe that she was already dead except for the low sputter coming from the slack hole of her mouth. Somehow I'd imagined her as possessing at least enough spirit to stay in command of Esmerelda. I'd heard the tinkling bell, Esmerelda spoke of it often in reference to the old woman, so the only way I'd been able to imagine her was as someone implacable, domineering, and though I knew it couldn't strictly be true, weirdly it entered my mind that Esmerelda had been coming up and tinkling the bell herself.

I made myself wipe the woman's face and neck with a washcloth from the basin Esmerelda had provided me. The cloth clung to the woman's neck, catching in every fold, dragging against her impossibly dry skin. I couldn't bring myself to wash the rest of her, or even to imagine what half-liquid spectacle might lie beneath the crumpled gown. I made myself cradle her head while I spooned out the medicine and listened to her choke on it. I made soothing sounds. I even whispered, stupidly, that everything was going to be all right, as if she could hear me, as if I had the power or authority to give that assurance to an anonymous heap of flesh.

When I slipped back into the sheets downstairs, after washing my hands several times with the bowl and pitcher on the woman's dresser, Esmerelda asked me how she was doing, how she looked, and vacuously, I again said fine, offering my benediction and blessed assurance. I listened to Esmerelda slip into an unaccustomed smooth slumber, the kind of sleep I didn't think her capable of. She simply relaxed her whole being and began to give off deep and regular sighs.

Then I was possessed by a thrilling sensation that at first I couldn't explain to myself. I only knew that it was making me wakeful. After listening to the wall clock bong three more times on the quarter hour, I understood what it was. The old woman would die soon. No one would be the wiser, if we didn't tell anybody. Her offspring never came to visit. As for me, the slave-catchers would stop looking for me after a while. Possibly I had been reported as dead by drowning.

150

I would set to repairing the door hinges, clear the brush out of the garden, build chicken-coops, maybe put a weathervane atop the barn so that I could be reminded each time I crossed the dooryard on my way to the fields which way was north and which was south. I didn't have to be Jacob Pingrim any longer. People could call me Elmer, Peter, Ishmael, Gabriel, or Roscoe Junior, for all I cared. I would have no problem inventing a new past for myself, as a natural-born freedman, an amateur botanist. As far as any neighbors I might encounter, I would endeavor to come across to them as eccentric in ideas and deferential in manner.

I rubbed my face across Esmerelda's back to experience another draught of bitter wintergreen. The dusky smell of sleep, with a light layer of dried sweat from the times she ran up and down the stairs, clung to her body. I liked to think that Rye, so sensible about everything, would encourage me to find a new life. But if I believed Rye and I had been meant for each other, like loam for wheat, like gray skies for geese, like rust for metal, like embers for skin, like undertow for shale, like a plank for my back, like snow for tombstones, like inchworms for eternity, like Greek for coons, like bricks for hooves, and I did believe it, then by definition it was impossible that any other being, including Esmerelda, could be meant for me. Knowing how possessive Rye was, she might be jealous, even in death. Perhaps she had become a ghost rather than a soul. Perhaps that's who I had felt pursuing me through the woods.

I lay there listening to the same night wind push its way through the off-kilter jambs, so in need of grease. It showed no signs of ceasing or dying down. The wardrobe against one wall of the study, with its pale wood, began to take on the sinister aspect of an upright coffin, as ungainly as it was clichéd, constructed all wrong, wide enough to encompass two or even three bodies. I mocked myself for an idiot, but I couldn't put the notion out of my mind. All I had to do was creep out of bed and go touch the wood. But I couldn't make myself do it. I, who had slept these previous nights in isolated woods full of bats, mice, foxes, earthworms, skunks, raccoons, cougars, without the slightest nerves, couldn't touch the wood of the wardrobe lest Rye's decomposed and stinking yet incensed corpse fling itself out to smear its juices over me, the same juices I used to suck with pleasure, before they turned noxious and vile and jellylike.

The housecat must have been in heat, and I must have been giving off some reek of substance, because it had entered the room, hopped on the pallet in the dark, padded up my legs and hip, then squeezed itself between the muttering Esmerelda and me. The cat kept insisting its furry bulk, sending an electric spark into the air. I pushed the cat away, but it only came back, two or three times, until at last I seized its nape and flung it across the room to hit the wardrobe with a dejected yowl.

Esmerelda sat up with a jerk. "Was that the old woman crying out?"

"No, the cat fell. Go back to sleep."

She sat in the dark in silence for another moment. "Is you cold?"

"No."

"You trembling all over, baby. Maybe you caught fever from touching dem ole white bones upstairs."

"Not any such. I was having a bad dream."

"Put your arms around me and I'll chase the bad dream away."

I did as she asked, mechanically, but she was too sleepy to notice how rigid I remained. Long before the quarter-hour bonged once more, she slumbered again. I couldn't hear the housecat any longer. Possibly I'd delivered it a mortal blow, and just as likely, it was bruised and sulky in a corner, furtive, waiting for me to fall asleep so it could repay me with its claws. Would the old woman die tonight, tomorrow night? In a fortnight? Or would she cling to her life in a stubborn coma for months, or even years? Was she even alive to begin with? Can you die if you're already dead? A sensation surged in me, the like of which I hadn't felt since the time I almost flung Creech into the fireplace. I was contemplating going upstairs and smothering the old woman with her own pillow. She needed to die. She deserved to die. She was keeping us from fulfilling our destiny. Now I was really shaking. I could hear a throb in the room, growing larger, possibly the cat's purr as its physique expanded its boundaries to those of its feline ancestors, so that its tiger-like form could stalk the room until it found its meet object. I jumped out of bed, lurched to the wardrobe, and ran my palms along its smooth surface.

"Egg-head, what in the hell is you doing?" Now Esmerelda sat up, displeased and wide awake. She struck a match to light a lamp, seeming to know beforehand exactly where everything was in the room—match, lamp, wardrobe, me. To her, even groggy, dimensions were exact. They never changed shape or size, night or day. Even the cat ran over and jumped into her lap for protection, its gray-green eyes shooting me a reflected rebuke in the flame-light.

"I'm restless, that's all."

"Last time I send a man up to do a woman's job. If you gets all jittery like dis when you has to wash dat slacked-out skin, you ain doin me no service."

Her speech fluctuated, making it hard for me to comprehend, but at last I made out its meaning. "It wasn't that. I let my mind get carried away."

"You a big baby, if you ask me. Come lay down and if de old woman call, you let me handle it. I thought she might have up and died in the night, way you carrying on."

"Okay."

"Now, no more foolishness."

"There will be none."

"There better not be."

Esmerelda was trying to wake me. I felt hungover, thick with sleep. Was it midday? The room had plenty of light but the sky outside was overcast, so it was hard to tell the time and my blurry, resinous eyes couldn't make out the clock on the wall.

"You knew."

"I knew what?"

"You knew. That she had died. That's why you was so fidgety."

"She's dead?"

Esmerelda was crying so hard she could hardly talk. "You must forgive me."

"For what?"

"When I seen her face, all lopsided and stiff, like she been real scared in de last moment, I believed you had gone up and smothered her last night, or choked her. This morning, I looked for bruises on her throat. Didn't find none, but I stayed plenty mad anyway. I didn't dare wake you up until I calmed down. Spent about two hours at her bedside watching a corpse do nothin."

"All I did was give her medicine and wash her face and neck." I put my arms around her and she started to relax into me. Her weeping subsided, and she blew her nose on a fold of her skirt.

"Esmerelda, my name is Jacob Pingrim."

She stumbled, and flew halfway up the flight of stairs with a piercing shriek, as if I had stabbed her. From above, she glowered down on me. "I tole you not to say your name."

"Why shouldn't I? I have a name, and you need to know what it is."

"Okay. Now you told me. Mister Pingrim."

"Jacob."

"Jacob, then."

"I want to live here always. With you."

"That can't be. Them childs of her been waiting a long time to take over these rickety acres."

"Those children, as you call them, despite the fact they're probably forty years old at a minimum, nearly twice your age, won't know their mother is dead unless we tell them."

"You gonna dig a hole on the far acre an jus throw her in it like a muskrat who got run over by a wagon wheel?"

"I'll build a coffin. I fashioned the coffins of my own wife and child when they died. In fact, there are all kinds of improvements I could make on this place, if I had reason."

"I cain't—cain't think bout any such. In fact, you had best move off this ground before another sun sets. You been here nigh on three weeks, I'll guess. We been pushing our luck already and you ain't no way out of harm. Just when you think you got away, a slave-catcher shows up and drags a nigger right back into the swamp ooze."

"That is a chance I'm willing to take."

"This runaway who came through last year, in the fall, they caught him and beat him senseless. I seen him after they got done with him."

"Come away with me. Right now, today. What's keeping you?"

"I won't leave a dead woman to rot in her bed. I'll dress out dis body. Hold a burial, and a minister say words over her."

"Who is her?"

"What you mean, who is her? She right upstairs and you seen her too."

"I mean what is her name?"

"You ain't knowing her. But her name is—was—Miss—Mrs.—Heath."

"These are nothing but excuses. Nobody is coming to the funeral of Mrs. Heath. It will be you and a parson, standing alone in a field of sod and not knowing what to say to one another."

"All the same."

"I'll hide in the woods for a few days, until the funeral is over and all the mourners have dispersed."

"Don't talk that way."

"Her children won't even know their mother is dead unless they're summoned. We'll keep the windows open at night, and if somebody is approaching, we'll flee."

"And in the winter? You gon' leave a window open when the frost run in to give us lung spells like what she died from?"

"If that's what it takes to keep you, yes."

"Ain't you tired of being hunted, looking over yo shoulder?"

"Are you afraid you'll be blamed, or held captive, or beaten senseless and dragged back into the swamp ooze like a nigger? Like a slave?"

"City boy, it ain't—"

"My name is Jacob."

"Jacob, I is not afeared of getting caught. If I had been, how could I invite you into this house?"

"You tell me. Why did you take that risk?"

"Because I knew it would only be for a spell of days. Then you would move on."

I felt as if she'd slapped me hard, without provocation. I leaned against the wall, suddenly weak-jointed. She came down the stairs toward me, as if to take the words back. She wanted to touch me, but I moved behind a table where she couldn't reach me.

"Jacob, I'm sorry."

"Don't call me Jacob."

She tried to muster a playful look on her naturally stern face.

"Everything begin and end. I been kind to you. Ain't I fed you and loved you up when you needed it?"

"That was before we lay down together."

"You think that change the world? Laying down in a mess of hay and wallering and thrashing, purely because that's how God made us and we can't be no other way?"

"Yes. Doesn't it change yours?"

"You isn't gonna stay wid me, over the long run. I don't have enough love to keep you. What little sack of meal I got to give, I promise I emptied it out before yo feet. But that sack is too puny for somebody like you. Who got a big soul. Who gone closer to God than I'll ever go. Who had a big love. That woman you lost—"

"Her name is Rye. I told you that."

"Did you? One time. See, I forgot her name already."

"Rye."

"Okay, Rye. She's in your eyes every time you look at me. I can't be somebody's spook woman, the walking image of the one he lost and keep trying to get back. I'm too jealous."

"Jealous of a dead person? That's absurd."

"You lost her in some bad way. That's why you got them scars on your back."

"Can't you forget them? They're evidence of human brutality and cruelty, its arbitrariness, and in truth they have nothing whatsoever to do with me personally. Okay, you want to know what happened?"

"No. But you gots to tell me anyway."

"You're right, I do. They were going to be sold, her and my child Creech as a unit, and me kept on in Lexington because of my value to the owner. So after they were hauled to Cheapside, as they awaited sale, I prayed to God, despite myself, to have a disease kill them. I changed my mind back right away, but they took a fever and died right after."

"Baby, baby." She had moved close enough to brush the side of my face with the back of her hand. "I feels bad about what you had to go through."

"Aren't you going to tell me it wasn't my fault?"

"Would you believe me if I said it?"

"No."

"Because we don't know. Not you and not me. Maybe it was going to happen anyway. But you made the wish, and you can't always wish your wish away. You have a mighty power inside you, Jacob. Like none I ever seed. I'm afraid of it myself. It jolted me when you covered my body with yours. I ain't saying you bad or anything. I know you is real good. All the same, loving you killed one woman, might have, and loving you might kill me as well."

"Over time, all my sentiment about Creech and Rye will fade. That process has begun. Yes, you remind me of her. Uncannily. There's nothing wrong with that. It's part of the sweetness of you. I never thought I'd find another woman like her."

"I got to stay here and put flowers on Roscoe's grave once in a while."

"You're going to give up a whole future over superstition? If I'm being unfaithful to anyone, it's to her, not you."

"That's right. To her."

"Christ! Do you realize that I lay awake wrestling with myself half the night because I wanted to go up and kill that useless woman, hurry up her inevitable dying, so that you and I could be together? "

"Of course I knowed. I almost decided to strangle her myself, so you wouldn't have to feel bad. I been going kind of crazy ever since you arrived and I laid eyes on you. I'm about halfway to a madwoman, really. I had the pillow in my hand. Only I couldn't go through with it."

"I'm leaving right now. Unless you want me to fashion a pine box before I go."

"Make love on me before you light out."

"I can't bear the thought of touching you. I can't even stand the sight of you. You repulse me, and I wish I'd never met you."

"That ain't none of it true. You wants me real bad right this minute. I know you're in a fury. Use my body to spend the fury. At least my smell will cling to you a while when you is running through the woods again."

I did as she asked. I tried to shatter Esmerelda's body into a thousand pieces, but only so that I might have the pleasure someday, wherever I might be, of putting them back together again.

His mind was clear as the cloudless sky. The ether shimmered, yet each star hung distinct. Still, he could not read the constellations— strange, given his scientific bent, but he simply never bothered to look up at them much. Any field Negro could decipher them better than him. All the same, he, the last of the least, veered east by following the road, sometimes walking right on it, while dogs barked in the far darkness, their woof-coughs scooping out the air as they tried to protect the universe with the sound coming from their mouths. A single drop of river water left in his skull from the crossing at Maysville dripped down his nasal fossa until he could lick it with his tongue. It tasted like him, mixed with the tang of every dead carp that ever dissolved into salt paste in the Ohio. Halting his gait, he savored himself, dank, as he was, as she had tasted him, the drip at the tip of his loins, what she called his spunk. Maybe his soul would get distilled to a single drop as he swam the current. Perhaps no matter how small it got, the drop couldn't disappear completely, only condense until it became almost nothing. Then the drop ran down his nostril; he licked, involuntarily, and reincorporated it into himself. Now there were more drops running down his fossa, out of his eyes, lots and lots of them, plenitude, and he'd lost track of which exact one contained his soul.

Her smell lingered on him, like she promised it would, or had that been a threat, except he couldn't smell because his nose was clotted with the inalienable smell of him. He blew snot through his fingers into the weeds, trying to smell her again, with luck he'd blow his soul right out with it, a clot to cling to a stalk and tremble, but no, there was more snot right behind it, an endless supply, filling up the space in him. He'd already swallowed his soul, where it would grow again in a ferment of mucous and utter burning blackness, the same way it grew the first time. God made him sturdy for some purpose. Only, he didn't know what it was. Unless simply to live.

The scars kept hurting more and more, turned into wounds again. She had enlivened them. He became aware of the wounds oozing and weeping into the back of his shirt, or was it only sweat? No, the fluid felt thicker, like pus, like the paste of existence. It had substance and stuck to his skin. He hung from the scaffolding of scars, a lank skeleton. Those scars might be all that held him upright.

Was Esmerelda correct? Did he have them coming? How many crickets had he stepped on? He didn't want to crush them, but from time to time, heard a crunch underfoot, as several crickets tried to make their way up his trousers and got stuck in the cuff. Speak like you speak, she said, think like you think, which is all de time. Vowels of de earth and a crack in his tooth. Give him a walking cane an a gold filling and on de sudden dat gimpy sumbitch game for anything.

Big country, so big it run in all direction at de same time so you ain know where you is, maybe you run true same groun ten time o ten time ten time ten, out of plums, mouth scorched, lookim fo dat vineyard, prodigal, belated parable, abacus sassafrass, dynamite and hoof splinter, wintergreen residue masks the breath of death, the funk of stunk.

He still felt her skin, the sensuous membrane, how she avoided diphtheria when her whole clan succumbed to it, leaving only her and him, for a magic spell, happy to be superficial, to dumb down so he could be as smart as her, but that was all gone, now he was moving.

He twisted the licorice of his sweetest memory until its braid reached the sky. Scratch dat name on a patch of slate, of a woman broke down to a stutter. Her eye open an shut time an again as she watch him stuff a rucksack. She ain say nothin only hold close your last jizm and burn her last glance of him to ashes with the prism of her eye. She blink. She blink. Starlight. Abyss. Starlight. Abyss. Celestial orb doan mean nothin except a pulse, a throb. Now scratch him pate all he want until him figure it out. You got a big brain. Live wid it. Cause it gon' stay beside you, wheresoever you wander. Wide awake, shake another cricket off the cuff. Onward, then, egghead. Let the mind become incandescent, if it must. Where else you think light gon' come from? Its short flash runs someplace yet unseen through the deep shaft of midnight because it has no choice.

PART FOUR:
THE IVORY RING

MAY 1833
LEXINGTON, KENTUCKY
DAN BASKIN

RAE WAS QUIET THE WHOLE ride back. I expected her to try to talk me out of returning her, but I guess she had seed too much at the riverbank. I whistled an imitation of a mockingbird, but it didn't lift her spirits none. I strayed into a field for sweet apples, and bragged to her it was the most daring theft of my career, yet she took nary a bite. They was even a flash of rainbow, as the rain and sun wrangled for the day. It might as well have been hailing on Rae's head.

Stalker seemed downhearted too. He fairly dragged his hooves against the stones. He'd have to be newly shod. Rae pointed me down a thistle lane that led to her mammy's place. The bungalow showed dishevel from every angle. Not a spot of paint on the naked boards. They had been weathered down to where you could scarcely see the grain. Cripple grass grew to the porch top. Several cats twanged and stretched their sinews as I scraped my boots toward the plank sag. The door was out of plumb and wedged in the frame so it wouldn't hang loose.

Inside, flies hovered enough to cover a mule. I thought maybe a person had died. Rae stood well behind as if using me for a shield. A woman's body, maybe her corpse, set in a chair swathed in a horse blanket. It stunk awful. But then the corpse moved. She let out a groan and lolled her head. "Rae," she said. "Fetch Mommy the poppy juice, and stir in molasses and sarsaparilla. Not too much, honey. All I need is a spot. This hip joint is a-killing me." Rae shook her head and backed up liken she was going to bolt. I motioned for her to do as her mammy said. In a moment Rae appeared from the kitchen with a cup full of a milky brew, held the woman's head and poured it down. A trickle ran off the woman's lips and onto her dressing gown. She didn't seem to care. She closed her eyes, and we watched the orbits hop beneath the sockets like ladybugs trying to find their way out. Then she opened her lids and fixed on me.

"Howdy, missus," I said. "I apologize that I up and left with your daughter."

"That's all right. What time is it?"

"Late afternoon. We'll be twilit soon."

"Lordy, lordy. And here I thought she had been gone for days. Sometimes she runs off to the woods for a spell. Well, I'm sorry, stranger. I haven't a thing to offer for supper. Them mean cats ran in and snatched off my fatback."

"It's okay, ma'am. We both done supped." Rae had cowered back against the sill of a window with a split shade. It looked drier than an old man's fingernail. Her quail-egg face hurled at me every manner of silent insult. "I don't want to leave the two of ye in bad repair. Will your husband be along soon?"

"Oh, honey, he died on me a couple year ago. The poor soul. Got stabbed in a knife fight."

"I see."

"Since he died, that hellion of a girl has run me ragged. Her brother is off to the penitentiary for every foul act you can imagine, so he's no help at all. I'd give her a thrashing only I can't find the strength." Behind the woman was a fireplace without a grate, and an andiron leaned up against the hearth. I turned toward Rae and held out my arms. She shook her head, rattling that mess of red hair, harder and harder, as if a demon spell was a-coming on. Then she runned straight into my embrace. Rae cried and cried into my flesh. It sounded more like hollering.

"Missus, what say ye I take this little lady on a vacation a few days in Lexington? My name is Dan Baskin. My address is 15 Market Street. Everybody at the Phoenix Hotel knows whar I live, in case you forget. I could bring her back Tuesday week."

Rae's mother had slumped back in her seat, and commenced to quiver. Whatever her age was, she would pass for twice as much. "You can take her permanent if ye want. I been praying to Jesus for someone to lift her off my hands. I don't know who will stir my poppy juice, but I can manage."

I left Rae busy inside my place on Market Street, running her hands over every last object. She cradled the pewter coffee pot as if it was made of gold.

"I have to go out for a short while. Don't steal none of my stuff."

"I'll smash it, instead."

"It's good to see you got your sass back, pipsqueak."

"Who are you going to see?"

"Never you mind. Get yourself cleaned up and put us on some stew with the meat and taters I brung. You can do that much on your own, I reckon."

"And a lot more."

On the way over, I picked up a chocolate bar at the sundry and stashed it in my jacket pocket. The wind, with a hint of autumn on its tail, was as fresh as it ever gets in this part of town, less mixed than usual with dung and seed. I busted into Leora's place. She had a young buck in bed with her, hair all stood up like a porcupine's. He was going at it like prodding a crawdad hole, jabbering words he thought was going to make her skin hot. When I kicked the bedstead, he jumped up like he thought I'd come to recruit him for an Indian war. He was a sight younger than me, his muscles bunched. If he'd given the matter much thought, he might have beat me to a pulp. But I wasn't going to give him the chance to gather whatever slender wits he possessed.

"Get out of here, junior. Or your mammy will be crying into a bouquet on the morrow."

"Who in hell are you?" His attention was already roaming to see whar he'd tossed his britches.

"I'm Leora's husband."

"She didn't say nothing about no husband. This lady is a whore. I paid her a full five dollars in advance."

"Are you calling my wife a whore?"

"No sir. That's what she claimed to be. But I guess she was mistaken."

"Run on off right quick, and I'll beat her instead of you. Otherwise, it's the both of ye."

"I'd rather you just pummel the lady, if it's all the same. They's other—I mean, they's plenty of whores in this town. No offense to your wife."

"None taken."

He lit out the door with his britches unfastened, treading on his cuffs. He didn't bother about the rest of his getup. I flung myself down on the bed and busted out laughing. She had her face fixed in a frown.

"That's the most fun I've had in I don't know when. It feels good to laugh that hard about anything."

"I don't mind so much that you ran him off. But did ye have to be so ornery?"

"If I had acted a gentleman, he'd still be in your bed."

"True enough."

"And I didn't thrash him."

"No, you did not. But what call have you to go saying you're my husband? You know it's a sore spot with me. Not a matter for a prank."

"Well, what if I was your husband?"

Leora sunk down on the very floor. "Don't fun with me, Dan. I'm almost sure you're not cruel. Though sometimes I do wonder."

"I'm not joking. I thought about us on the trip home, and I want to get married." I handed her the bar of chocolate. "Here's the candy you ast for."

"Is that meant as a troth?"

"I suppose. It's all I've got in hand at the moment."

She hopped up and nearly squashed me with her naked bosom. "Oh yes, Dan. Of course I will. Let's do it today. I don't need but a nickel ring. They's one at the corner shop I've gandered at many a time."

"We'll pick it up in the course of the week and have it engraved. Later on, I'll find you something better."

"I told you I don't care about any such."

"To marry me, you have to give up the life."

"That was my last customer just run out the door. But what about you? What about that woman?"

"Which?"

"If you and me is going to get along as man and wife, you have to stop treating me like I'm stupid. Which woman? The one you leapt out of bed to hunt down."

"She's dead."

"I'm sorry. Not that sorry, to be honest, but a little bit. Kind of happy-sorry. What about the slave?"

"He's dead too. He drowned in the Ohio River. They'll find his body, soon or late, but it won't look like him."

"I guess you won't get your reward money. Now I truly am sorry about that, as you can imagine. What are we to live on?"

"Some fellows I know cuts timber. I've a good hand with a saw. We'll have to live close."

"Close is how I want to live, Dan. A single small detail troubles my mind, though."

"What?"

"Do I have to wear the white shift?"

"No, that's all over. We'll throw it away at the first haste."

"We don't have to do that. I'll cut the cloth up and use it as mop rags."

"Whatever suits your mood. There is one more little item."

"Ain't there always?"

"In my house at this moment is a feisty redhead, thirteen years old, or so she says. She's got a good heart, but she is also sometimes a liar and a thief."

"A lot of them are at that age. Is she going to be living in your house?"

"For a while. We'll see what happens. I wanted you to know beforehand that there will be three of us."

"Is she your honey?"

"Of course not. Didn't I say she was thirteen? What goes through your mind, woman?"

"Reality. Does she want to be your honey?"

"That is not a question I am even going to ask myself."

"No matter. If the little hussy don't act right, I'll pull her hair straight out by the roots, as if I was harvesting carrots."

"I'll leave that chore to you. Tomorrow I'll come to fetch whatever possessions you want to move from here. Let's wait a few days to get hitched. I want you to grow comfortable with the idea."

"I was comfortable with the idea two years ago."

"Then give me a few days."

"That's fine. I want all ghost women fled from your life when we wed. And the real ones, too."

"They're gone already."

"We'll see about that. And Dan."

"Yeah?"

"I ain't gonna ask you for much. I never had much. But they is one special thing I require, and it matters more to me than a ring or a house or a handful of jonquils."

"What?"

"I was a prostitute. For five years. You know full well, because you yourself paid me many a night and day. I'll gauge that a hundred men has laid atop of me. A few of them you know, most you probably don't. I'm telling you at the start facts that should come as naught surprise. Don't ask me about them customers later. You might as well be jealous of a room full of horseflies that took turns stinging me. I can't do nothing about what I was, or did. Living clean of all that won't cost me a button."

"Yeah. I understand."

"Do ye? For true and ever?"

"I do, Leora."

"And one last thing. Of them scads of men, you was the only one I ever offered to bed for free. That's God's truth."

"Not even Fontenot?"

"Not him neither. That scoundrel makes too much money as it is."

"Okay." I give her a kiss on the lips, and that was all. I noticed for the first time the rings under her eyes. She was way too young for those. Maybe over time, with the right things, they would soften. I run my hand over the rings. "I got to get back before the pipsqueak burns down the house. She's making a stew."

"That sounds lovely."

"Why don't you come over and share the supper? I want her to meet you."

"If you like."

"I'm going to break the news to her about our marriage."

"I know she'll be thrilled to all get."

"Rae might surprise you. She don't have much of a mother. And I don't believe you've ever had a child."

"No, Dan. I ain't never had no child. Only you, and that for about ten minutes."

166

The nickel ring was at a tinsmith's shop on Limestone. He wasn't a jeweler, just had a case of sundry gewgaws set on the counter. Leora had let him know I'd be a-coming. "Have ye the ring for my betrothed?"

The smith was a slender chap who looked like he supped broth. His beard likely made up half his weight. He took out the ring and held it high. "Thar she is. A beauty to behold."

"How much, then?"

He eyed me careful before speaking. "Twenty dollar."

"That's a jest."

"I snip and hammer tin. It ain't really a humorous bidness."

"That's two full weeks' wages."

"Ye can give me half now, and half in a month."

As a slave tracker, twenty dollars was as nothing to me. I sometimes earned two hundred dollars in a month. And I hadn't saved a scrap.

"You know full well Leora wants this particular one and you're holding that over me. I could buy a gold ring almost for that price."

"Then it's what you ought to do. But every ring has got a story. I'll bet that ivory ring you sport on yer pinky has got a tale behind it. This yar item was brought to me by an itinerant Swede. Don't know what business he had down in these parts. Frankly, I believe he'd lost his way. But he said that this ring once belonged to a princess down by the Cumberland Gap."

"And you believed him?"

"I take a man at his word."

"For your information, there ain't no princesses in this whole wide country, much less at the Cumberland Gap."

"Well I ain't been down that way myself, but that's what he swore. She was a servant girl whose mammy had died, and her jest mopping the floors and slopping the stock. And the elder sister meantime a-running wild, spending a penny whar she ought not."

"Don't say."

"I do say. The older one a spendthrift, and this girl had nothing to wear. They called her Catskin, because she sewed the hides of cats together, which was all the garment she could get. She ast her pappy could she cut down the wedding dress of her dead mother for everyday

167

use. And he said absolutely not. So naturally, being a woman, she wouldn't take no for an answer."

"That part I believe."

"Catskin ast him for a dress made of all the colors of the birds that flew, and all the shades of the clouds that floated past on an October day. And blamed if he didn't up and have one sewed."

"I'm guessing he purchased it at a tinsmith shop."

"No, it was a tailor. The long of the short is that she wore it to the king's house."

"The King of Cumberland, you mean?"

"The very one. Now he was set to marry a princess of high birth, but one who was a peck of trouble. She hollered at the servants and complained about every dish set before her. They served her pheasant and she called it buzzard. When the king spied at his house party the girl with the dress of colors, why he plumb lost his head and slipped Catskin this yar nickel ring out of his vest pocket."

"You'd think he could afford better, being a king and all."

"There's no accounting for taste, friend. I guess he knowed quality when he seed it. Long of the short, Catskin received it on her finger and the next time she come back to the manse, why it was as a baker for the king's wedding with the wicked princess. The princess wanted to know whar was the troth ring, she made quite a racket and throwed a bowl of perfectly good gravy to the ground, and as he was a hemming and hawing, Catskin slipped the nickel ring off her pretty finger to him in a piece of cake. He chomped down and cracked a tooth, and when he pulled out the nickel ring, his eyes met with Catskin's green ones. In spite that she was wearing a pair of britches, he recognized her as the girl who had wore the dress of many colors. And so they wed."

"Thanks for the tale. You solved my problem."

"So you'll take the nickel ring?"

"Not a bit." I walked out and softly closed the shop door behind me.

I removed the ivory ring from my pinky and give it Leora. It fit her ring finger perfect. "I want you to bear a part of me. I can't stand to buy junk from a shop. This is more personal and I know it has value."

"I love it, Dan. I had admired it on your hand. But I didn't know whar it was from."

"Being wore by you is what makes it new."

"You wasn't married before, was you Dan? Tell me true."

"I wasn't."

"Well, whar's it from? It looks like a woman's ring."

"It's an heirloom what needs to be renewed."

"You allus got a mystery to be cracked. But all right. Truth is, more than once I wanted to snatch it off your pinky and didn't know why. Now I'll have it for myself, and I'll wear it with pride."

We got married by a justice of the peace and Leora was in the mood to go straight to the house and eat liver and onions after, so that's what we did. After two weeks of back-busting labor, I could barely climb on Tracker at the end of each day. I had forgot what it was to work a real job. It was a different wise of being in the forest. I wasn't peeping at no animal tracks. The man at the other end of the timber saw had never heard of me, and didn't care who I was. He was more concerned to stand clear of a falling oak. That suited me fine.

On the whole, each of us had adjusted. I didn't bounce on the bedsprings too hard of a night, as so many times in yore. First, I was wore out. And second, I thought Leora might want a small rest from her five years of labor. When we fallen together, I took it slow, and she seemed to appreciate it. The woman would flat-out coo and her words would drip as with sorghum. I won't say I paid much attention to the talk across the pillow, but betimes I would commence to stroke the very back of her neck, under the hair, until she sighed and dropped off into slumber. Leora took up the habit of touching me all through the night, with the tips of her fingers, which deprived me of sleep, but I didn't complain. A couple of times, she turned over in a sound snore and walloped me in the face.

August 1833
Central Ohio
Jacob Pingrim

A FTER ESMERELDA SHOVED ME OFF, I spent several days some ten miles from Strawberry Farm, again in the woods, eating muskrat instead of chicken, wild greens instead of mashed turnips, choke cherries instead of strawberries. Before, I could stand them; now, they offended me. I should have brought food from the farm with me in a rucksack, but I was too proud for that under the circumstances. The cardinals in the trees above quarreled so much that I began to recognize each one's distinct chatter. I wished I knew bird language so I could join in. I had the feeling they understood my situation and were commenting on it, one to the other. I argued with myself that I should push on, at least to a good stream where I could catch trout. But I couldn't seem to move. I lay in a bed of interwoven sticks I'd fashioned to keep clear of the ground moisture. I went two days without eating. I do believe that in better weather, without showers of rain that only served to make the air stickier, I could have lain there indefinitely. Mosquitoes saved me. They bit so fiercely, I was forced to take shelter.

I stumbled out of the woods and onto a road of clay and gravel. A pile of split logs lay by the wayside, skinned of bark. I discerned several houses in the distance. I sat on the pile, thirsty, and with the strangest craving for pigs' knuckles in vinegar water, a morsel I hadn't eaten for years. A bumblebee kept circling my head, disappearing for a while, then coming back to do the same again. A stand of goldenrod lay at my feet.

The silhouette of a person came walking down the road, the gait deliberate and slow. I was too tired to run back into the woods. Surely Walter Brathwaite had stopped pursuing me by now. There was even a chance he might think me dead. Several people had seen me swept downriver, and only by luck had I survived.

The silhouette had become the figure of a man. His narrow face was burned by wind, cheekbones prominent. His hair was blacker than mine had ever been. He had a knapsack slung on his shoulders and was dressed in a suit of cloth with a string tie.

"Jesus is coming," he said.

"Is he far behind?"

The man smiled as if he'd heard that one before. He put down the knapsack and took from it a pamphlet. "Can you read?"

"Only English, Latin, and Greek."

He handed me a religious tract all about the Second Coming, wars, and rumors of wars. "What's your name?"

"Robert Maples. They used to call me Black Antler."

"Are you a Shawnee?"

"I don't advertise it. Almost all of my tribe has been relocated to Kansas and Oklahoma these past two years. Those of us who managed not to go keep a low profile."

"I know something myself about keeping a low profile."

As I was skimming the tract of dire prognostications, the man took out a loaf of bread and broke off a chunk. Robert Maples bowed his head. "*Meleto velawa yeama kesheke nelawa thwawapuka.*" He held out the chunk to me.

"I didn't understand what you said."

"'Give us this day our daily bread.' I wanted to bless the grain for you. That way it nourishes you twice. And here is some water." I ate and drank, in reverent silence, except for my slurping. He waited without haste for me to finish.

"Now you're going to save me, I guess."

"Not at all. I only wanted you to know that He is coming. I couldn't just pass by. 'Always give a word or a sign of salute when meeting or passing a friend, even a stranger, when in a lonely place.'"

"Is that from Proverbs?"

"Tecumseh said it. My grandmother used to repeat it."

"My gratitude for the bread and the salute. As you can perhaps imagine, I haven't shared much polite society these last days."

"Things will go better for you if you stop living like a savage. The Shawnees lost at Tippecanoe, yes, but we were civilized all the way up to defeat. When my wife died of smallpox, I was bitter. I killed three white men, for no reason, in the woods one night. I hacked them to death with a small axe. No one caught me, and I was never brought to justice. I drank too much, and eventually I became a Christian. No one saved me; it was just gradual. In fact, I first joined a Baptist church only so the whites wouldn't be so hostile toward me. I didn't believe in Jesus. Then little by little, I did."

"I should have killed a white man in Kentucky when my woman and child died, instead of blaming myself."

"Maybe you should have. It feels good at first. You enjoy the blood on your hands. But I don't recommend that course of action. However, I do believe you will not be taken for an escaped slave so easily if you clean up. Why is a man who speaks Latin and Greek living in the woods and eating bugs? It doesn't make sense." He removed a roll of clothing from his knapsack. "This is my second suit. I want to give it to you. We're about the same size. Clean up and act like a free man. Otherwise, you might as well go back to Kentucky. You have the expression of a slave in your eyes."

I was going to protest, but I ended up saying "Thank you" to Robert Maples.

"Put them on."

"Right now?"

"Yes, why not?"

I did as he said. The clothes hung off me a little, but with a few days of decent food, they would fit. "You'll look fine after you wash your face and comb your hair and the mosquito bites subside. You know, Chillicothe is only a couple days' walk from here. I just came from there. All the free blacks are helping each other out, and aiding the ones like you who escaped. The town is full of abolitionists too. Some people will hate you there, but most will treat you right. Follow this road and ask as you go. Try not to mistrust everyone. No one walking along this path has done you a wrong. They might, but they haven't yet."

"And you think the blacks in Chillicothe will succeed? You can say that after the whites forcibly relocated your entire people from this same state?"

172

Robert Maples offered an enigmatic smile. "It's too late for us, but not for you." He gave me a wink. "Believe me. Jesus is coming." He shouldered his knapsack anew and continued his slow gait down the road. I wondered where the bumblebee had gone.

I wasn't ready for Chillicothe. The very thought of all those people, even if they might work in my favor, put me in a panic. I made my way back to the farm. Wild strawberries covered the south hill, each tiny body of fruit uneaten and ripe to bursting. I walked right in the house. There sat Esmerelda on the sofa, looking at a half-peeled apple, its flesh brown. I took the knife from her hand. She let herself be embraced. No protests leapt to her lips. I asked her where the dead woman was. She took me to a shallow hollow. The body was pitched in, rolled in burlap, and brush had been thrown atop it. I cleared the brush, dug a grave of proper depth, which took me half the day, and made a coffin, which took the other half. It was almost midnight when I finished shoveling the dirt back in. Abejidé flitted through my mind. I wished that I'd had the chance to dig her such a grave, one of proper depth.

Esmerelda cooked a meal at that late hour. She seemed to know fried fish was what I craved. I'd gotten into the habit of catching brook trout not far from the farm and there were a few still on hand. I lay against a seat back in the kitchen, watching her dredge a filet through the flour, listening to the hot pan sizzle, taking in the vivid scent of ticking cast iron, the flour as it caramelized into crust, the oil as it spattered. I kept eating, and she kept cooking. There were no side dishes, just a stack of breaded filets. When I was done, she heated water, stripped off my suit and washed me down. She took a long gander at the jacket and pants, but said nothing about them.

The entire time since I'd arrived, we hadn't spoken. We lay on the pallet together. I fell asleep quickly and didn't wake until late the next morning. A cow was in distress, probably not having been milked in a couple of days. It bawled from a distance. Esmerelda lay fast in my arms, both of us in a sweat. When we arose, she went to tend to the heifer. Things got quiet, except for the incessant cluck of hens beneath the window, as if asking for slaughter. Esmerelda came back indoors. She then boiled a pan of coffee and laid out eggs, a slice of salted pork, and fresh milk, still warm. After breakfast, I walked through the fields until I found a slab of stone of sufficient size. With a chunk of flint, I scratched out the name MRS HEATH in block letters and embedded the stone in the grave. I said a prayer for her, one for Abejidé, and another for the infant of Mistress Brathwaite, who had only lived one day, and whose grave we'd searched out on that bitter winter afternoon. It occurred to me that we had not prayed over her at that time, only stood in mute witness to her brief existence.

I went to the shed and took an inventory of what tools were on hand. Some had rusted, but the set was fairly complete. I set about mending breaks in the fence. She fed a couple of hogs and the chickens that stayed underfoot. By pulling apart a leaning shed, I gave myself lumber and nails to replace rotten boards in the main house. In some cases, I cut chinks and made pegs. Luckily, there was no problem with termites. I had to crawl under and set new joists for the porch. I found lime and glue, mixed it with water to make a whitewash, and gave the house several coats. Esmerelda began to clean the premises in earnest with vinegar and lye and buckets of water she brought from the well. Together, we busted sod, pulled out weeds by the root, and got the garden in shape. I planted stakes and built trellises and frames to put it in order. I examined each plant for disease or neglect, and destroyed the ones that weren't thriving. The garden was good, but had become a victim of its own abundance.

Esmerelda raised no complaint, and in fact said very little. Work was what she was used to. It was the one thing she knew how to do. She hung up my suit and sewed me a couple of sets of clothes out of garments and spare cloth rummaged from a trunk. Probably some of it had belonged to Mister Heath at one time. She was a wizard with a needle. I wasn't going to complain about a few moth holes, but she darned every one to perfection. Torn curtains were repaired. Out of a root cellar she brought jars of conserves and out of a smokehouse, which also needed repair, she produced a ham.

I was astonished at the secret industry of this lone woman. For years she'd run the whole place with superhuman resolve, even as it did its best to fall apart. Yet it seemed that what she'd waited for was someone else like her, to labor alongside without much ado. She saw the slave in me—not the captive, but the beast of burden, who also had the ability to reason and solve problems—and she liked it. Before, I'd been a fugitive, wounded and weak, thin and helpless, needing to be satisfied by food and sex and nursing. Esmerelda had wanted to tend to that man, but not to keep him. She couldn't understand that it was just a circumstance. To her, I was a cripple. If I'd come back and tried to persuade her in words that I wasn't, she'd have run me off again.

The best thing I did for myself, and for us, was to keep my mouth shut and tend to business. We made no reference to anything that had happened before. After two weeks of us working steadily from the moment we woke until the spent twilight, stopping only to take meals, she produced a flask of spirits from a cabinet. It was a home-brewed brandy or whiskey with a noxious flavor. It tasted like one of those medicines that either kill you or make you better. Who knew whether it had been concocted by Mister Heath, years past, when he was desperate for a drink on the coldest day of the year, with the wind running high and his spirits low. As we sat on the porch on a bench I'd built, I made myself drink the stuff without betraying my disgust by any expression. After a few draughts, it wasn't so bad, just a continuous burn in the throat that made its way to my extremities. Our bodies came together. She and I kissed for a while, then dragged ourselves upstairs and with a candle lit, crossed the threshold into Mrs. Heath's bedroom. Esmerelda lit several more candles and the room filled with a tallow scent. Esmerelda had cleaned and disinfected every inch of the quarters, and the sheets had been boiled and hung to dry and returned to the mattress. She turned down the bedspread and we fell onto those fresh sheets for the first time. "This is where we live now," she said.

We entered into one another, with every muscle aching. Our limbs were too weary for anything more than a long, slow, ongoing exploration of each other. She'd done her best before never to be entirely naked in my sight. Now she was. I touched her protruding ribs, one of them punctuated with a large mole. A small scar on her stomach made me realize just how smooth her skin was, all except for her hands. She had the squarest feet I'd ever seen, the toes as if hacked straight with a cleaver. Only the round of her hips betrayed the curve of this woman who wanted to live by the rule. When at last we copulated, she began to buck against me with lids squinched. I asked her to slow down and open her eyes. She accused me of putting a bit on her like you would to check a mule, but I said I only wanted her to look at me. We lay still for a spell, and the clenched quality in her relaxed. I wanted to tell Esmerelda I loved her, but I knew better. So I said, instead, "You're quite a woman. I never saw any other wield a pick axe like you do."

She stroked my nose, her arm moving in and out of shadow. "Does that mean you loves me?"

"It might."

"Well, I never seed a man what had such a hand with a plank and saw."

"Does that mean you love me?"

"It means you has good hands."

We took to sitting on the porch in the evenings and listening to the sounds of small creatures at the edge of the wood. To maintain the insects at bay, I kept a log fire burning in a pit I'd dug and lined with slate. There were plenty of felled trees to feed the flames. Esmerelda had a flair for rolling cigarettes. She didn't smoke, but on one of her occasional ventures beyond the farm, she had traded with a neighbor who grew and cured tobacco. So she bequeathed the habit to me. I smoked to please her, and pleasing her in turn made the tobacco enjoyable. In the end, by that strange process, it tasted good. A whip-poor-will called from a nearby branch.

Summer began its transition into fall. One morning I got up to salve the foot of a lamed calf. A hard frost lay on the ground. The crops, such as we'd been able to grow, were in. By the time I got back from the barn, Esmerelda was canning squash.

"I had a dream las night."

"If it's some kind of superstitious dream, please don't tell me about it."

"Somebody was dead in de dream."

"If it was me, please keep that information to yourself."

"I couldn't make out the face fo sho."

"But it could have been me, right?"

"I didn't say dat. Cause you tole me not to say it."

"I get the picture anyway."

"I thought you say it was superstition and you don believe it."

"Just because it's superstition doesn't mean it won't happen."

"Don't mean it will, either."

"Okay, so am I going to die, or not?"

"Not before you salve that lame calf. I can't afford you to die dis day."

"In that case, I'll be off to the barn."

"Soon as I finish dis squash, I'll get started on breakfast."

"Good, because it may be my last meal."

I pushed two cows apart to get to the back of the barn. The lamed calf was cowering morosely in the corner, clearly in pain. It must have stepped on a scrap of metal yesterday, or a sharp stone. I laved the wound; it meekly let me hold and dress the hoof in one of Esmerelda's stockings, which was smeared inside with some herbal goo, the recipe for which only she knew. The smell of it made me glad I'd never cut my foot in the line of duty. But it seemed to content the calf, which knelt down and in no time began to drowse. The harness for the mule on the wall was past repairing. My barrel of nails was almost empty. The feed sacks, too, no longer bulged. I returned to the house and told Esmerelda that I was going to take a trip into town, because we needed supplies.

She looked apprehensive, but she kept canning squash. "You gone go into town?"

"That's what I said."

"I knows what you said. I jes don believe it."

"Aren't you low on meal as well?"

"How bout I go? Dat mule like me better than you."

"I've been thinking about the fact that I can't hide out here forever. I'm free now."

"After I jes tole you about my dream. And you ain pay it no mine."

"On my way back here, after you kicked me out, a Shawnee I met on the road told me to stop acting like a slave, and to get the scared look out of my eyes. I plan to follow his advice."

"We can argue about it de livelong day, but you's gone go no matter what. So I mought as well make a list. I need thread. Needles.

Lard." She continued to tick off items. "You ain writing it down. Or has you got de memory of a storyteller?"

I put on the suit I'd been given by the Shawnee. I'd filled out since then, and the suit fit me snugly. My shoulders had become broad, and my chest deeper. She wrapped salted meat and cheese in cloth. I readied the saddlebags. The mule, as predicted, didn't want to come out of the field, and I had to spend half an hour pulling on a rope. Once I sat atop him, he seemed resigned. Since the harness was busted, I had to tie complicated knots in the rope, produce a makeshift bridle, and hope for the best.

"If you has to stay overnight, fine de board house for color people. Owner is Miss Jameson. Doan tell nobody where you come from. Jes say you hear about her long de way."

By the time I was two hours into the trip, I felt giddy. It was an entirely different sense of being on the road. The path seemed mine. Almost no one was upon it. I even tipped my hat to a lone horseman as he passed, and though he squinted, he tipped his hat to me as well. Sparrows foraged the ground, and some flew alongside my progress. Their clipped notes and trills thrilled my soul. I remembered some of the words of a song Felicia used to sing as she churned butter and I sang them to the air with my rusty voice.

Mule's shoulder is sore and so is mine
Churn, butter, churn.
Poppies in the field and grapes on the vine
Churn, butter, churn
Baby's asleep and the prophet is blind
Churn, butter, churn
Hands on the handle still beating time
Churn, butter, churn.

The mule seemed to enjoy the tune, and picked up his pace. As I continued to sing, I even let myself slide into a Negro dialect, since Esmerelda wasn't around to reprimand me for "not speakin de way I speaks." The wind stayed still, so only my hands and feet turned cold. I wondered what the mule's name was, and decided to name him Able, short for Despicable, which was his nature. In that abbreviation lay the secret of existence: to take something bad and find the good hidden inside. I remembered with regret how patronizing I'd always been to my fellow slave Felicia. I took her placid ways to mean she accepted our common state. But she'd just been making the best of things. If I'd told her I was escaping, and asked her to come along, who knew what she might have said? I had a hankering for some of that creamy butter, which floated into one's mouth as if borne on a cloud.

I made town by mid-afternoon. It wasn't much; a few stores and houses with a steeple hastily nailed atop a roof to make a church. A sole elderberry tree with stones laid around it tied the proposition together. The stones were stained with berry juice as if a casual crucifixion had taken place there, and no one had bothered to clean up after.

Inside the dry goods store, a man in an apron sporting an exceptionally neat beard stood rearranging canisters on the counter. I stood a few feet away, waiting for him to take notice of me. I was just beginning to take offense at the slight, when it occurred to me that maybe he was simply busy. I decided it was best to step up to the counter and announce myself. "Good morning," I said.

He looked up and set down a canister lid. "Hey there, wayfarer. I don't believe I've seen you before. Welcome to my shop."

I almost gave the man my name, but thought better of it. "I'm new to the area."

"Whereabouts you live?"

"Oh—a good drive from here."

"Then I guess you better load up. What can I get for you?"

"Here's a list I wrote."

"Fair enough. I only learned to read last week, but I'll sound it out." He kept a deadpan look straight on me. It took me a minute to realize he was making a joke, and my laugh came all on the sudden. "That's more like it, wayfarer. You seem tense. Try to enjoy this blessed day. There's coffee in the storeroom if you want some. Just walk on back."

I was as incredulous as if he'd offered me the key to the cash register. I gathered myself and walked almost on tiptoe back to the storeroom, as if I expected someone to be waiting with a plank to knock me down. There sat a pan of coffee, to be sure, and clay mugs. I poured a cup and drank it with savor. It seemed to have the mellowest flavor of any coffee I'd ever tasted. I didn't even mind that it was lukewarm. I remembered Robert Maples saying that no one on the road had done me harm, and that I shouldn't assume they would. The storekeeper called out to me when he'd gathered my purchases. He gave me the price and I began to count through our closely hoarded cache of coins.

"If it's a stretch, I'll extend credit. All's I need is your name."

"That's all right. I think I can cover it, with enough left over for the boarding house."

"Well, in future, I don't mind giving a line to good customers who pay up on the month."

Outside, I loaded the saddlebags and slung them on the mule. As I was tying them down, a man came riding up alongside me, his horse's flank almost touching me. The first thing I saw was his spur. I looked up and he had on a hat with the broadest brim I believe I've ever seen. He rode a half circle around me.

"All stocked up, I see. Got far to go?"

"Just back to the homestead. I'd like the supplies to last me for a while."

"Which direction is that?"

"Oh, the road meanders."

"I don't know any roads as meanders out of here."

"That's because you're used to riding them. They probably all seem straight to you."

"Could be." He removed the broad-brimmed hat with a sweep and dropped it to his hip. I couldn't help notice that he was missing three fingers. "Lost those in the Canada War," he said at once. "It could have been worse. They could have scalped me. But as you can see, I've still got a full head of hair."

"That you do."

"What did you say your name was?"

"Attila," I lied. The absurd name had popped right out of me. Now there was no taking it back.

"Attila. Never heard that one before. I have a cousin named Atticus, though. So, you're a free man, I take it."

"We're all free here, are we not?"

"In a sense. But I figure you have your papers."

"Papers?"

"I assume you know about the Black Laws. You have to post $500 bond and have court papers that state you're a free man. Lots of escaped slaves running around, thick as crows, it's caused problems in Cincinnati, and folks are sick and tired of it."

I decided to brazen it out. "In all the time I've lived in Ohio, I've never once heard of anyone being asked to produce papers."

"That may be true. Out here in the sticks, nobody seems much to care. That doesn't mean it don't apply. The law is the law."

"I'm not in the habit of carrying papers on my person."

"Well, you better get in the habit if you're going to be strutting about in town like a citizen. The next time I see you, I expect you to show papers. And if not, for two hundred dollars I can get you some. I know a few people at the court. It's that or jail. Or worse." He put on the hat with his two fingers, gave me a salute and rode off.

I'd looked forward to staying at the boarding house. It had seemed almost an adventure, eating pork chops and cobbler around a table with other "wayfarers," as the store keeper had called me, shaving in front of a hand-held mirror, and lying down on a groaning bed where many had slept over the years, bringing their cares to the pillow, perhaps crying, making love, or simply drowsing off into a profound sleep that released them from the burdens of that day. Although they wouldn't know it, my life would intersect invisibly with theirs.

But now, on account of some seven-fingered stranger's threat, possibly idle, possibly real, I was inclined to ride Able into the night, pitching down in an open field, once again among the burrs, when I could no longer stay awake swaying astride the mule. I hadn't even brought a bedroll. I found myself getting angry. Robert Maples was right. I still was acting like a slave. I made my way with determination to the boarding house, a neat structure surrounded by gardenias and azaleas planted in perfect rows.

I'd expected a structure big, rowdy, and ramshackle, busting with cowboys, gamblers, speculators, and lonely schoolteachers. Instead, it was someone's home with three spare bedrooms and a table right inside the kitchen. Miss Jameson herself came out to receive me, wearing a yellow dress and an azalea in her hair. She didn't look more than eighteen years old, with the face of a child who'd never seen misfortune. She was even wearing a bib, for reasons unclear to me. I'm not sure I'd ever seen such an expression of placid innocence on a black woman's face before. Even Rye's good spirits had been a quiet, stubborn contrariness to the torment she knew to exist in the world.

"You're the proprietress?"

"Long as my fortune lasts."

"I need a room," I said, looking around with unnecessary defiance.

"We have three. Have a look around and pick the one you like."

"No one else is here?"

"Not today. Business is slow."

"That's better for me."

"How come?"

"No reason. I'm tired from the road."

"I didn't make supper, except a pot of beans for myself and corn bread. I was just sitting down to eat. I'll share my meal with you."

"Are you sure?"

"Well, this is a boarding house. If I didn't provide supper, that wouldn't be good business sense." We sat at the table, her right next to me. "You'll excuse the bib. I don't want to stain this dress. Sometimes the beans I make taste so good that I get excited and start flinging them all over myself."

I couldn't help but let loose a robust laugh, which was just what she wanted. I didn't expect such a sly humor to accompany that child's face. She seemed to understand the incongruity of her own being, and knew how to exploit it. I could imagine her charming an entire table of hungry and cantankerous travelers, and in truth, Miss Jameson seemed to pick up on the tension in me, and smooth out the wrinkles in it like an iron pressing on a shirt.

"What's your first name?"

"Miss." Her eyes sparkled as she lifted another spoonful of beans.

"I see. Then Miss it shall be. Mine is Jacob."

"That's not the name you signed in the guest book."

"I was feeling cautious."

"Afraid, you mean."

"Yes, afraid. Have you ever heard of the Black Laws?"

"I see you've been speaking with Jomblit."

"I'm not sure what his name was."

"Seven fingers and a face like George Washington after a bar fight?"

"That's him. Is he some sort of authority?"

"He's nobody, who thinks he's somebody. He runs liquor to farmers all around the county. Prides himself on bringing service right to your door. He says he was in the war of 1812, up by Canada, and still thinks of himself as a commissioned officer. We all have to hear his battle stories. But I heard he lost those fingers setting a wolf trap. I don't think he was ever a soldier. It bothers him to see black people walking around free. He can't stand it that I operate a boarding house, and less that I come from an educated family. Twice he tried to get my property condemned for being 'unsafe and unsanitary.' For a while, it cost me money to stay open. He bad-mouthed my place so much that the census fell off. I had to hire a lawyer. He and I had words over it. I told him he should move across the river to Kentucky, so he could walk around with his hands in his pockets all day enjoying the sight of slaves at work."

"I was a slave in Kentucky. I escaped about four months ago."

"I thought you were some kind of teacher or businessman. You don't speak like a slave, that's for sure."

"Neither do you."

"Touché."

"Sometimes I'm terrified they're going to take me back. I'll be fine for a while, then I wake up in a sweat and hear dogs barking when there are none."

"I've seen an attempt at an illegal return happen, but only once. A group of men took it into their head they were going to spirit someone across the river and collect a bounty."

"Did they succeed?"

"Not really. He broke free, then they gave chase and beat him to death."

"Thanks for the inspirational tale."

"Sorry. It's the truth. But it was only one man. You're smart. I believe you could outwit any attempt on you." As if to apologize for putting a scare into me, she brought out a cigar, a bottle of port wine, and two glasses. I'd never smoked a cigar, but the tobacco suited my mouth. It was a long step up from the harsh hand-rolled cigarettes I smoked to please Esmerelda. The port wine was of quality, comparable to what Mistress Brathwaite sometimes allowed me to partake of on the sly when Walter Brathwaite was off the premises and out of sight.

"What about the Black Laws? Did the wolf-trapper make that up too?"

"No, they exist. My parents, before they drowned in a boat accident, insisted on getting me registered. The main reason the law came into being is because there were too many slaves moving into the cities, and they were trying to discourage the migration. But as I understand it, hundreds of laws are passed every year by half-drunken legislators. And most of them aren't enforced, especially this far out."

"So you don't think this Jomblit could make trouble for me?"

"If he really wanted to, he could. But even though he tried to get me evicted from my own house, he can't make good on all his threats. I've heard that he's going broke from suing neighbors and former friends and so-called business partners. And he's been married six times, so they say, and every single one of those women has a death grudge against him. So he's pretty busy hating lots of other people, and you'll probably have to wait your turn. Have some more port."

"I'm sorry about your parents."

"Don't be. They were the happiest people I've ever known. They died in the river before anything tragic could happen to them." Her eyes smiled. "That's how my dad would have put it. He had a light-hearted wit about everything. It was as though no prejudice or misfortune existed in the world, and he and my mother lived the way they wanted without asking anyone's permission. When someone said a hateful word, my father would laugh the insult off, or brush it aside with a kind or witty remark. I used to get really frustrated by him because he wouldn't fight back. But now I realize how wise he was."

"Some of that spirit seems to have rubbed off on you."

"Except when I get fighting mad. Then I want to run a sword through all my imagined enemies."

"Are you eighteen?"

"I'm thirty, for your information. I just don't look it. Why do you ask?"

"No reason."

"Because you're not in the habit of seducing little girls?"

"I wasn't seducing you, I promise. It's hard to be flirtatious when you're discussing the Black Laws."

"Would you like to share my bed tonight?"

"In another life, yes. But I live out on Strawberry Farm with a woman named Esmerelda. She's the one who recommended you."

"Ah, Esmerelda. The one who lives at that remote place over the hills beyond Standing Stone. I didn't know she'd sent you. She seldom comes to town, and keeps to herself. Nobody knows her by name, except me I suppose. She stayed here a couple of times. That's a very good woman. Fierce, I'd say. And she'd surely wallop both of us if she heard us having this conversation."

"No doubt."

"Well, I'm not going up against Esmerelda. I'll only say that she's lucky to have you." She took my hand into hers and with the whorl of her fingertip she touched the whorls of each of mine and put my hand back on the table. "By the way, that's not a proposition I've made before. I've never met anyone quite like you. You're my equal, in every way. Or so you seem on short acquaintance. Take it as a compliment and forget about it."

"I do. And I will."

I chose the room furthest from Miss Jameson's and spent the entire night wallowing in the sheets, having erotic fantasies about her. I should have been fretting over seven-fingered Jomblit, but instead, I undressed Miss Jameson in my fantasy seventeen times and possessed her twenty-seven times. My whole scalp was soaked in spite of the nippy air in the room. I got so thirsty I drank directly out of the pitcher set on my night table for me to wash with. I heard her up walking the floorboards with her ghost step, several times, but I kept my door closed. When I finally slept, I dreamed of being swept downriver at the crossing, my body tangled up in branches, leaves, and the corpses of Miss Jameson's parents.

The next morning she'd laid out a beautiful breakfast of fried eggs and sausages, impossibly light and flaky biscuits, fig jam, and black tea. The cost of it definitely wasn't covered in the meager coins I'd handed her. We ate in a silent reverie, both of us half-asleep and yet alert. Miss Jameson set down her teacup. Her eyes were a little swollen. She looked, if temporarily, closer to thirty that morning than to eighteen. "If Jomblit, or anyone like him, ever comes after you, do what you can to escape. But if you don't have any other choice, kill him. Or die trying to kill him."

"I promise that I will."

"If you ever let yourself be captured, I'll never forgive you." She got up, unlocked a cabinet, and removed from it a musket and packets of shot, which she set before me. "Here. These belonged to my grandfather. I have no use for this gun, or at least less use than you. I know it's serviceable, because I cleaned it myself and went to the woods to try it out."

"You're giving me this musket as a present? Because I have no money left."

"Yes. No one knows for sure what happened to my parents. But I believe a mob chased them to a bluff at the river's edge. Why, I don't know. The usual reasons, I guess. Either they pushed them in, or my father jumped alongside my mother to survive. Or else he just committed suicide. I don't discard that possibility."

"And your mother?"

"However he went, she followed behind. That was her nature."

This time, I took her hand in mine. "I apologize that I didn't keep you company last night. I heard you walking around. I should have gone in and held you so you wouldn't feel so apart."

"No, that wouldn't have been enough. Only your lust would have pacified me. I was in a wild mood. It's better that you stayed behind a closed door."

We shook hands and parted. I strapped the musket to Able, and we set out for Strawberry Farm.

FEBRUARY 1834
LEXINGTON, KENTUCKY
DAN BASKIN

LEORA WORE THE IVORY RING as if it was a diamond. Each day she polished it and would hold it up to the light coming through the south window. I returned from the timber stand with sawdust in my ears. Leora enjoyed having my supper ready, tucking a napkin in my shirt front as if we was at a banquet, and she turned out to have quite a hand as a cook. Then the boss moved me to the lumberyard to strip bark and to plane and shiver logs. Leora and I took to walking around town in the evening until purple streaks dragged across the sky. Rae kept to herself, moody. We invited her sometimes to stroll with us, and I'd tempt her with the prospect of sugar candy, but mostly she said no. Town folk stopped staring at us and moved on to the latest scurry. All I wished for was what I had— days so buried in toil and sweat I hardly had time to think or even sit, except to gnaw on a hunk of roast beef and a sour roll that Leora had packed for me. Evenings were to stroll and quaff ale together.

Rae was put into a local school. She didn't like it one bit. The first days, they had her sitting with the smaller chaps, but she was so bright that she quickly showed she belonged at the top of the class. Only once did she drag a girl around the room by her hair. I had to go and smooth things over with the teacher so she wouldn't get kicked out. It helped that Leora sent along a plate of pork and a fudge cake. Leora did her best to accommodate Rae. She wanted to teach her to cook and stitch and other feminine arts, but Rae it seemed would burn the pot on purpose and Leora would end up scouring the black bottom with tears at the edge of her eyes. It was a battle of wills, and though at times I wanted to shake Rae until her very teeth fell out, I kept apart in those moments, because I knew Leora had to win the battle by herself. Me interfering would only make Rae more attached to me, and more contrary to my wife.

The only times they really seemed to understand one another was when Leora would draw a hopscotch in the dirt with a stick in the alley. They'd throw stones and skip from one square to the next, and forget for a while that they was mortal rivals. When Leora and I repaired to bed, Rae would rattle around the house, dropping things on purpose to make a racket. She would raise the iron and drop it three of four times for no reason. Leora wanted to leap from the bed and scratch the girl's eyes out her head, but I would lay a hand on her and tell her to be still, as Rae would grow bored if we paid her no mind. And sure enough, after a stretch of days, Rae lost interest in her pranks and more or less settled down, only occasionally whittling on the furniture with a knife.

Leora wanted so bad for Rae to treat her like a mother that she begun to pine for a child of her own. Now and again, I'd catch her moony eyes roving over me, as if to pose a remark, but none came. She got real melancholy and plumb give up on bringing Rae around to the woman's world. The best solution, as I saw it, was to make her a child, since I could see her fever growing apace. I loaded up on beef, liver, and taters at supper of an evening, we'd climb to bed early, and Leora loved on me like steel on a stone wheel. Sometimes she would sob and grapple, like a soul in the middle of drowning. Her hair grew wild and once she even ripped her garment and had to sew it back later. She dug her nails into me at times as if she wished to extract a substance from my skin.

At morn, she would arise and make breakfast as if nothing unusual had happened. As I saddled Stalker, she'd be hanging a rug to beat or mixing vinegar and water to clean the mirrors and the glass. She begun to speak real soft to Rae, and Rae begun to listen. I don't know whether it was persuasion or whether Rae was bewitched by my wife's transformation. Leora's cheeks and hair took on such a luster you would have mistook her for a girl sprung to her first initial blossom what had never knowed a man. She could of been Rae's older sister. When I returned of a late afternoon, she would wait for me at the very door to receive me as I passed the threshold. She'd ask me to tell every detail of my day, the names of the men in the lumberyard, how each one worked at his task, his peculiar ways, what had we talked about during lunch break. Rae, too, would sit and listen, entranced by the most banal goings-on that I myself found boring in the telling. I was cloistered by them two females, who hung on me like brambles. They even follered me from one room to the other and back again. I brought them puzzles, knitting needles, and finally, a kitten that scratched my trouser legs and walked over our faces in the nighttime as we slept.

The kitten distracted Leora's mind as an early frost fell over Lexington. Rae named him Mister Tumbles. When she wasn't tormenting the kitten with a stick, Rae loved to sit and pet its fur for a long spell. I had to caulk the seams of the walls and the door and window frames to keep cold air from pushing through. I found Leora a big wool coat at auction. It had belonged to a fine dead matron of the town. She complained that the coat didn't flatter her figure and I said that was fine with me; I was just as happy her rump wasn't to be paraded for inspection every time she sashayed to market. I got one for Rae too, sewed out of an Indian blanket, the type I had seed brought up from the Mexico territory.

One afternoon in the midst of February, I come to the front door, watching my breath precede me as it mingled with the fragrance of an oak fire. There stood Leora outside in her big wool coat, looking for all the world like a Cossack I'd spied on the deck of a wheel boat in the dead of winter. "Why air ye out here asking for death by chill?"

"A man named Cyril has come looking for you. He's inside. Says he's down from Ohio way."

"I don't know any such. Tell him to be gone. I want supper, more like, and am in no mood to share it with a stranger."

"He's been waiting all afternoon. I offered him a glass of water, but he would have none."

"Then let's see what mischief he's up to. I know I don't owe anybody money and them as owes me ain't him."

I entered and thar was a sort of wrangler, except the boots were too shiny and without the expected wear. He had a smell of pomade upon him. He'd sat down in my chair, and that I didn't like one bit.

"Have we had truck betwixt us? I think not."

"That's no greeting, cousin."

"Nor was meant to be. Cousins we ain't."

"Just a manner of speaking." He stood up and twirled a straw hat in one hand, as if about to do a trick with it. The other he extended to me. I didn't take it. I'm not one to disparage a handshake, but in this case I made an exception. Rae had come in and perched herself on the back of a kitchen chair, doing one of her strange balancing acts as she settled in to witness. Her red hair stood up all about her crown. She needed a trim. "My name is Cyril."

"So I gather."

He twirled the hat to all get out, until he run out of spin, trying to come up with a new pleasantry all the while. When he seed it was no use, and that I wasn't partial to his charm, he got right to business. "I was wanting to hire you for a job."

"What's the job and what's the pay?" Leora set down crackers and tea, but none of us made a lunge fer it.

"The pay isn't coming direct from me. It will arrive after, depending on how everything goes."

"Then I'm not interested. Sound like a bank robbery."

"Many would say it's perfectly legal. Or ought to be."

"I've already got a job."

"There's a bounty. Split among three men, it comes to two hundred each."

"Just out of curiosity, who is the third man?"

"Name of Jomblit."

"Don't know any such."

"Nor he you. But he found a notice in the papers of a slave escaped from Lexington and he saw in person the man they described."

"Then what does he need me for?"

"It's not so simple. At the time he saw the man, he didn't know he was a slave. He claimed to be a free black with papers. He was buying supplies, but wouldn't say where he was from. But we know he's a day's ride from there, because all he had was a mule and no bedroll and he was wearing a suit, like as if he was a preacher. He must be residing on a farm somewhere right in that area. We figured him to be in Sunfish or Camp Creek. We heard a report that he'd been spotted in Poplar Grove."

"So go get him."

"The truth is, Mister Baskin, we tried. We traipsed from house to house and farm to farm for several days straight. We searched, we bullied, we bribed, and we scoured, even through the woods until our hides were scratched. But we found no sign. If we happened on the place where he is staying, he gave us the slip or was so well hid we just couldn't turn him up."

Rae and Leora was watching me intent-like. "I don't do that labor any more. You could even say I come to revile it. Besides which, if the slave is in Ohio, why it ain't legal to bring him back."

"Oh, come on. You and me both know how things work. If we bring him back unhurt, nobody will raise a cry."

"That don't make it right."

"If somebody stole your horse and took it to Ohio, they would perfectly expect you to bring it back and would brand you a fool if you knew where he lay and didn't try. What's the difference?"

"Out of curiosity, what was this slave's description and name?"

"Six foot of stature, light-skinned almost like a white man. So he could pass if you weren't looking close. Thirty-five years of age, flecks of iron in dark, nappy hair. Walks slightly pigeon-toed. Extremely well spoken, as if he had formal education. Many scars crisscrossed on his back. I'm sure the owner wasn't proud to put that last part, but it will make him easy to identify once he's tracked down." I almost blurted out the name, but Cyril did it for me. "He's called by Jacob Pingrim. A mulatto is what he sounds like, with that Dutch surname." I tried to stay calm, but Cyril, who was not unobservant, must have seen a spark rise to my eye. And once it rose, there was no sense trying to quell it. "Do you know him, or know of him?"

"The news is general in Lexington. We all know he escaped, about three months back. I know, and so does the barber. Everybody can tell you who Pingrim is. He's famous locally fer being so smart and fer crossing plants together to whar they won't die without a hard fight. Like what the Shakers done at Pleasant Hill."

He begun to work on me, his voice dropping down soft like he was soothing an ornery hunting dog. "Everybody also knows you as the most famous trapper of these parts."

"Tracker, you mean."

"Same difference. Jomblit says it's like trapping a wolf, and you have to think like a wolf."

"Sounds like horse shit to me. I sure don't think like a wolf, and I caught plenty. I think like a person scared to death who is living by his wits. A human reduced to an animal."

"We need you, Baskin. We'll never find him without you. I talked to several people, and even up in Ohio, they all know you by reputation, though none had met you in person."

"I don't need your compliments. Or Walter Brathwaite's money. I'm a lumberjack now. Besides, that slave is dead."

Cyril took out a note pad and begun to scratch on it. "I spoke with Brathwaite this morning, and he never mentioned any such. I'm sure he would have known about that."

Leora was casting nervous glances my way, but I paid her no mind. "If you must know, I was at the river crossing when he died. I saw him swept downriver in a current that would drown any man living. And he looked none too strong. Leave him be, and let his ghost walk the banks."

"I see. 'Ghost walks the banks.'" He kept taking notes, or maybe he was just doodling to make himself look important and smart as a lawyer. "So Brathwaite hired you?"

"Nobody hired me. I am a free agent, and do as I see fit. Anybody puts out a reward is asking the whole world to do what they can."

"The locale we want to keep quiet. We don't want an all-out manhunt that will rob us of the bounty, when we're so close to trapping him. Why didn't you shoot Pingrim at the crossing?"

"Was it really necessary? Didn't I just say that we watched him die?"

"We?"

"I did."

He put the notepaper back in his pocket, somehow satisfied. "Well, I'm afraid I don't believe you. The man Jomblit met in Sunfish Township buying feed matches the description in every respect. You might have seen Pingrim go under, but it's possible that he resurfaced, got lucky, and made his way to the bank. Those currents are unpredictable. I know, because I used to run whiskey across the river from here to there."

"Suit yourself. But count me out. I am not leaving my home and job for a wild chase after a dead man. Brathwaite won't let loose of two nickels for a corpse."

Rae jumped from the chair back to the floor. "Go after him, Baskin. You know ye want to. Stop living here under roof and sleeping each night in a soft bed like a woman."

"You mean 'with a woman,' don't you, Rae? Is that what's got your dander still up? After all these weeks?"

In return, she give me a peppery frown. "I hain't got no grudge. Yer wife isn't the worst woman in the world. I'm only saying let's have us an adventure. You and me. I'm bored as hell. Ye know yer a tracker by blood." She turned to Cyril. "He could find Pingrim quicker than fifteen of ye banded together. He's a damned bloodhound tarted up in a hat and clothes to look like a regular man. He's half Apache, half Creek, half nigger, and half white. His great granddaddy was the mayor of Yoruba."

Cyril took a step toward her, with a smile like a deadbeat uncle's. "Is that so?"

"I was with him at Maysville when that slave crossed. I got a good long look. The current caught him hard, yes, but Pingrim is a tough son of a bitch. I dreamed twice that he's still alive, and that he woke up in a hayloft. I even found a piece of straw in my hair."

"Did you, now?"

"I'll go along if Baskin won't. I only require fifty dollars as payment if I catch Pingrim by the toe. I ain't got no Creek blood, but my granddaddy mated with a coyote, then my daddy with a saluki greyhound, and that's how I come to be."

Cyril chuckled in a way that made me want to knock him down, but I stayed my hand. "Little lady, when you grow up, come to Ohio and look up Cyril Connor, yours truly, and I'm sure we can find gainful employment for a greyhound such as yourself." He twirled her hair in his fingers and let the hand drop to her neck and brush the skin before removing it.

"I'm a deadeye with a pistol. I borried Dan's a few times, as he don't take it to work, and I can shoot the bung-hole out of a dog as he runs away."

"You did what?"

"Sorry, Dan. I didn't hurt nobody. Was only glass bottles. But I hit four of five straight on at the first trigger."

Cyril put on his hat and looked relaxed and sleepy-eyed. "Honey, you're a sparkler. Wish you were my daughter. We'll find him with or without you, Baskin. It's a matter of time. Just thought you could speed matters up, and that's worth a smaller cut to me. If you change your mind between now and tomorrow afternoon, I'll be at the Phoenix Hotel. I understand that is where Pingrim used to shine shoes. I'm hoping to find useful information there. Room nineteen."

That night the wind howled round the corners, through a crack in the sill, and into my ear pouches. It sounded like the whistle of an insane man come to claim kinship with me. A piece of loose tin from the roof kept beating the side of the house. I cussed and swore I'd get up to fix it, but I never did rouse from the bed. Finally I slept for a stretch. When I awoke and padded into the kitchen, Leora sat in the milky light by the window, worrying a porcelain cup with a little hairline crack down the side. Mister Tumbles walked along the edge of a cabinet. I fetched a strip of jerky and begun to gnaw on it.

"What's the trouble, woman?"

"My ivory ring is gone."

"You must have misplaced it. Don't fret; it will turn up."

"I never take it off, Dan. Only after that discussion last night between you and the visitor, I just pulled it off and laid it on the counter to rub beeswax on my hands. I was dead gone and I forgot to put the ring back on. I crawled on hands and knees all over this floor, but it's not to be found."

"We'll purchase another."

"That's all ye have to say?"

"Yeah."

"The least you could do is backhand me like a proper husband fer being a thoughtless wife."

"As if I would."

"There ain't no other ring like that. Carved of bird-life. Besides, it was yours and that's what made it special and true."

I pulled my chair right acrost from Leora, set down, stroked her hair. "I'm late for the bark yard. But listen. That ring has a history. It started in Africa and carried bad luck then."

"I thought you didn't believe in bad luck."

"That was yesterday. Maybe it's for the best it's gone."

"Don't say that."

"It belonged to Abejidé."

"The Yoruba gal."

"The same."

"How could you give me another woman's ring?"

"Foolhardy, I guess. I was trying to break a spell. At the crossing, I had Pingrim in hand and could of put him in chains. He told me she drowned herself after I let her get sold away. She was cousin to him. That's why I let him go. In my mind, giving you the ring was like banishing a ghost from our lives. And her ghost really was banished, for me."

"Maybe she has rose up in her wrath and sorrow."

"Maybe you need a diamond now."

"Dan, there's one more thing."

"Ain't there always?"

"Rae is gone."

"To school. She must have left early."

"No, it's Saturday. Only a work day for you. She's run off somewhere. And I do believe she stole that ring."

"You can't keep that girl on a short leash on her free day. You might as well put a lasso on a bobcat. She'll turn up once she's done whatever mischief she set out to do. When she comes back, I'll whale on her until she tells whither she sold that ring to the pawnbroker, or tossed it in a field for spite."

"Don't say that. You'd never raise a hand to Rae."

"Wait and see if I don't."

"You love her as if she bore your very blood."

At the bark yard, the first thing I did was drive a big splinter right up under my fingernail. I let out such a holler that the other fellows stopped planing to gander.

"Yer a mite sloppy there, Baskin. Was ye bad with the poison last night?"

"Go to hell. I drunk naught but well water. Ye've all slipped up with the shaver before."

"All of us except you. You won't make another mistake for years, so we got to jump on ye when we can." They all laughed themselves shed of breath while I muffled my sour mood by pulling a cap down over my brow. Something was eating at me. Tiny snowflakes, barely grains, danced around my face and hands. Any other time I might have stopped to wonder on the flakes for a spell, but this day they were as gnats to my cheeks. I worked the shaver hard, stripping a log in no time, and moving right on to another felled tree without a rest.

"Dan is here to compete today, boys. We'd better step it up with the planers." One of the men, a big, tough cutter who liked to play the harmonica on his work breaks, pitched into the task with long swoops and begun to sing.

They found a slipknot round her neck
And from her bosom a note they took
How the butcher boy her bereft
As if a knife her breast had cleft.

"Shut the hell up."

"Make me. Everybody but you enjoys a good love song."

He let the words fly with such gusto you'd a thought he was calling a barn dance. The song had about twenty verses, and he sung them, on purpose I think, out of order. The woman died off in the first verse and come back to life many more times than Jesus did. At lunch the singer shared coffee with me to make clear he hadn't meant no harm, nor was a-mocking me. I couldn't eat the meatloaf sandwich Leora had made me, and gave it to him. He swallowed the bread in two bites and went to work on the harmonica. I didn't dare ask the name of the tune, as it was probably about a murder or a train wreck, or some slave being hacked to pieces right after he proposed marriage to a gal. He stopped honking the harmonica, come out of his crouch and stretched to his six and a half foot frame.

"What's eating you, Dan? I'm busting hell out my gut to lighten your mood. You are not yourself, and that's no lie."

"I can't tell, Charlie. Some thought bedevils my mind, as if I couldn't remember my own birth day, nor my mother's name."

"What is your mother's name?"

"Janice."

"Mine is named Wanda. If I was a girl, they was going to call me Wanda too."

"You is the ugliest damned girl I ever saw," cracked one featherweight layabout who leaned against a stump.

"You pipe down, Rich, or I'll wring your neck. It's so scrawny I'll just wrap my pinky finger around it, and crack my knuckles. You'll be dead before a hummingbird touches the next flower."

It wasn't until I was riding home that the bubble in my mind popped. "Hell, she went with them." I busted through the door. "Leora, I don't mean to be brisk. But I've got change my shirt, jump on Stalker, and ride like hell to Ohio."

"I thought you wasn't going to get caught up in that man's scheme for bounty."

"I'm not. Don't you know that ornery little bitch has gone to the Phoenix, searched out Cyril, and talked him into taking her along for help?"

"You can't be serious, Dan. They wouldn't take a slip of a girl along on such a journey."

"Didn't I? And I'm no fool. The truth is, the girl has a nose for tracking. And that wild gift of gab—I cain't explain it, she's out of her gourd, but she could coax a rooted tree off a cliff."

"You've got your mind in a whirl. Give the matter thought on this night and if ye feel the same tomorrow, well then okay."

"I'll tell you what. Go to the bureau. If my Colt pistol is in the middle drawer, and a box of bullets alongside, I'll sit down to supper. And if it's missing, I'll splash my face with a handful of water and be off."

Leora walked to the next room and I heard the clunk of her footsteps stop and the slide of the drawer that allus stuck halfway. A long minute passed and her heels scraped their way back. "If yer a-goin, so am I."

I was about to explain that she would only slow me down, but Leora was already up and pulling off her dress for a stouter garment.

I was in too much of an immediate fix to stand agin her. Rather than argue, for at such a time a woman can wear you down to a nub more worser than a Philadelphia lawyer, I hasted a few streets over and hired a gig from a man who owed me a favor. By the time I returned, she was got up in warm duds and her big coat. She had a basket of food and a bag at her side, and Mister Tumbles in her hands.

"I reckon that cat is for warmth?"

"Of course."

Given that I had no pistol, I cleaned and bound up my rifle, which was my only other arm. I had six cartridges, which was more than I'd ever needed on any occasion. I attached Stalker to the gig. He wasn't really made to pull, as he's not a dray in nature or spirit. Besides, and I hate to say it, he's getting on, the more so as all he mostly does is carry me to the lumber yard and back of a day. But I knew he'd be mad if I didn't bring him along. He wants an adventure, and likes to feel he's still man enough to make the journey. I run my finger along his nap and felt how thick it had growed. I told Leora it would be a cold ride. I made her as comfortable as I could, throwing blankets over her coat, and I brought along a stoppered jug of hot mint tea and a flask of whiskey to take the bite off. She swathed her face in a scarf and pushed a hat with no brim over her crown.

"What about you?" she spoke through a muffle.

"I've got this pair of gloves and sheepskin jacket. I'm used to worse."

"Sometimes I think you just like to suffer, Dan. You should have been a Christian after all."

I patted the blanket round her shoulders and hopped in the gig. A neighbor had agreed to tell my boss I'd been called away for a few days. I'd work any grievance out with him when I got back.

"I'll stop at the Phoenix first and sound out the matter." When we arrived at Main Street, I helped Leora out and told her to wait in the lobby. She took quite a gander at the chandelier as we walked in. I realized she'd never set foot inside for the simple fact that wasn't her price range. Men came to her quarters through word of mouth. The doorman recognized me and gave a greeting. I slipped him a couple bills and asked him to get the lady a warm toddy and keep an eye on her until I finished my business. He called her 'Ma'am' about six times before I went out of earshot.

I bounded to the dining room and my eye fell on Blackie, an Irishman whose name had always struck me as ironical because he was the palest white man I'd ever seen. I believe he was albino, but yet he'd served as the headwaiter for many a year. At least he was easy to spot. We set at a back table and I sketched out the situation as quick as I could. I asked him had a redhead with a quail-egg face almost as white as his showed around the hotel this day.

"Surely she did, Baskin. I know the very maid. She engaged with a man who sported a wealth of pomade in his locks right at that table opposite."

"And you eavesdropped."

"As always when it bears the stamp of intrigue. I informed Corliss I'd take over that table personally."

"So?"

"The parley was passing strange. This girl went on in with vigor about her capable shot with a pistol she claimed to own. She spake with her mouth full of braised fish. Said she warn't afeared of slaying in cold blood. And that so keen was her eye she had found the boat at the crossing the first time, and knew how to navigate southern Ohio as well as walking around a horse's stall. Her lit-up face put me in a wonder, so much so that I brought her a slab of chocolate cake for free, just to watch her cram it inside her head."

"And the man?"

"Well, at first he was amused, is all. I think he bought her dinner more for the sport of hearing her wax on. But the more she talked, the more he listed. By the end, he said he had nothing to lose and that he'd teach her how a real trapper worked. I couldn't make out whether they were bound to hunt foxes or men."

"Did he touch her?"

"How do you mean?"

"Caress her."

"Well, he rubbed her shoulder and played with her hair a bit, now that I think of it. He wanted to order her a glass of wine, but I said that was prohibited, and he didn't insist."

"Thanks, Blackie. I'll repay you when I can."

"You owe me nay, Dan. Your company has ever been a pleasure."

We set out in the gig. The air was so clear you could have rung it like a chime. The wheels gave a smart bounce off the cobbles. Seemed like I was destined to allus be setting off in the middle of the night while other folk hove down into dreams. The moon showed crisp as we careered onto the turnpike. Stalker felt the journey and leaned in to it. He give three full whinnies as a signal. I would certainly never try to explain to Stalker the reasons for this sudden journey, as I had no desire to dampen his spirits. I had qualms about subjecting Leora to this ordeal, but I had come to realize that I had to cease conjuring her as a soft body upon a soft bed. That's how I'd come to know her first, but she was much more than that. Her eyes shined through the slit between her scarf and hat. It could have been merely the wind, but I reckoned she was crying for Rae, in spite of all.

"Dan, how can you run the gig apace in the pure dark?"

"Is it too fast?"

"No, I want to get there quicker as you do. I only wondered."

"I'm used to a rumble beneath me. Hit don't feel nary strange. And there ain't no person to strike in the road in the dead of a chill night. Every fool but us has trundled to a bed long since."

"Feels like we're flying through a void of sky. The sensation is right peculiar." The whoosh of the trees and rills as we swept along kept us company. The moon peeped betwixt stark branches. "What will we do if she's hurt or kilt?"

"What makes you say that?"

"Naught but a premonition."

"I'd like to leave you at a hotel in the township. In case blood is spilt."

"I'll face whatever spectacle happens, Dan. You needn't worry. I watched my sister die as a child. It was my job to bathe her with water. She moaned and begged me to bring her out of the spell. I didn't know what to say except to mop her neck. But I didn't shiver. I kept to my post."

"Then we'll go to the end together." I lain my hand upon hers. "My voice ain't but a croak. Still, I'll sing ye a swatch of a tune my mother used to offer me at cradle.

O! Mor siriol gwena'r seren
Ar hyd y nos.
I oleuo'i chwaer ddaearen,
Ar hyd y nos."

"Seems you know every sort of a language. It's a wonder they never put you in a larning college."

"Did you like it?"

"It's pretty enough. Only I don't understand the words."

"My mother was from the Welsh land."

"You never said anything about her before."

"I hadn't thought on her for the longest while until Charlie asked me her name this morning."

"Well, what does the song say? Or did she only sing it in the Welsh way?"

"It means while the moon keeps watch and the weary world slumbers, the child is at peace. And then it says fate may sever our lives, but it won't be forever."

"I wonder why they'd say all them words to a mere child. I don't believe she'd have the first idea what a fate was."

"Even that cat in yer arms knows what fate is. He only don't know what to call it."

"Maybe. You'll have to sing it to him again when the light falls, and see if the expression on his face changes."

"When he heard me yowl, he thought I was his mother, that much is for sure."

Leora hunkered down into her blankets and nudged Mister Tumbles back beneath them, but in time, the coffee run dry and my hands had gone numb beneath the leather. I seen Leora crouch as if trying to pull her body inside itself, and knowed she was suffering. We come to a farm with an outlying hay barn, and I decided to pull in for the rest of the night. My plan was to roll back one door enough to bring the gig and horse inside, whar we could at least soften the clime. It set up a fierce creak soon as I moved it. Then I thought, why not knock at the farm door? The farmer would be waked up with a jar, but that was all the harm, and Leora might sleep indoors. In my travels,

I'd always felt on the fringe, as if I myself was a criminal or a slave. Somehow I felt more comfortable on a bedroll with the hard ground beneath, whar I didn't have to talk to nobody.

I alighted from the gig and rapped at the door. The gent what opened, while not old, sported the longest whiskers I'd ever seed. I would have thought them a prank except they suited his face so well. I explained that we was traveling north but shocked by the frost, and without no more words than that, he waved us in, hollering to his wife to put on her house slippers and fetch a kettle. Leora throwed off her blankets like Lazarus from the grave and hurried inside. I got Stalker situated and fed, and assured him we'd be along on the morrow. He turned three full circles in the barn and scratched his withers on the planks before nipping at a bale of hay.

The couple said their names was Dab and Chelsea. She bundled around cutting pound cake and opening a jar of beans and chow-chow like it was somebody's birthday. Their hospitality made me so abashed that when I spoke, I began to stutter. She figured it was the cold, and rushed to serve me a cup of tea. They had lit three lanterns strung from the rafters. The hiss was right pleasant, like the sound of a summer rain. Hooked rugs lay underfoot and the chairs, made of cane, had nary a snag. The paintings on the wall were not even portraits, rather fields of flowers, birds, and insects, drawed by hand to make you think on life itself. I'd never seed the like. I'd passed through the atriums of a few fine houses when I went to take payment for a slaving job, whar all the furniture come over in a crate from England. But none like this. It was homey, I guess that's what they call it. It was like they had made or collected each thing theirselves, and it had some meaning for them, whar they could look back and remember a moment long past.

I suppose this house and its innards was the dream of Leora, though she would never say so. She put to her cheek a wool afghan that Chelsea give her for cover. They was already in a parley about their grand-aunts, which was a wonderful seamstress and which could pickle beets. Just two women gabbing. It give me comfort to know that this couple would never have a call to think on Leora as a whore. Sometimes as we walked in town, I'd see her cringe when a man passed by. Though I never let on I'd noticed, there was always something to remind her. I understood, as my brushes with men I'd knowed from the trade, even before today, kept trying to pull me back that way. I even come upon the brother of a man I killed eight years ago. And here was Chelsea apologizing that the spice tea was too weak.

"It suits my soul," I said, now managing not to stutter. That seemed to smooth her cap, and she offered me another cup.

"What's bringing you north at this hard hour of the season?" asked Dab.

I could see Leora's brain working over the situation, wanting to explain what she and Rae and I was each to the next, in words that wouldn't lay open to question. "Our stepdaughter. She has been visiting a relative in Ohio, and is poorly all on the sudden."

Their eyebrows raised ever so scant at the word *step*. I had an impish desire to blurt out that a slave-tracker and a harlot was running down a piss-ant who'd fled with a pistol to threaten an escaped nigger slave after the tracker stole the girl from her narcotic-addicted mother. "Was you a widow, then? I know some as has lost their men in the Indian wars."

"No, we adopted."

"Ain't that something? They is so many younguns running around without a mama or a daddy, just languishing."

"Did she get the cholera? They say there's a lot of that in Ohio just this autumn."

"We're not sure what's wrong with her," I said. There was a long pause as they took my words, and Dab plucked at one side of his whiskers.

"That cholera is serious business. A man who brought me staples last week said several has passed already, and that it's a plague upon the land. Is your daughter at least still—is she okay?"

"We'll know when we get there."

Chelsea had cast an apron to her face, breathing into it with labor, as if she might be protecting herself from the cholera right that minute.

"Air ye all right?" Leora asked her.

"Pay no mind," said Dab. "It strikes a chord is all. Our daughter kilt herself last spring right after planting. Took a poison I laid out in the barns for rodents."

Chelsea burst into sobs. "Do you have to tell our sorrows to strangers?"

"They ain't strangers. Not now. We've not said a word to anybody about our grief. Not at the funeral. Not to our kin, or the pastor, or even to one another. I'm busting with it. These two, maybe they can understand what we feel. For all we know, the Lord sent them to our door on the briskest of nights for that sole reason, so that the four of us can keep company and stave off the gloom. Their faces are kind. That's got more power than my pride." He reached out to touch her limp hand.

She dropped her apron and made herself look at us full on. "We don't even know why she did it. I swear we weren't mean. The usual quarrels between a mother and a daughter. She said I was too strict."

"I'm sorry for your loss," said Leora. "I'm sure you was a good mother. Us girls is sometimes born contrary. I know I beviled my mother until she'd fly to fury, whup me good, and mope for the rest of the day."

"Honey, if I could wrangle you from your husband, I'd adopt you right now. Me and Colette hooked that rug beneath your feet together. Some days I want to burn it in the fire, so I don't have to look at it. Only I know I'd regret after. So there the thing lays, getting caked with mud."

"Y'all better get a rest. I have to get up early for the mere sake of three ornery cows, so I'll make sure your steed is hitched and ready. She'll lay out a good breakfast and slice ham and bread for the road."

"No need to tend us so. I'm an early riser."

Dab stared me down. "Pilgrim. You done already disturbed me rudely in the middle of the night, so don't be putting no conditions. I'll wait on your royal self when I take a notion. You've got more melancholy in your visage than me, and you ain't even lost a child. Let us help you fly to her side."

The next morning, we set out early, toting a wicker of victuals, courtesy of Chelsea. The clouds had lowered close over the valley, and had squeezed out much of the cold. The warming air lay still about us. Even the birds seem to doze in the trees, scant of song. Stalker made good speed, now that daylight helped. They was traffic a-plenty, most of it southbound. We lunched under a spread of pin oaks, ones I believed had been growing upwards of a hundred years. They was the tallest I'd ever seed. Fox squirrels scrambled along the branches, showing us their orange bellies and swishing their yaller-tipped tails. They set up to chitter as if they wished to jump down and enjoy the cold chicken, but none dared.

"I don't care if I have a child, Dan. I'm going to win that girl over. At the speed she's going, she'll be spending a stretch of her life in jail."

"I'm afeared she's a-laying upon a mattress with Cyril at this very moment. And realizing she don't want what she thought she wanted. That man's pomade smells the same as a man who bought Rae a drink in Maysville. The aroma of honeysuckle when it's overripe and about to die off."

"Us girls reach an age whar we get crazed to have a man's touch upon us. And if thar ain't one fitten, or if the one we desire won't pay us no mind, why we let ourselves be fondled by such as will."

"At Maysville, she wanted to share a bed with me and was furious when I refused."

"I figured as much. My first time was at the age of twelve. The man was a vagrant. He ended up in prison for setting a house on fire."

"Yours?"

She smiled and handed me a plate of cobbler. "No, nothing so bad as that. It was his mother's."

"That's a relief. Otherways I wouldn't be eating this dessert."

February 1834
Strawberry Farm
Jacob Pingrim

W HEN I REACHED STRAWBERRY FARM, I unloaded the supplies, carrying them to the barn and kitchen. Esmerelda ignored them all except the musket, which she took in hand as if handling a snake.

"Where you get dis gun? You spend my money on such a trinket?"

"It was given to me."

"Who by?"

"A sympathizer."

"Ain't nobody simplify me so much he gone gib me a gun."

"Well that's how it happened." I heard my voice coming out sharp, almost for the first time with Esmerelda. It was her job to cut the air, and mine to stitch it. She was so bewildered by my tone that for a moment she couldn't speak.

"You gambled?"

"I did not gamble. Did it ever occur to you that I'm a charming person, and that there are good souls in the world who want me to prosper? Who don't want me to cringe like a dirty nigger for the rest of my born days?"

"I thought you wasn't going to talk to nobody about what you did and where we is."

"I unburdened myself a little. That's simply how it went down."

Esmerelda began to put away the kitchen supplies, slamming the pantry doors shut.

"If you needs a musket, den you must have said a-plenty, and afraid it gone get out."

"A man threatened me with something called the Black Laws. He said that I had to have papers and put down some kind of deposit. Did you ever hear of those?"

"Only law of de black is keep yo mouth shut an do yo work an doan complain. And den nobody gone bother you. I should of gone into town myself, like I said."

"I cannot live in a monastery the rest of my life. Sooner or later, there was going to be a brush with someone. Now it's happened."

"Mus be a bad brush if you needs a gun."

"The gun is for safety, just in case."

"An you knows how to shoot a musket?"

"I used to hunt on occasion."

"Seem like you know how to do everything. It's a wonder you ain't join a carnival."

Esmerelda had returned to a soup on the stove, which she stirred faster and faster. My joints ached from the hours atop the mule.

"Do you have to keep cooking? Could we please just talk like people?"

"We is talking. And I doan see you makin no lunch."

"Suit yourself."

"You stay wid Miss Jameson?"

"Isn't that where you sent me?"

"Hm."

"Meaning?"

"Yeah, I guess I did. She give you dat musket?"

"Yes, she did."

"Why you didn't just say so at de first sip of water?"

"What of it?"

"I knew it was her. She young and pretty."

"You are pretty."

"Says you."

"And young."

"I ain't so young."

"Didn't you say you were twenty-six?"

"I ain't sure. Somewhere around dat."

"Well, she's thirty. Older than you."

"So you was talking about personal things. Did she ask you to sleep with her?"

"I did not sleep with Miss Jameson. I slept alone in a room, like any other boarder."

"Dat ain't what I asked. Was de house full?"

"If you must know, it was empty except for me. I wish to hell I had slept in a ditch full of stagnant water and woken up encased in a rime of ice."

"Me too."

"I'm being punished for receiving a musket. I did nothing wrong. You'll be happy someday that we have it on hand."

"I'm happy now. Because dis soup is turning out exactly like I planned. You just puts in tomatoes and pole beans and such, and it come out de same way every time, unless you don't stir it. Den it burn and leave a bad taste in yo mouth."

"I'm going to lie down. Suddenly I'm exhausted."

"Dat mule need a bath. He come a long way an broke a hard sweat."

"I'll do it when I'm ready. Or maybe never." I left the room, and this time it was me who slammed a door.

Esmerelda slept on the couch that night, or somewhere in the house. All I know is she didn't visit the bedroom. Perhaps she didn't sleep at all. When I woke the next morning, dressed, and walked into the kitchen, she was stirring the pot again. Only this time it was boiled oats. Neither of us spoke. When the oats were almost a paste, she glopped some into a wooden bowl and set it before me with a rude *splat*. I didn't touch the stuff, just watched the steam rise before me like the specter of husbands past.

The cat, which had taken an extreme aversion to me since the time I flung it against the wardrobe, spent most of its time hiding. Now it had decided to mew and rub itself against my leg as if in heat. I didn't dare even nudge it away, as I would only be accused of animal cruelty. Yet every desperate meow seemed to inflame Esmerelda, as if I were rutting on the floor before her eyes with a strumpet I'd brought home.

Finally, I said, "The only reason Miss Jameson knows where I'm living is because I mentioned you. She asked me if I'd like to share her bed. And I said I couldn't, because I was attached to Esmerelda."

Esmerelda grabbed a chunk of molasses sugar and whacked it against the stone counter. It shattered into pieces, some of them crumbling onto the floor. She took a good-size hunk and flung it across the kitchen, where it landed squarely in my bowl and spattered my clean shirt with flecks of gooey oats.

"I had a mine to put pepper in dem oats. But you gone get sugar today because you spoke my name to Miss Jameson. And it's lucky for both of you dat you did. Now she remember where I live, and now she know where you live."

FEBRUARY 1834
SUNFISH TOWNSHIP, OHIO
DAN BASKIN

I DROVE THE GIG STRAIGHT ON until we reached Sunfish Township, moving at top speed. I'd never pushed Stalker so hard for so long, even in the most extreme chases. When we reached Sunfish Township, sun slatted the oaks of the western hills, and shot light over a little square with an elderberry tree at the center what looked lonesome for company. I entered a store to buy us cheese and bread, a bottle of spirits, and chow for Mister Tumbles, as well as apples and oats for Stalker. The place had closed, but the bearded man on the other side of the door opened without much trouble. There is two ways to investigate: the roundabout way, asking questions that don't stir nobody up nor make them question your motives, and the direct way. I had no time for the first.

"You seen a black man around here what fits the description of tall, some gray in his hair, and speaks real well?"

"Yes, such a man did buy supplies from me. Not that it's anyone's business, but I have no reason to deny it. He seemed right pleasant. I never got his name. I hear he's being sought for, but that nobody has turned him up."

"That's right. And so nobody knows yet where he lives?"

"Are you after a reward as well? They say he is an escaped slave."

"I mean him no harm. If anything, I'd like to stop the harm. He's free. But if them as wants him catches up with him, they may beat him out of his senses trying to drag him back."

"I say live and let live. I don't wish to know any man's past, as long as he behaves himself. Jomblit and Connolly went on their own search party earlier today. They had a redheaded girl with them. She ate quite a lot of licorice while they loaded up with enough jerky and flour for a week. They're not going to stop until they run him down. They're obsessed. I don't know why they're dragging that little creature along. She seemed jumpy. And she ate the licorice almost whole, as if she wanted to choke herself. Though she didn't look too innocent to me, I must say. She had the foulest mouth on her I've ever heard on a girl."

"That's my stepdaughter."

"I'm sorry. I didn't mean to offend."

"No offense taken. She can be mean as hell, but I got to round her up anyway."

"So it's really her you're after."

"You might say so."

"I don't mean to alarm you. But Cyril has a reputation around here that is real unsavory. His partner Jomblit is worse."

"And?"

"Cyril is the one who kept bringing your daughter candy. At first I thought he was her uncle. But he fondled her like—well, I wouldn't want my child handled that way. She pushed him away, and he would insist again. Do you know him?"

"He visited my house a couple of days ago and took her with him."

"He kidnapped her?"

"He catched her mind, and her body follered."

"If I knew where the black man lived, I'd tell you. But no one knows. At least no white man does."

"My wife is exhausted and trembling. Is thar a boarding house nearby?"

"We have two, one for whites and one for blacks."

"The one for blacks. Whar is it?"

"You don't mean to stay there."

"Is it illegal?"

"Why, no. It just isn't done."

"It is tonight."

"Two blocks north there's a neat little board house with a white fence around it. Fresh paint."

The Miss Jameson what opened the door a crack most surely did not want us to stay. At first she said the lodging was full. But once she seen the state Leora was in, why she bid us come in for stewed beef, at which point I tried to pay her, at which point she allowed as how she had a spare room. She asked me was thar no room at the other one for such as ourselves. I said I had not even bothered to check, for this is whar I aimed to spend the night. The stew was tender as babe's breath. Leora excused herself from the dinner table and crashed to sleep. The other guests, a traveling banjo player and a young couple on thar honeymoon, looked nervous as deacons in a duck blind at my presence. To break the tension, I ast the banjo player could he strum whilst I sung. Miss Jameson bade us sit together in her parlor and the banjer man perched on a stool too short for his legs, all a-spindle. She brought us a yaller tea too sweet for my tongue, but I drunk it for favor.

Into my mind come a Yoruba song I'd heard down by Cheapside one night when a group was frying gizzards and passing a gourd of liquor from hand to hand. I could only remember two lines, and I sung them over and over. At first the banjer man was so stunned, as if a goat had commenced to whistle, that he let the instrument hang from his arm. By and by, he brought it close to his vest and begun to strum, then he banged upon the banjer, catching up the rhythm of my husky syllables.

> E mariwo yan ya
> Ogun ofomo de onile

The banjer man smiled and begun to pick, with intricate flicks of his fingers. He plucked each note sure out of the air like black cherries to the beak of a jay.

"Where did you learn it?" ast Miss Jameson.

"In another life."

"What does it mean?"

"I've no idea."

The banjer man put down his instrument. "The hunter has been scrubbed clean, and the swaying palm trees banter the news."

"And Ogun? Isn't he a deity?" Miss Jameson wanted to know.

"The god of war and rage, partial to tobacco and rum. He carries a machete."

"The only God I might consider follering."

The newlywed couple said good night. They thanked us for the song, and give me a ginger handshake. The banjer man stared me down. "So has the hunter been blessed by Ogun?"

"Whatever do ye mean?"

"I'm seventy years old. Born on a riverbank of the Fuuta Jalon. I should have stayed among those grasslands instead of migrating south, looking for fame. I've been hunted, and I know a hunter when I see one."

"I'm looking for a former slave named Jacob Pingrim."

Miss Jameson's eyes danced when I spoke his name. "We're not a safe house. You're in free territory."

"I'm aware of that. You may see me as a hunter. And I'll be straight. I was one. I used to run down slaves like dogs run down jackrabbits. But them days is well over. I'm on a special mission. I've come to save Pingrim's skin if I can."

"You cannot do that unless you change his skin."

"I'll do whatever I have to."

"What reason could you have for wanting to help him? Are you an abolitionist?"

"I've never called myself any such thing. I don't get mixed up in politics."

"Then?"

"I can stop Jomblit and Cyril this night. That's all I have to offer; a rifle and six cartridges. What comes after don't depend just on me."

"Did it ever occur to you that Jacob Pingrim can defend himself?"

"Yes, it did. But I came anyway. He'll have to slay two men, and maybe a little girl, if he goes it alone. Unless he has a band of rogues I don't know about."

"If you were to kill those men, you'd be tried."

"If I'm found out, yes. So far, just the three of us knows my plan. So I'm putting my fate in your hands, with no more assurance than a bowl of stew."

I watched her doubt, looking to the banjer man for some sign of what to do. He ducked his head and plucked. I reckon he didn't want to be blamed later. "And if I did happen to know, who is to say you won't betray us? You could as easily be seeking the same reward as the others. I've never seen a white man sing in the African tongue. But it could all be a ruse."

"It could. You'll have to trust me. Or we can sit in this parlor waiting for your friend to be captured."

She explained the route, over a set of hills to Standing Stone Ridge, and out a trail called Slate Run.

"You may have trouble finding it at night."

"I'll find it."

The banjer man looked up from his string labor, as if he now dared speak. "I was at the square today, picking and minding my own business, and nobody pays attention to an old Negro anyway. The two men and a redheaded child came out of the store. She struck up a conversation with a laborer and pulled out an ivory ring. It seems this laborer saw Pingrim riding a mule out Slate Run. The girl told him the ring was carved out of three birds by a sorceress who flew over the world from the dark land. And the girl said that she had to give the ring back to Jacob Pingrim, because it had been taken from the finger of a princess who threw herself down a well, and if Pingrim didn't slip it on his finger before nightfall tomorrow, the world would come to an end under a blood moon. The laborer looked up at the sky, took the ring, examined the markings on it, and I guess he recognized it as real. For that's when he up and told them what he'd seen. So now they are able to track Pingrim as far as Slate Run."

FEBRUARY 1834
STRAWBERRY FARM
JACOB PINGRIM

I STAYED IN THE ROOT CELLAR for two days, among the field mice and spiders. At least the woods hadn't smelled of ancient potatoes. Jomblit came by twice during that time. According to Esmerelda, he and the other man pretended to be looking for an escaped criminal who had killed a white man. She didn't put up resistance, or question their claim that they were agents of the law who had to apprehend this light-skinned black and take him to Cincinnati for questioning. She let them look everywhere they wanted. On the first visit, they'd caught us unawares, but had first insisted on searching the hayloft, giving me time to get down to the cellar. Then they looked through the main floors of the house and immediate grounds. Esmerelda even offered them teacake, but they said they were in a hurry. When they had gone, she insisted on putting a couple of pounds of spoiled meat beneath the stairs to the cellar, and made me a bedroll in the far corner. She said she knew they'd be back before long.

I told her I hadn't done anything wrong, and that those men had no authority of any kind to be on the premises. She said, "Doan make no matter who right if you is dead. I seed dat man face. He crazy." Sure enough, they came back early the next morning, took another look around, and insisted on entering the cellar. A few steps down, they began to gag.

"Jesus God, woman. Did you bury a corpse down here?"

"I believe a possum been stuck down dere an he die. I ain got no man to fetch him out. Maybe you kin hep."

"That's not what we came for. We're on an errand of the greatest importance." And the door closed. When they were gone, I came storming out. "I'm not cowering there anymore. I'll die of lung poisoning."

"Saved yo neck, didn't I?"

"That's a matter of opinion. Anyway, if they come back again at this point, it will be because they know I'm here. And come what may, I am not descending those stairs again, even to bring you an armful of potatoes."

Without comment, Esmerelda carried the spoiled meat out with a stick, dug a hole and covered it with earth. She turned to me with a deadpan gaze. "Ain't you gone scratch a headstone, like you did for Miz Heath?"

"Yes, I'll inscribe 'Meat Me In Heaven.'" Esmerelda boiled water and gave me a bath, scented with dried flowers she'd kept in a jar. The first whiff of their aroma brought me back to those first days on the farm, when I slept in the hayloft. I took out the musket, loaded it with powder, and tamped it down with the rod. Esmerelda said nothing. I walked by her, down the front steps, a few feet from the nearest tree, and set the trigger. I lifted the musket. It was ridiculously heavy. I pointed it at the tree. It took several tries before I could get it to fire. I spent the afternoon loading, tamping, setting and firing. Sometimes the musket worked, and sometimes it didn't.

When I'd satisfied myself, I came to the steps of the porch, where Esmerelda had sat watching me. "Less us leave dis farm," she said.

"What?"

"I don care if I lives here or not. I jus rather live wid a man who alive."

"Don't be ridiculous. I'm going to defend this property. With my life, if necessary."

"Don even belong to us. Dem children gone come to claim it some day. An den what?"

"We'll fight them in court. In fact, my plan is to go to Chillicothe soon and see what can be done legally to give us title. It has been abandoned. Those children are no more real than the bogeyman. They probably all died of influenza, or moved to South America."

"Maybe. But I been thinking about my sister Malika. I remembered dat where she live called Hickory Town, in Pennsylvania. Says lots of people is from a Dutch land, and dey makes iron there. Maybe you can work in de iron factory."

"I'm a farmer. I can make the most stubborn plant live."

"Well, you made me live. So I guess you kin. Now you jus make sure you make you live."

"That's exactly what I intend to do."

February 1834
Sunfish Township, Ohio
Dan Baskin

For a quarter-hour I watched Leora sleep. I didn't have the heart to wake her up. Neither did I really want her along. I gathered my gun, hat, and a few other things I needed. Before I could turn for the door, she sat bolt upright.

"I'm a-coming with ye, Dan. Don't try to gainsay me."

"Woman, you could die."

"So could you."

"Don't get philosophical, Leora."

"Will if I want to."

"I need to move fast."

"So do I."

"Ye don't even know how to use a gun."

"I shot my daddy in the shoulder once, when he tried to lay a hand on me. Besides, it's a moot point, because you ain't got no second gun. Rae stole it."

"*Moot.* That's a mighty fancy word for a little lady."

"I done told you, I'm big whar it counts and little whar it counts. Now let's get a move on. My rump has surely kept me in comfort on the back of your saddle, and I can bear a few more bounces."

We trotted along Standing Stone Ridge under a blood moon. Stalker's hooves scraped the flint so regular I thought sparks would fly up. Rae had been right about the state of the heavens on this eve. I don't know how I missed it before. I myself called it a hunter's moon. That phrase I learnt from an Ojibwa that time him and me hunted elk for five straight nights under its light, beginning two days waxing to the full and carrying on two days after, on the wane. We could see well under its light, but that is also when I begun to develop a keen night vision, and learnt how to read the contrast between light and shadow.

Leora complained nary a whit on the ride. I couldn't stop this time to worry whether she was cold. This was to be a rude journey. A screech owl floated its long trills and upsails from way up a pine tree. Stones underfoot jumped out in profile under the moon's light. On the southerly side of the ridge, thickets of cypress and spruce swooped down into the distance. I half-hoped Jacob was lost amongst them. A body larns to make do a long while in the forest when the alternative is death. Even a grasshopper can taste like toasted corn under the right circumstances.

"Ye can see a fur way along the blue spruces, cain't ye, Dan? What must this scene look like of a day?"

"Green."

"You're a hell of a poet, Dan."

"Well, it is green by day."

"A one-word poet."

"I'll show ye. I'll make up a love poem on the spot."

"Let's hear it."

"Okay. Nighthawk lays two eggs—stead of one—hunts all night—let's see, now—um, past the crack of dawn."

"That ain't no love poem."

"It's poetry, isn't it? Them bastards changes direction all the time as they swoop and soar. If ye ever tried to watch a nighthawk run the sky while you're on horseback, ye'd fall right to the ground."

"How come ye ain't a-feared of what's to come?"

"Don't worry, I'm afraid."

"You don't look it."

"How would you know? You're staring at my back."

"You don't smell scared."

"How does that smell?"

"Like a branch the next morning after it done burnt to ashes."

"Well if I start to smell like that, dump a bucket of cold water over me."

"I will."

We passed the Standing Stone. Leora wanted to climb off and look at it, but I told her we wasn't on holiday. I spotted Slate Run right quick. It was easy, cause they was slate all scattered around. A quarry lay on the west side that made for quite a drop-off. Miss Jameson hadn't mentioned that detail. If ye was to slip into the quarry, you'd surely break many a rib and maybe your skull too. I skirted the pass real ginger, and we begun to descend to the lowland. The cypresses loomed up and catched us in a moon shadow. They was crickets a-plenty to make a show. Stalker drank from a stream we had to cross. I could hear the water rush in the dark, as if it wished to sweep us away, only it was too shallow for that job.

We come to the fringe of the farm whar Jacob was supposed to be. The forest went right up to its edge, which wasn't so good for him, because a man could hide within plain sight of the farmhouse. On the other hand, it made for a quick escape. I waited for the bark of a dog to betray us, but they weren't none. Had I been him, I surely would have got me a dog for the purpose of setting up a racket if somebody was to approach. This night, his oversight worked in my favor.

I pulled a rolled blanket off the saddle, stamped down the springy underbrush and laid it across fer Leora to sit. She lay down at once and curled up on the blanket as sleep gained on her again. A time passed and I figured her to be out. Then she spoke up. "Dan, ain't ye going in to fetch out Jacob Pingrim?"

"No. We'll wait for Jomblit and Cyril to appear."

"I ain't no tracker. But wouldn't it be simpler to warn him right away?"

"It would. But first I want to see if Rae is with the ransom seekers."

"What if she is? Trot up and take her first thing."

"Rae may not want to come back. All she knows how to do in a situation like this is cause trouble. If anybody is going to get me killed, it will be her by opening that damned mouth and saying heaven knows what. Besides, they say Jomblit is pure crazy. No telling what he might do. Try to shoot her, me, who knows? So you're going to lay low, right in this spot. We'll let them bring out Pingrim from the house first, if he's inside. Then I'll ask them for Rae, in exchange for Pingrim. At that point, they'll want to gallop off for their pay with no problems."

"Yer using Pingrim as bait?"

"Yes, you could say that."

"That ain't right."

"He forced my hand to let him go the first time, when he really was a slave. He owes me this."

"Didn't you promise that innkeeper that ye'd try to save Pingrim?"

"And I will. Only Rae comes first. Once she's safe with you, I'll chase them two scoundrels down. They won't get far. They can't outrun me, even if I give them a half hour's head start. I'm too quick and too silent."

"That's braggart talk."

"No, it's the truth."

"Who knows what they'll do to Pingrim in the meantime?"

"They ain't gonna harm him, after all the time they spent catching him. He's worth too much money. Rae ain't worth nothing, not in cash. She's the one they're most likely to harm, if there's a stand-off. They'll use her as a hostage."

"And if you catch up to them, then what? It's two agin one."

"Whatever needs to be done."

"You mean you'll kill them?"

"If I have to."

"That's murder."

"If they have apprehended a free man, I'll stand a better chance in court, if it ever comes to that."

"I see you done thought out all the angles."

"Pretty much."

"What about God?"

"He ain't never done nothing for me, nor I for him. So I guess we're even."

"Don't do it, Dan. I don't want ye as a corpse."

"I don't plan to be one. But don't talk agin me, Leora, not at this late hour. I brought you along contrary to my best judgment. That means a lot more than a pretty poem. Only you have to accept things as they are, and not interfere. This is the way it's going to play out, exactly as I said."

"All right, Dan. I'll look on in quiet."

Not long after daybreak, I heard a whisper against the grass. It was Rae, on horseback. Though I'd seen her only a few days before, she looked thinner, and spectral, liken her skin had watered down to milk, and her bones was a-floating inside the broth. Her eyes was pure black, with no depth. I had to admire how she dismounted without noise. She was barefoot and holding my pistol in her hand, almost careless. I was afraid the safety was off and that it would misfire and shoot her in the foot. I thought about making a lunge for her, and to hell with the rest of it, but I figured her escort was right behind the stand of oaks. They'd kill me before I laid a hand on her. Rae slipped around the house, peering in windows. I took the chance of their focus being on the house to move up from behind the barn to within a few yards. She disappeared around one side and after a long moment, come out on the far side of the porch. She give a short bird whistle and waved. I reckon she'd spotted him inside one of the rooms. Jomblit and Cyril poked out of the stand, their horse's muzzles leading the way. They looked at one another and Cyril decided he'd dismount. His horse was shooed back into the trees. Nobody spoke a word.

A sudden wind rustled up the branches and died down again. I could hear Cyril's soft footfalls crunch across the late ground frost. I worked my fingers to get the blood moving inside them. There was Jomblit a-smiling as if he'd just won at a dice table. Cyril kept a serious face. He seemed all business. Jomblit nodded to Cyril, who then stood on the first step to check would it creak. It was solid built, as if newly repaired. He walked up the three remaining steps and approached the door, laying a hand on the screen. It opened on oiled hinges. I guess Pingrim was too fine a repairman for his own good.

Cyril waited a good spell with his hand on the latch of the main door. At last he clicked it down and let it go. The wood door swung open a couple of inches, and he waited to see if there would be any response from inside. After a short pause, Cyril turned to Jomblit for the final signal. As he swiveled back around to enter, I saw the end of a musket come through the opening in the door and a flash of fire followed by a blast. The charge tore open Cyril's chest and he fell to the ground. There was a lot of blood, but it looked pale in the morning light as it run across the frost.

The door closed and Jomblit barely reacted, except to back up. "Go inside," he said to Rae. "They're not going to shoot a little girl." She took two steps toward Jomblit's horse, raised her pistol and shot at him point blank. She only managed to wound the horse, a much bigger target, who threw him off as it recoiled. He hit the ground at an odd angle and I heard a crack as he slammed against the dirt hard and howled. The wounded horse ran off into the glade. It looked like Jomblit was trying to reach for his gun, but it seemed his arm had broke. His other hand, with the two fingers, wouldn't be much good for shooting anyway. He let loose a string of curses the like of which I'd never heard all one on top of the other.

I walked forward with my rifle raised and called Rae's name, keeping out of range of her shot. That was my pistol and I knew how far the bullets would go without erring. I wasn't going to trust in her missing with her second shot at Jomblit, no matter she had missed before. Sometimes you just get lucky. Rae whirled around and recognized me with them flat black eyes of hers, with all the green drained out.

Her whole body had gone a-tremble, and yet she kept the pistol raised over that man. "Hey, Baskin."

"Hey, pip."

"Jomblit put it to me, Baskin. Exactly like my brother did. So did that dead man over there."

Jacob Pingrim had walked out onto the porch. He seemed mighty surprised, but he said nothing. He set the musket down, looking astonished that it had even fired at all.

"Come here, Rae. It's all over now," I coaxed.

"No it ain't. Remember when I blowed the rabbit's legs off along the trace, and you finished him off for me?"

"Nobody is finishing anybody else today. I'm going to bind Jomblit's hands. He can't hurt you."

"He already hurt me. He has to die."

"No, he won't. He'll go to jail."

"Which of us is the child, me or you? It's the nigger who allus goes to jail, except in the story books. I thought you said you'd killed men before."

"When I had to."

"Now is that time. You let Pingrim go at the crossing, all right. That was fer the best. But now? I think you just don't know how to kill. I said then you was a coward, and I was right. Did you really ever kill a man, Baskin?"

"I did, Rae. On several occasions. But that don't make me a man."

Rae took three more steps until she stood directly over Jomblit. As she pointed her pistol at his face, Jomblit tripped her with his foot and she fell on top of him as he grabbed the gun from her hand. Whether it was more the danger, or the sight of his body lying under hers, I couldn't abide it and I shot him in the throat. Thar was a brief chug, then a sob, after which the man lay still.

I hoped Jomblit's body in the mud would be enough to atone for both our sins. I wondered whose were greater, his or mine, if you added them up over a lifetime, or a hundred lifetimes. I did know I was free from Abejidé. She was as dead as Jomblit, she wasn't coming back. I had done what I could. It wasn't enough, but then again, it never is. I wasn't sorry I had met her. I was only sorry that she had ever met me.

Rae stood up, her eyes wet, but she was smiling. "I knew you could do it, Baskin. I knew you would save me."

FEBRUARY 1834
STRAWBERRY FARM
JACOB PINGRIM

BASKIN AND I DRAGGED THE two bodies to the same gully where Esmerelda had once left Mrs. Heath in my absence. I asked him whether he'd come to catch me or to save me. "No," he answered, and that was all. Rae tried to cozy with Baskin, but he was having none of it.

"Where did you get your saddle, Baskin? I bet you won it in a contest of skill." He just narrowed his eyes at her and turned back away. "When are you going to fix that split boot. If somebody gives me a needle and thread, I'll sew it right up. I don't mind." This time, he didn't even turn his head to acknowledge her chatter. All I knew is that he didn't want the redheaded girl around him. She kept crushing pinecones with her foot. I told her to come with me. I gathered the wood shakes for the roof project I'd had to abandon. Dan's woman kept quiet, and Esmerelda just seemed moody. I didn't want to know exactly why. I needed to do something. I motioned for Rae to follow, placed a wooden ladder against the house and pointed to the roof.

"I'll go up and down the ladder and bring you the shakes. All you have to do is nail them in place. Four to a side."

The redhead said nothing but we set to work. I brought each shake to her and stayed alongside to show her how to place and secure. Half her attention was on me, and half on an old bird's nest she spotted in a branch overhead.

"Don't let your mind wander."

Rae picked up a shake with two hands and dangled it in front of herself. "You made these?"

"Yes."

"How?"

"You split bark to heart, crosswise to the grain."

"With what?"

"A blade and a mallet and whole lot of muscle."

Despite her skinny arms, once Rae caught the rhythm, she could drive each nail in two strokes. Her accuracy would be the envy of any carpenter. When she was good and tired, I helped her down the ladder. Rae asked if she could have a meal. Esmerelda wiped the dried blood off her hands and face, from where she'd stood close to the man when she fired and set a plate of mashed turnips, ham, and cornbread in front of her. I asked where Baskin and his woman were.

"Dey's asleep."

"In the middle of that racket?"

"I guess so. I put them in our bed."

"If I'd known that, we wouldn't have worked on the roof. They're right underneath the patch we were working on."

"Sometime a man and a woman so tired, dem strokes jes sound like somebody drove a nail in yo coffin an you mighty glad about it."

Rae looked up from a forkful of mashed turnips. I'd never seen eyes so green. In truth, I was afraid of them. "I'm sorry I led them men to your home, Pingrim. It was me who figgered out whar ye was."

She took from her breast pocket a ring carved of ivory. It was made of three interlocking birds. "This is what I used to find you, after we got to Sunfish." She held it out in her palm and handed it to me.

"Where did you get it?"

"I seen that yer woman don't have no ring."

The ring was beautiful and without flaws. "All right. I shall." I took Esmerelda's hand and slipped the ring on it. It took some pushing to get it on her work-muscled hand.

The couple came down looking worse than before, their hair sticking out every which way, faces puffy with sleep.

Baskin's wife caught sight of the ring on Esmerelda's hand and asked if she could look at it. With shyness and caution, she held it up. The wife gazed at it, her face serious, for a long moment. Turning her head, she glanced first at Baskin, then at the redhead, as if for some sort of corroboration. No one said anything. She broke into a sudden smile, said, "Oh, that's pretty," and let go of Esmerelda's hand.

Baskin put on his slouch hat. "We need to bury those bodies." Rae stood up. "You sit down, pip, and finish your meal."

"Okay, we'll dig. And then you'll be on your way?"

"What else do ye require?"

"What will you tell the authorities when they come looking for these men?"

Baskin paced the floor. "If the subject comes up, I'll say I shot them both. One with a musket I pulled from your arms, and one with one of my own pistols."

"You don't have to take responsibility for what I did," I said.

"What do you care? Was the law ever on your side? Me and you ain't friends. I'm a practical man. Nobody is going to put me in jail on account of these scoundrels, or if they do, it will be for a couple of months. I been through worse. They ain't worth it, and everybody knows it. I'll tell them we was after the same prey, and they tried to take the free nigger away from me and cheat me out of my illegal reward. People will understand."

"And what about that free nigger," I said. "Where did he get to?"

"Right now he's on this farm. But what I suspect is that he's going to head further north and get lost for a good spell, until this blows over."

"Amen," said Esmerelda.

"And leave this farm behind?"

"It ain't my property," said Baskin. "So I can't really say. But if they stick you in the hoosegow, ye ain't gonna be farming it anyway."

"I guess we'll roam then, northward."

Esmerelda took my hand in hers, the one bearing the ivory ring. "Dat's right, city boy. To Hickory Town, with Malika."

"Maybe we can come back eventually. It will be overgrown."

Baskin was gazing at the window. "These fields ain't going anywhere. You'll cut it back to shape."

FEBRUARY 1834
STAWEBERRY FARM
DAN BASKIN

AFTER SUPPER, PINGRIM BUILT A fire of split hickory logs inside the stone hearth. They had not had time to season, so they was a little green, but they smelled good anyway. Rae throwed down on the floor like a rag doll. So profound was her slumber on the floorboards that I reckon she forgot where she was even in her dreams. Leora conversed with Esmerelda every bit as natural as she had with Chelsea. I guess when it's kitchen and board, nobody's that far apart. Ye can argue about the right way to make beans, but that's about as far as the disagreements will go. Leora is easy with people. She can make ye talk even before ye know what it is you want to relate.

After Pingrim and I had smoked together and nipped a glass of brew, we hadn't much to say to one another. I barely knew the man, except by reputation, and I suppose he could say the same about me. I excused myself to go to the barn and feed Stalker. That damn beast understood me better than anyone, by his wits alone, and I didn't ever have to make explanations. When I examined his hooves, I saw they had begun to bleed, as I suspected they would after running over several miles of scattered slate. I apologized, but he didn't make me feel bad about it either, only nickered a time or two. I cleaned the hooves as best I could and promised I'd find a salve and do better tomorrow. There was no question of him running us upland as a dray. Rest was in order.

The stars had come out by the time I emerged from the barn. The smoke of the hickory logs smelled right fine drifting from the chimney. I had an urge to leave the four of them inside, and ride Stalker the livelong night, bloody hooves and all, to an unknown destination. If I saddled him up, he'd go without complaint. Knowing that was enough for me. I ducked my head to get under the doorframe, as if I'd arrived home after a long day's work.

ABOUT THE AUTHOR

JOHNNY PAYNE is the author of five plays, eight novels, and two books of poetry. His plays have been staged in NYC, Los Angeles, Chicago, Virginia, and Texas on both professional and university stages. Payne directs the MFA in Creative Writing at Mount Saint Mary's University, Los Angeles.

CONNECT WITH JOHNNY

Sign up for Johnny's newsletter at
www.johnnypayne.com/free

To find out more information visit his website:
www.johnnypayne.com

Twitter:
@johnnyPayne7

Instagram:
@johnnypayne7

Facebook:
www.facebook.com/profile.php?id=100030082134319

Get Book Discounts and Deals

One Last Thing ...

Thank you for reading! If you enjoyed this book, I'd be very grateful if you'd post a short review on Amazon. I read every comment personally and am always learning how to make this book even better. Your support really does make a difference.

Search for *The Hard Side of the River* by Johnny Payne to leave your review.

Thanks again for your support!

Made in the USA
Lexington, KY
15 December 2019